HER MISSING HUSBAND

AJ CAMPBELL

Her Missing Husband

by

AJ Campbell

Copyright © AJ Campbell 2023

ISBN 978-1-8381091-5-8

Cover design © Tim Barber, Dissect Designs 2023

ALSO BY AJ CAMPBELL

Leave Well Alone

Don't Come Looking

Search No Further

The Phone Call

The Wrong Key

All books are available at Amazon and Kindle Unlimited

A FREE GIFT FOR YOU

Warning signs presented themselves from the start. Flashing like the neon displays in Piccadilly Circus, they couldn't have advertised things more clearly. But Abbie was too troubled to see clearly. Too damaged to see the dangers Tony Sharpe brought into her life. Until the day he pushed her too far.

See the back of the book for details on how to get your copy.

For all my readers.
I couldn't continue writing without you.
Thank you for choosing to read my books.
AJ x

SEVEN YEARS AGO

'Why the obsession?' The bald, black-eyed man slouches over his mug of tea, his voice no more than a whisper. Those eyes, how they bore into Lori's.

Unfazed, Lori straightens her back. 'Justice, Frankie. Justice for Betty Tailor.' She sips her coffee, the charcoal taste as bitter as her feelings for the monster sitting opposite her.

'To put me behind bars, you mean.' Frankie taps his packet of cigarettes on the table. 'So you can climb the career ladder. That's all you're interested in.'

'You're guilty as hell. You know it. I know it. And I have the proof. And so do the police now.'

'You're so wrong.' Frankie Evans sneers as he pushes his plastic chair away from the table and stands up. Its metal legs scrape along the tiled floor. The sound, so loud against the din of the surrounding diners, grates on Lori's overtaxed nerves. His immense body dwarfs her petite frame. He smirks at her. 'I need to take a leak.'

Lori feels her top lip involuntarily lift to the left. Her nostrils flare. The hulk of the man she hates swaggers across the rundown café that smells of fried food and cut-price coffee: a popular go-to place for workers grabbing early morning breakfasts or lunchtime sandwiches. When he disappears around the corner to the toilets, she glances around the shabby surroundings, noticing how the yellow Formica tabletops match the nicotine-stained walls. The owners need to call the decorators in.

A phone buzzes. Lori pats the pocket of her camel coat. It's hers. She fishes it out, seeing her best friend's name scrolling across the screen – as it has roughly this time every afternoon for the past three months. 'Just checking in,' April says. 'You OK?'

Lori tries to keep her voice normal. 'I'm fine. I can't talk.'

'Where are you?'

'Out and about. I'll catch up with you later.'

'Sure. I'm here all day. Call me any time.' Lori ends the call as Frankie returns.

He sits down, puffing out his chest. 'You have no idea who you're dealing with.'

'I'm not frightened of you,' Lori says. 'What do they say about bullies, Frankie? All cowards, the lot of you. You just don't know it. And if you did, you certainly wouldn't admit it.'

His laugh exudes malevolence. 'You're way out of your depth, missy. Way out.'

A group of men dressed in white overalls caked with paint leave the café, laughing and berating each other in jest. Most of the tables remain occupied though: a security blanket for Lori. 'You're going down for a very long time, Frankie. And with what I have, they're going to throw away the key.'

'You need to back off or you'll be looking over your shoulder for the rest of your life.'

It's Lori's turn to laugh, although she's not sure how convincing she sounds. She repositions herself in the uncomfortable chair. 'So, come on, tell me, what did you really bring me here to talk about today?'

He pauses. For effect, she knows. He picks up a set of cutlery wrapped in a napkin as thin as tissue paper and pulls the edge. A knife and fork clatter onto the table. Frankie grabs the knife and points the blade at Lori. 'Your husband.'

Lori feels a rush of blood through her head. His words hit a nerve already exposed. 'What about him?'

'How long is it now since you last saw him? Three months? What happened to him, Lori? The world wants to know as much as you do. What happened to Howie Mortimer?'

Lori sits up straight once more, her cool composure lost in the fire he has ignited within her. One that has been burning low for the past few weeks but is now set to rage once more.

Frankie's spiteful laugh returns: an evil, menacing cackle. 'Now I have your attention. Tell me. Have you plans to see him any time soon?'

'What do you know?'

'Look at the pain in those pretty blue eyes. The

sadness. Oh, Lori, Lori, I could perhaps feel sorry for you if you didn't have it in for me.' He jabs the blade of the knife at her again. 'Why don't you back off and crawl back into your hole? Then I'll think about what I'm prepared to share with you about your husband's disappearance.'

Lori's back teeth clench like the jaws of a vice, her voice urgent. 'You're bluffing.'

His goading continues, smiting her where he knows it hurts. 'It's no consequence to me either way.' He shrugs his broad shoulders. 'But for you...' He pokes the knife once more in her direction. 'For you, Lori, that's a different story. See, you really don't know who you're dealing with here.'

It's so out of character, but she wants to strike out at him – dig her fingers into his tanned face and twist his ugliness, like he has her twisted heart.

'Poor Lori. Her husband disappears.' Frankie raises a hand. 'Puff!' His fist explodes in the air. His hand falls to the table with a thud as his stare leaves Lori and he glances over her shoulder to the door of the café. Two police officers bound in accompanied by a gust of cold air. Lori follows Frankie's gaze and shivers as the chill bites. They head for the spot vacated by the decorators.

Frankie's hand reaches across the table and swallows Lori's tiny fist. 'Looks like you're out of luck. Out of time.' He lowers his voice. 'I'm not sure what I'm going to enjoy more. Knowing the pain you're suffering from not having a clue where your darling husband is or wreaking my revenge on you when I'm found not guilty of these ridiculous charges. You're a dead woman walking, Lori. Live with it.'

1

TODAY

'However did that happen?' Ray asks, staring at Lori's palms revealing several jagged punctures where she has lost a layer of skin. 'We need to get them cleaned. You don't want them getting infected. I'll get the first aid kit.'

He gently steers Lori towards her favourite seat at the back of his small but thriving café. Situated in a small village in North Wales, it's perfectly positioned to catch the footfall from visitors to the nearby nature reserve and impressive Amberside Falls. The last customers have left, and it looks as if Ray is cleaning up ready for another day.

'I fell at the final hurdle. The dogs were keen to see you,' Lori says, forcing a laugh but wincing as she removes her small backpack and plonks it on the floral PVC-covered table. 'No big deal. I just need to get cleaned up.'

Ray takes the leads of her faithful springer spaniels, Misty and Shadow. 'What have you and your mother been up to?' he asks the dogs, tying Shadow's lead around a leg of the table as he glances up at Lori. 'Don't tell me. The slope leading down to the turnstile. It's torturous. That loose slate is a nightmare.' Ray tries to tie Misty's lead around the table leg too, but she refuses. Silly dog. She can be as obstinate as a stubborn child these days. But Lori's dogs aren't that young any more. They will be seven this Christmas.

Seven years.

Ray coaxes Misty to comply then pulls out a chair. 'Sit down, and I'll get the first aid kit. Then I'll get you a drink. How about one of my Scarlett O'Haras?' The café provides an essential meeting place for the local community. Everyone loves Ray. His extensive range of coffee is something else. It's what drives people to the café from miles around.

Lori forces a smile, taking a seat on the cross-backed chair, upholstered with a PVC- covered cushion that matches the tablecloths. Ray is forever experimenting with innovative ideas for his coffees and naming them after famous people or the mood of the day. His Scarlett O'Hara is his take on a red velvet cake. Its delectable taste is second to none, but with a helping of whipped cream and chocolate shavings, it's too rich for Lori right now. She still feels queasy from her earlier tumble. 'A double espresso will do, and a large glass of water, please.'

Ray glances at his watch. 'At this time of day?'

Lori nods. A busy night stretches ahead of her, and caffeine is essential. She wants to make as much hay as she can while the sun is still shining. This morning she scrapped her current work in progress. Despite her efforts over the past few months, the story simply isn't working.

She isn't feeling it. 'I need a new story idea by Friday. Otherwise, I'll be searching for a new agent.' A humorous tone coats her words, but there's no joke in her message. She gives her trademark smile. A smile that is as engaging as it is endearing. Her eyes are alive, but somewhere deep within them, a sadness is forever present for those who know her well.

'That bad?'

'That bad.'

Ray disappears behind the low cooler that usually displays the cakes of the day that he makes early each morning, or later in the day if there's a lull in customers. He retreats into the kitchen.

Lori glances at the dogs looking dotingly at her before turning her attention to the news broadcasting from a flatscreen attached to the side wall. There's a bulletin about the unprecedented heatwave that has descended upon the UK, which has sparked fires across the country. Firefighters are tackling a grass fire at a nearby farm that has spread to two local properties. There's been a substantial disruption to transport. Drought has been declared in many regions. There are people dying from heat exhaustion across the country. The UK can't cope with this blistering heat.

Lori wipes the sweat dripping down her temple, wincing at the increasing pain from her hands and knees.

Ray returns, rummaging in a green box. 'This should do for now.' He removes medical wipes and a tube of antiseptic cream. 'Let me. I've washed my hands.' He tears open one of the packets of wipes and cleans the dust and dirt from her hands. His touch is so tender; soothing and calming. Apart from a nudge as they've shared a joke, or an accidental brushing of shoulders as they've passed each other in the café, it's the only physical contact they've had since they met when Lori moved to the village at the beginning of the year.

He looks up and catches her eye as he applies a layer of antiseptic cream. A wide smile appears between his moustache and scruffy beard. She winces as he cleans her knees. 'Sorry,' he whispers. 'Pity you're wearing shorts. You'd have been more protected in jeans.' He reaches into the first aid box and removes two large square dressings. 'Keep these on until you go to bed, then best you allow some air to help the healing.' He secures the dressings with surgical tape. 'Now let me get you that drink.'

Lori wipes more sweat from her brow, throwing her head back. When is this weather going to let up? Picking up the menu, she fans her face, still sweating from the airless evening heat. When Ray returns with a bottle of water, a double espresso and a glass full of what looks like a black slushy, he places Lori's drinks in front of her, along with a mini Biscoff biscuit, which half hangs off the saucer. He takes the chair next to her and holds up the glass. 'What do you think of this?' He describes the new addition to his elaborate coffee menu: a matt black mixture of cacao powder, milk, espresso, and coconut charcoal. 'Dark and chilling. I think I'll call it The Goth.'

Its bitter smell is intoxicating, but Lori isn't listening to Ray. A weekly news summary currently on the TV has seized her attention. Her jaw drops open, unable to believe the words flowing from the reporter's mouth or the shot of a man on the TV screen. His menacing features haven't changed. The bald head and bullet eyes. It's a face Lori will never forget. Ray's eyes follow her gaze to the screen.

The newsreader continues. 'After what appears to be the work of his exceptional lawyers, who have worked tirelessly to reduce his sentence from murder to burglary, Evans has finally walked free from prison. He was convicted in 2015 for aggravated burglary that left a woman dead. But Frankie has always claimed his innocence. The judge sentenced him to a minimum term of thirty-five years for what he described as, "the unforgivable, ruthless and meaningless attack on a vulnerable woman". Having served his time for the part he played in the burglary, Frankie Evans is now a free man.'

Ray puffs out his cheeks. 'Crikey! There's the face of someone looking for revenge if ever I saw one.'

2

'Did you know coconut charcoal aids detoxification?' Ray turns his attention to his drink. 'Perhaps The Barbarian would be a better name. What do you think?'

This can't be true. Frankie Evans was guilty. The newsreader moves to the next story. Lori stares at her cup, her stomach flipping somersaults. This can't have happened. Frankie Evans can't have been released from prison.

But he has been.

According to the news, Frankie Evans is a free man.

'The Barbarian or The Goth?' Ray scoops a spoonful of the black mixture and offers it to Lori. 'Try some. Give me your honest opinion.'

In a daze, Lori takes the spoon and samples his drink. It tastes as bitter as it smells. 'It needs sweetening,' she says, her voice wavering.

'Are you OK?' he asks. 'You look like Chucky has just walked in.'

No! she wants to scream. *I am not OK. Frankie Evans has*

wangled a get-out-of-jail-free card. She loops her fingers through the small handle of the cup, trying to control her shaking hand. *How the hell did he manage that?*

It was her big break – the breaking news story that launched her career as an investigative journalist. Lori's dogged determination to achieve justice prevailed and, unfortunately for Frankie Evans, he was the recipient of the full weight of the law due to her findings. Findings that he has always vehemently contested, and it now appears he has been vindicated.

The plaudits and awards came raining in. From then on in, she could have had any job she wanted. The world of journalistic opportunities was her oyster. Headhunters called, offering roles she could only have dreamt of securing later in her career.

It was a particularly nasty case, an aggravated burglary that spiralled out of control. A seventy-one-year-old, Betty Tailor, was beaten in her home, tied up, and robbed. The intruder then inexplicably set fire to her house, leaving her to perish in the most abhorrent way imaginable. The story grabbed the nation, and Lori's heart. Betty Tailor was an author. One that Lori had much admired. Lori had interviewed her once in her reporting days for an article on prolific writers. Betty Tailor was the sweetest of souls. Lori will never forget the tea Betty served in dainty cups and saucers from an antique teapot. And Betty lived in Chester, only streets away from Lori and Howie's family home.

The home Lori hasn't set foot in for nearly seven years after she realised she could no longer live with the memories it held of her missing husband. So she secured a lease for a two-bedroom cottage in Cornwall where she moved to with her daughter Molly for a year. One of the biggest mistakes of her life. She had thought that by freeing Molly from the constant memories of Howie and getting her away from the delinquent gang she had fallen in with would set her daughter back on the straight and narrow. How wrong could Lori have been? The so-called friends Molly made in Cornwall turned out to be even worse than her former spurious friends. Molly quit school and moved to London with her new boyfriend, despite Lori dropping to her knees and begging her not to. Molly was still only seventeen, but she didn't care. She wasn't listening. In her eyes, she was months shy of her eighteenth birthday, and she could do what the hell she liked. Lori was distraught, but nothing she could do or say could change her determined daughter's mind.

Each year since, Lori has lived the life of a nomad, renting a house in a different location around the UK, before settling nearer to the family home this year and taking the cottage in North Wales.

Lori downs the coffee in one. The double caffeine shot offers a luxurious aftertaste but fails to calm her nerves. She needs to get home. It's stifling in there. 'I must go.'

Ray frowns. 'So soon?' He looks hurt.

Almost every evening for the past month, after her evening walk, Lori has stayed to chat with him after his last customers have left for the day. And in the mornings, after she has walked the dogs, she stops for one of his coffees and a chat before his morning influx of customers begins trickling through the door. But right now, she needs to be on her own. 'Sorry. I must get on. Molly's coming to stay tomorrow. Do you remember me telling you? To look after the dogs while I'm away for the weekend.' She also reminds him of her agent's deadline that is coming at her like a speed train without brakes.

'I'll drive you home.'

She stifles a wave of emotion. He is one of the kindest men she has ever met. 'I'm fine.' She stands up. An excruciating pain in her knee unbalances her momentarily.

'I insist. The car is parked around the side.' He leaps up and unties the dogs' leads. 'I'll go get it. Are you OK to meet me at the bottom of the steps?'

Lori takes the leads, forgetting her injuries and cursing as the strap catches her knee. She walks outside, letting the dogs have another drink from the bowl Ray leaves at the door for his canine visitors. It's even hotter outside. Her stomach is turning. Frankie Evans is out of jail. She still can't believe this has happened.

Ray pulls up in front of the café in his beaten-up Land Rover Defender. He is wearing the cricket hat that he always puts on when he is out and about. The clip strap dangles on his chest. The passenger door is already ajar. He reaches across and pushes it to open it fully. Lori helps Misty and Shadow inside and climbs in after them, while Ray pops back to lock the café door.

'Belt up,' Ray says when he reappears. She doesn't know why he bothers. No seatbelt will protect them if this thing crashes. It will disintegrate on impact and explode, rather like her thoughts do as she thinks of Frankie Evans being freed. Ray dips his head and peers over his circular-framed glasses. Only when she pulls the strap across her shaking body and clicks the end into the buckle does he ram the gearstick into first and head out of the village.

'Hold on,' Ray instructs. Lori tucks her fingers carefully around the grab handle to stabilise herself as the anti-quated 4x4 bumps and rattles down the narrow single-track road. Within a minute, he takes the pothole-infested lane that leads to her house, sending them bouncing around like stones in a tin can. 'Hey, I meant to ask you,' he shouts over the noise of the car bumping along. 'One of my regulars is holding a charity event for Cancer Research in the café next month. Would you be able to donate one of your books for the raffle?'

'Sure. I'll get you the first three I wrote. They are part of a series.'

'That's kind of you. She'll be pleased.'

The diesel fumes settle when he pulls up outside her grey stone cottage with its matching flint roof nestled within a boundary of hedgerows. Ray leaps out of the car and strides around to the passenger side to open the door. The dogs spring out. 'Are you going to be OK with those hands?' Ray takes Lori's arm and helps her out. 'Want me to come in and help with anything?'

'I'm fine.' He has become a good friend these past few months, and she doesn't want to offend him. She could invite him in, but she needs to be alone. Frankie Evans is out of prison, and she needs to find out precisely when this happened and more about the circumstances of his release. If she got this all so horribly wrong, which she certainly doesn't think is the case, then she wouldn't be able to live with herself. What were his final words to her the day she last saw him? "Dead woman walking". And if she did get it wrong, that brute of a man certainly isn't one to take it lying down.

3

Ray leans his elbow along the top of the car door. 'I'm going shopping. We've run out of a few things at the café, and I don't want to leave it until the morning. Do you need anything?'

Lori smiles. She's never known anyone to work so hard. Apart from Howie, that is. A self-confessed workaholic, her husband never stopped grafting. Not that she could complain because back then, she worked every hour she could, too. Fresh out of university, Howie set up a video and film production business with his best mate Paul Bennett, who later married April. It could have been incestuous, but it wasn't. All four of them had strong work/friendship boundaries, and apart from a few minor fallouts over the years, they made it work. Lori couldn't have lived without April and Paul's faithful friendship these past seven years.

'I might grab a carton of milk from you in the morning. I'll pick it up after my walk.'

'You sure you'll be walking in the morning?' Ray gives a sympathetic nod at her hands and knees.

'Of course. Dogs aren't just for Christmas and all that.'

With a flick of his hand, he mock salutes like an RAF squadron leader. 'Your wish is my command. You know where I am. Just call.' He swings the passenger door shut. It doesn't close properly, so he thrusts his butt against it to give it extra help.

Lori waves as he reverses down the lane. Misty and Shadow bounce towards the cottage. She follows them as fast as her injuries will allow, desperate to get to her computer. When she gets around the back, she is deep in thought when she stops. Are her eyes deceiving her, or did she just see a figure in her garden? It must be her eyes, or her mind, playing games. The dogs would be going crazy if there was anyone there. The news of Frankie Evans is playing with her head. That man has always excelled at doing that.

She opens the stable door at the far side of the house and walks to the small dining area that overlooks the garden. Darkness is falling, but no one is in sight as far as she can tell. She sighs. It must have been another figment of her imagination, as many things have been for the past seven years. That's what happens when your husband leaves for work one day, and you never see or hear from him again.

Switching on the light, Lori fills the dogs' bowls with water. The lighting in the cottage is the only thing she doesn't like about it. The windows are small for the size of the house, so there's very little natural light, apart from the

AJ CAMPBELL

dining area, an extension to the main part of the property, which has floor-to-ceiling patio doors. Parched herself, she grabs a large glass from the wooden draining board and fills it from the kitchen tap. Her knee is throbbing. She finds a packet of painkillers in a drawer and takes two tablets with her water. The dressing on one of her hands is coming loose. Leaning against the kitchen sink, she peels away the adhesive edges and removes both dressings. She turns on the tap and runs her hands under the water. It stings like hell.

Usually, she would leave both the upper and lower halves of the stable door open. Any breeze is welcome in this weather, and she enjoys the view out to the garden. But her sixth sense that seldom lets her down is telling her to close it completely tonight, despite the stifling heat. She swings both halves shut and locks them before heading to the lounge, a heavy-beamed, low-ceilinged room she seldom uses. It's lonely watching TV on your own every night. A good book and her bed are far more appealing. She opens the cast iron latch of the black door that leads to the narrow staircase and makes her way upstairs. The night stretches ahead and she needs to freshen up.

Halfway up, she stops to straighten a photo of Howie and Molly. The one that saddens her the most; it's been harrowing seeing her daughter suffer so much. Molly is posing in a head-turning red gown – a ruched bandeau maxi – by the front door of their house in Chester. She looks so beautiful. It was the night of her school prom when her enormous potential was only a grasp away. Her head is resting on her dad's shoulder, her corkscrew curls tumbling across his chest. Curls she'd chopped off when they moved to Cornwall. Then she'd had her head shaved. The camera caught the pride in the twinkle of Howie's eyes perfectly that night. She loves his eyes: a striking violet, such a rare colour.

Lori wipes her thumb across the glass, brushing the dust that has collected over the past few months as she has spent hours drumming her fingers on her antique desk while staring at a blank screen. Writer's block has struck her hard this year. She's in the worst creative slump of her career. Usually, she can count on her writing to get her through the bouts of anxiety that have struck her since Howie's disappearance. Which is why she is suffering at the moment. The words just won't come. A lump fills her throat. It always does when she looks at this photo for too long. It's so damn depressing thinking about the what-ifs and what-could-have-beens.

Turning the dial to the coldest temperature, she steps into the shower. Ice-cold water blasts her body. She lathers a dollop of lavender gel into her clammy skin with her fingers, inhaling the fresh and cleansing scent. She often takes a cold shower. A ritual Howie taught her when they first met at university. To begin with, she thought he was stark raving bonkers. Who would want to endure that? 'It's good for the circulation. Your immune system gets a boost, and it makes you feel more alert afterwards. Don't knock it until you've tried it,' he told her. And she did. And he was right. As he always was about everything.

She digs a tube of antiseptic cream and two bandage dressings out of the bottom drawer of the vanity unit where she stores items without a natural home. It's the only muddled spot in the whole cottage. Tidy house, tidy mind: one of the mantras she has to live by. She used to be a messy person. The way she left washing-up in the sink and clothes draped over the chaise longue at the bottom of their bed drove Howie nuts. He would be delighted by her neatness now. She goes to throw the cream back in the drawer when a box catches her eye. She picks it up. The anti-depressants that were first prescribed to her nearly seven years ago that she stopped taking when she moved to the cottage at the beginning of the year. But she keeps a supply just in case. She throws the box back inside the drawer. She can't play that game again: the tug of war between her heart and her head. Her heart forcing her to stay in the past, her head telling her to move on.

Frankie Evans continues invading her thoughts as she throws on a pair of white cotton pyjamas and rushes downstairs, desperate to get to her computer.

Three men were initially arrested for the abhorrent murder of Betty Tailor. Two of them, the Bright brothers – a modern-day dupe of Britain's notorious gangster Kray twins – were unequivocally placed at the scene. On the advice of their lawyers, they admitted their part in the heinous crime in a futile attempt to gain favour with the judge under the premise of not causing Mrs Tailor's family further suffering. There was too much evidence against them. The Bright brothers incriminated Evans, saying he was present and was the one who set fire to the house. Evans, however, claimed he was never there and with the lack of forensics, he was released without charge.

Lori's tenacious digging and craving for the truth swung the hammer on the final nail of Frankie Evans' coffin. And boy, did the face of that hammer hit with an almighty blow. After dragging up misdemeanours from Frankie's youth, where he had a particular persuasion to lighting fires, Lori finally got him placed at the scene by accounting for the crucial twenty minutes he claimed he was elsewhere. Largely circumstantial, but it stuck. Frankie finally admitted that while he was party to the initial burglary, he left prior to the assault of Betty Tailor and the subsequent fire. The jury didn't buy Frankie's claims, and the judge sentenced him to life imprisonment.

Frankie's menacing words echo in her ears. "You need to back off or you'll be looking over your shoulder for the rest of your life."

4

The buzz from Ray's double espresso has worn off. Lori needs more caffeine. And lots of it. She fills the kettle, carefully avoiding anything touching her palms. While waiting for the water to boil, she grabs her laptop from the central island and fires it up. Browsing the news pages, she learns that Frankie Evans was released just under a week ago. She is surprised this is the first she has heard of it. Why haven't the police, or one of her ex-work colleagues, warned her? Perhaps they sent an email. She's behind with her emails. There might be one sitting in her cluttered inbox. She'll have to check.

Unease creeps through her as she reads the most recent news story she can find. She searches again and reads other articles from the time he was arrested. Articles she has read so many times she could recite them. Clearly some people still think Frankie is guilty, but he is now a free man, and there is speculation that he intends to seek compensation for the loss of the prime years of his life. His mother fell ill around the time of his sentencing. An illness that resulted in a terminal diagnosis. The mother who raised him single-handedly, who he couldn't be with as she battled her short fight with ovarian cancer. Lori comes across another news story she's read before. One detailing an interview with Frankie's mother as she fought death. Lori had to stop herself repeatedly reading it at some point. It was too depressing thinking of a dying mother not being able to see her son. Lori scans it now, picking out the thinly veiled threats his mother weaved through the interview that her son would never forgive those who put him away.

A noise disturbs her thoughts. What was that? It sounded like a faint banging noise. Her mind races. Has Frankie Evans found her already? Lori tells herself to get a grip. She's being stupid and paranoid. How could Frankie Evans possibly find her here? She knows it's one of the subconscious reasons she has chosen such secluded locations as she has moved from house to house these past seven years. She knows men like Frankie Evans have a network of people on the outside to carry out their dirty work, but she tells herself to toughen up. She is way stronger than this. The dogs would be going crazy if someone was here. She takes deep breaths, reminding herself of the promise she made years ago. She will not let that man play with her any more. But it's not that easy.

Lori clicks on Facebook. When she first started investigating him, Lori researched exhaustively, so she knows he was never one to engage in social media, but his wife Niamh was always on Facebook. Niamh was a fitness instructor and used her page to promote her business back then. Lori enters the name in the search bar. Many women called Niamh Evans appear, but it only takes Lori a short time to locate the page she is looking for. She remembers Niamh's photo of her and Frankie outside the nightclub where he worked as a bouncer before he was sent down. Lori browses Niamh's page. Frankie's release isn't mentioned. In fact, when Lori scrolls through the page, she can see Niamh has not posted anything personal for a few years. She uses the page solely to advertise her business.

Further down, Lori sees that Niamh moved to Tattenford, where her parents live, shortly after Frankie was put away. Progress posts back then show how they renovated some outbuildings on their land for their daughter and their grandson. Part of that conversion involved erecting a wooden structure for Niamh to run her personal training business from.

Lori sends the laptop to sleep. She has work to get on with. Especially since she's going away for the weekend to meet her agent and attend her friend Martha's fiftieth birthday celebration. Frankie Evans can't take up any more of her headspace. Despite her fall earlier, and the unsettling news, the stifling apathy that has plagued her in recent months has shifted. On the drive back from the café, an idea came to her. An encouraging feeling of inspiration she hasn't experienced for a while. It needs further exploration. And in Lori's world, when the bells of motivation toll, you prepare to focus and get your fingers typing.

It's airless in the cottage. She finally relents and opens

the top half of the stable door, the gentle cooling breeze a rapid welcome. She looks out into the darkness. A puff of cloud shrouds the full moon sitting atop the mountain. It's the only visible light down the lane where she lives. The seclusion of the place is palpable.

Over recent weeks, she has been trialling several writing spots in a desperate attempt to try to spark some inspiration. It's been warm enough for her to take her coffee, inspiration, and impetus to work at the small round metal table at the back of the house, beside the kitchen window, where she often drinks her morning coffee as she gazes at the idyllic backdrop of the mountains that dominate the skyline. In fact, she spends many an hour there. Sometimes trying to write, sometimes reading or mulling over ideas in the evening under the light of the old-fashioned lantern. But, no, not tonight. She feels the need for safety, to be locked indoors. And although she usually craves peace to write, she needs music.

She takes her coffee to the snug – a cosy room off the side of the lounge which she uses as her office. Although small, it's full of character with oak beams, a charming open hearth fireplace with a log burner and stone flooring. It's a little hideaway, housing her desk and a small sofa, and she adores working in there. Misty and Shadow obediently follow and take their spot on the large cushion beside her desk: an uncluttered workspace where most of her creativity occurs – when it occurs, that is. Switching on the adjustable desk light, she fires up her iMac and scrolls through her playlists on iTunes. Guns N' Roses. Perfect. Just what she needs to distract her mind. She clicks the play button and ramps up the volume until the rock beat fills the room.

She tidies her pen holder and checks her emails. Her usual procrastination rituals before she can find her way into the writing zone. A shuffling noise outside piques her attention. What was that? The dogs stir. She gets up and goes to the small window, cupping her hands around her eyes to look outside. It was probably just a fox.

She returns to her desk and reads her emails. There it is. She knew she would find it. The usual chaser email Hector always sends at this point in the process. His halfway check-in asking if everything is going to plan. She's up for delivering on the scheduled date – the first of October – isn't she? He's looking forward to discussing progress when they meet on Friday. If only he knew the evening she has just endured. He signs off by saying he looks forward to seeing her. It's been far too long.

Her current novel – her tenth – consists of a title and an unsatisfactory jumble of disjointed scenes. Wholly unsatisfactory and worrying. Not the almost-completed-but-rough first draft Hector expects at this stage. She doesn't yet have a half-decent synopsis either. But she has been struggling this year. The seventh anniversary, fast approaching, of when she last saw Howie has screwed with her mind and squeezed every drop of her creative juices dry. Seven years. How can it be? She stares at the screen, unaware she is singing along to the lyrics of her favourite Guns N' Roses song, 'Live and Let Die'.

If only she could.

5

———

Lori types a quick reply to Hector, remonstrating with him. Has she ever let him down? No. Every deadline he has imposed to date, she has met with a few days to spare, sometimes even a week. Even when it has meant completing final edits over forty-eight consecutive hours, breaking only to use the toilet, grab a quick bite, or make another cup of coffee. She signs off confirming their upcoming meeting and leaves it at that. She doesn't want to lie. Lori rarely lies.

She must start on something to give to Hector. Otherwise, what she said to Ray earlier will come true. She will need to find another agent. Hector has been supportive over the years, but Lori has seen him drop other authors who have failed to deliver. She can't afford to let that happen to her. Thankfully, her fingers weren't injured in the fall earlier. Banishing all thoughts of Frankie Evans – she can deal with those tomorrow – she opens a new Word document, which she saves as Another Book. She doesn't have a title yet. Not that she's worried. It will come at some point. Sometimes not until the eleventh hour, but it always does. It's not worth stressing over. Hector usually changes it anyway, as do the publishers.

The words come to her like ants to food, fast and furious, as she nurtures the seed planted earlier in her mind. *Finally*. Production at this level hasn't happened for weeks, months even. Her distracted mind, busy working the vivid prose that has built her a loyal fan base, absorbs the stinging pain from her hands and knees and the disturbing thoughts of Frankie Evans. When she glances at the bottom of the document, three hundred words have found their way from her mind and onto her new manuscript. She lets out a big sigh.

She can feel her characters' emotions and sympathise with their thoughts. They are evolving along with the plot she has in store for them. They may take a detour, but she's confident she'll be able to steer them back on track. The instinctive passion that tells her this idea will work thrills her like little else. She's on a roll of creativity. A comforting place where she can forget about her missing husband and Frankie Evans. After an hour, her word count totals seven hundred. That's more like it. She'll write a synopsis tomorrow. She allows herself a brief smile. This will keep Hector's fears at bay. Her own as well. Mercifully, she still has another book in her. The relief is immense.

Lori falls deeper into her trance-like state as she types fast, her fingers desperately trying to keep up with her creative mind. Her train of thought is running like a locomotive.

Until something in her peripheral vision tweaks her attention.

Misty and Shadow have awakened from a deep slumber and sit bolt upright. Their ears are pricked, and their heads slant from side to side, seemingly trying to absorb the disturbance their acute senses have felt. 'What's up with you two?' Lori lowers the volume of Guns N' Roses belting out their tunes. Shadow gives a gentle throaty rumble, only for Misty to copy her brother. They both give a cursory glance at their mistress before jerking their heads towards the threshold of the snug.

'Come on, you two. You're spooking me.' Despite the heat, a chill shoots down the length of Lori's spine. She settles the dogs and turns her attention back to the screen. But she's lost her thread. The dogs lift their heads. She follows their gaze, the low lighting throwing shadows through the opening to the lounge and up to the hallway. Suddenly, the two spaniels bolt in unison from their comfortable cushion in the direction of the front door. Lori gets up and darts after them. 'What the hell?!' she shouts to shut out the illogical feelings raking through her body.

Hurrying from the snug through the lounge to the narrow hallway leading to the front door, Lori catches up with Misty and Shadow. 'It's probably just a fox,' she calls out.

Who is she trying to kid?

Misty and Shadow are sniffing urgently around the base of the front door. The hallway lightbulb blew weeks ago, and Lori berates herself for neglecting to replace it. Apart from the landlord, postman, delivery people, or an occasional visit from April and Paul, no one comes here. She has never invited anyone. She always uses the back door as the main access to the cottage, so buying a new bulb has completely slipped down her list of priorities. Oh, how she wishes she had sourced that bulb now. She flicks a switch. The outside porch light offers a semblance of illumination, which only adds to the sinister feel of the atmosphere. The dogs' edginess increases, their growling morphing into outright barking. In the seven months she has lived here, she has never seen them act this way.

She attempts to calm them. 'What is it? What've you heard?' They are on their hind legs, scraping their paws on the wooden panels of the old door, and working themselves into a frenzy. 'Is anyone there?' she calls out. Not that anyone would be able to hear her. She stands on tiptoe to look through the pane of glass. She can't see anyone. Perhaps it *was* a fox. Or that puma-sized cat stalking the Welsh countryside that has been spotted several times. The one farmers report has been slaughtering their sheep.

She slowly raises her hand to the front door latch. She feels like she's in one of the horror films she and Howie ridiculed all those years ago, where the protagonist walks headlong into a terrifying situation putting their life in harm's way. Improbable, yes, impossible, of course, yet here she is about to open the door to an axe murderer. She laughs at herself. 'Just get back to your writing. Or go to bed!' she shouts aloud. But she knows she won't be able to sleep tonight in her current state unless she gets to the bottom of what has caused her beloved hounds to fret so much.

Slowly opening the door, she glances over the hedge into the darkness. But there's no one there. At least no one she can see. Stepping out onto the porch, she fully expects Misty and Shadow to bundle past her into the night in pursuit of the enemy. 'Hello, anyone there?' She looks down the unkepmt track that leads to the garage at the side of the house.

The dogs turn and beat a hasty retreat through the cottage towards the kitchen. Lori stands stock still. What has got into them? They are howling like wolves. Nervously, she closes the door and picks up the hiking pole she keeps in the umbrella stand in the corner. She bought it when she first moved to the cottage in the middle of nowhere in Cornwall. It's made from hazel wood with an oak top and has a metal end. Lori didn't buy it to take out walking, though. Her first thought when she saw it was that it was the next best thing to a baseball bat. She clenches the stick in her hand, ignoring the pain from her injuries. But she can't get a firm grip. The grease from the antiseptic cream causes it to slip. She wipes her hand on her pyjama top and grabs the stick further down its shaft. Wincing with the stinging pain from her cuts, she cautiously follows the dogs, sliding against the wall and peering around each nook and cranny for any intruder.

When she reaches the kitchen, the dogs are going crazy, barking at the open top half of the stable door. How could she have forgotten to close it when she went to her snug? She tells the dogs to calm, but they ignore her. She strains to see what has caused their ferocious outburst. The light is maddeningly and terrifyingly insufficient. But she knows her eyes are not fooling her this time. There is no mistaking it. A person, silhouetted against the backdrop of the moon, is standing outside her home.

6

Misty and Shadow's paws are scraping on the lower half of the stable door Lori locked earlier. No canine cowards, they bark aggressively at the would-be intruder. Fear twists Lori's stomach in knots. Thoughts return of the figure she believed she saw in her garden earlier when Ray dropped her home. She knew it wasn't her imagination. She did see someone. Visions of Frankie Evans flash through her mind. Has he found her? She grabs the wooden staff. With both hands, she takes aim to strike like a baseball player waiting for the pitcher to throw the ball. Nudging her shoulder against the switch to turn on the kitchen light, she stops.

'Lori, it's me,' a flat voice says.

The voice is familiar. But it doesn't register at first. Confusion blurs the limits of Lori's perception. She knows the voice, but the undertone disguises its owner. Where does she know it from? Lori squints, but the lighting is too low to see clearly. Cautiously, she steps closer until it finally registers. The person standing at the door shouldn't be here. Not at this time of night, unannounced. But there's no mistaking that it's her childhood friend, April, standing before her.

It's all wrong, though. Lori barely recognises her voice. That's what's confusing her. April is a person of sunny days and sandy beaches, bubble baths and freshly laundered sheets, flowers and picnics in the park. She is the person who possesses the ability to change Lori's mood within a minute of her company – the lightbulb in the dark. But the April at Lori's door is anything but. Her posture is drooped, and her shoulders slumped. Tears of mascara blacken her cheeks, and her cropped blonde hair is stuck to her forehead in strands.

Lori relaxes. But only partially. Something is troubling her about the menacing glare on her best friend's face. 'April, you scared the hell out of me.' The dogs' mood switches from guard dog to adorable pet at the excitement of smelling a familiar visitor. They leap up. Their paws land on April's thighs. 'Shadow, Misty, down.' Discarding her weapon against one of the pewter-grey coloured kitchen units, Lori unbolts the bottom half of the stable door, opening it wide to invite her friend in. 'Whatever are you doing here?'

April doesn't move. She stands rigid, a colourful designer handbag dangling from her bare arm. But her usually smiling features tell a different story from the one she usually portrays. This is a cross between disgust and sadness: a dystopian protagonist, unlike her usual look of a happy-go-lucky rom-com character. April doesn't even acknowledge the dogs. Her eyes are as dead as a corpse.

'Come on. Come in. What's happened?' Lori opens her arms to her friend, but still, April doesn't budge. She stands staring ahead as if in shock.

'I've left Paul,' April says, her voice monotone. She is clenching a bunch of the seersucker material of her pink gingham sundress. 'We're through.'

Lori's jaw opens. 'What?'

'You heard.'

'Don't be silly.'

Never did she expect to hear these words from her friend. April and Paul have been together forever. They are the perfect couple. They met in their late teens on a film set around the same time Lori met Howie at university. April was a trainee make-up artist. Paul was a runner. They immediately clicked and became inseparable like the Posh and Becks of the dating scene back then. Within a year, they were married. When Paul secured a directing role in a small film later the same year, April quit work, never to return. And during the following five consecutive years, they made four cute bundles of perfection. Lori and Howie are godparents to all of them. Lori panics. April and Paul can't split up. They are her foundation, the rock that has kept her sane these past seven years.

Lori steps forward and throws her arms around her friend. She notices the smell of alcohol on April's breath, and she didn't stop at one drink judging by the strong peaty smell of whisky. April doesn't reciprocate the embrace, standing as rigid as a statue as if the shock has filled her with cement and fixed her to the ground. 'Let's get you inside.' Lori slips the bag from her friend's arm and places it on the floor. 'And get you a drink.' Placing her hand on the small of April's back, Lori guides her towards the reclaimed wooden beams that create a partition between the kitchen and dining area.

Misty and Shadow follow them and spring onto the sofa. An old teal loveseat, it's the first item Lori and Howie bought when they purchased their first home. It's the only piece of furniture that Lori allows them on. Lori pulls out one of the chairs from the drop-leaf table for April to sit down. 'What happened?' Lori asks, frowning.

'Can you get me that drink?'

'What do you fancy? Coffee, tea, cocoa?'

April fingers the grout between the blue tiles of the tabletop. 'Make it something stronger.'

'Whisky? Gin?' Lori offers reluctantly. Actually, gin is not such a good idea. It can make April weep inconsolably. And if Lori isn't mistaken, April will be doing enough crying tonight. 'Or I've got some brandy,' Lori offers.

'Whisky,' April says, tapping her polished fingernails on the table. 'Make it a large one. On the rocks. You'd better have one as well.' If April wasn't Lori's bestie, Lori would swear there was malice, hatred even, in her friend's tone.

'You want something to eat?' Lori asks. 'I could make you a sandwich.'

April shakes her head. She looks so sad, yet so angry. 'Just get the drink.'

'I'll be right back.' Lori runs to her computer to pause

Guns N' Roses, ignoring the stinging pain jabbing her knees from her speedy movements.

Lori fetches two glasses of whisky. A small one for her, and a slightly larger one for April. She would still like to work more tonight. When an idea strikes, she needs to keep the flame burning. That's how she has always rolled. And with Hector's deadline only weeks away, she needs to keep the momentum going. Besides, she's never found alcohol and painkillers a good match. Judging by April's state, though, Lori knows she'll have to put her writing ambitions aside for the evening. Her friend needs her more.

Lori places the glasses on the table with a bowl of nuts. April probably hasn't eaten tonight, and, given the way she is acting and what she has just relayed, Lori wants to provide as much support as she can. 'How did you get here?' she asks.

'I drove,' April mumbles.

Surely she has not been driving under the influence? It has always been one of April's absolute no-nos, and Lori's. Yet here her friend is, obviously the worse for wear. Lori decides April will not be getting in her car again tonight. 'You didn't come here earlier, and I wasn't in, did you?' Lori asks.

April swirls the amber liquid around the glass. The ice clinks against the edge. She shakes her head. 'What do you mean?'

'It doesn't matter. What's gone on with Paul?'

Lori takes a sip of the whisky. It burns the back of her

throat, sending her taste buds reeling. She has forgotten how much she likes the sensation.

Still not looking at Lori, April says, 'I found out he cheated on me.'

'No way.' The revelation shocks Lori. Paul is as much in love with April as Howie was with her. 'I'm so sorry.'

'I bet you are.'

What's that meant to mean?

April lifts her glass to her trembling lips and downs her drink in one grimacing gulp. She pushes her glass across the table like a bartender slides drinks down a bar. 'I'll have another one of those.'

Lori hesitates. This is not the April she knows. April likes a drink, yes. They have spent many drunken nights together. But not like this. But then again, discovering your perfect husband of twenty-odd years has cheated on you is enough to drive anyone to the bottle. 'You sure that's a good idea?'

'Just get me the bloody drink.'

Further stunned by her friend's behaviour, Lori goes to fetch the bottle of whisky as ordered. Then, she thinks again. It's best she doesn't take the bottle to the table. The mood April's in, she may well ditch her glass and swig the whisky neat. Lori refills another glass with ice and a centimetre of whisky and returns to her friend. 'When did you find this out?'

'Today.'

'I don't know what to say.'

April traces her finger around the top of the glass. Eventually, after an uncomfortably long pause, April fills the void in the conversation. 'Why did you do it? What did I do wrong? Was I not good enough?'

Lori frowns. 'I'm not following you.' The drink has got to April. She's not making sense. 'Who did he cheat on you with?'

'What do you mean, who with?'

'Who did he cheat on you with?' Lori repeats, in as comforting a voice as possible, acutely aware of her friend's fragile state.

April's eyes lock onto Lori's for the first time since arriving. They are full of loathing, as if she is staring at the devil. 'You know who.'

Lori's shoulders press against the back of the chair. 'I'm sorry. You're not making sense, April. I don't get what you're trying to say.'

'Don't play the innocent with me, Lori *perfect little* Mortimer.' April spits. 'Acting all righteous.'

Lori doesn't like where this is going. Her friend is acting so out of character it's like another person is sitting opposite her. 'April, what *are* you talking about?'

April growls like one of the spaniels. 'Do I have to spell it out? I know it was you. You slept with my husband.'

7

April's accusation is like a sharp slap across the face. Lori clenches her hands, stunned. Is April referring to the night Lori thinks she is? No, please. The worst mistake of her life for which she has never forgiven herself. It meant nothing. It was a drunken fumble. She can't even remember how it came about. When she woke up the following morning, she had thought she was in a dream. The morning-after humiliation is still so vivid in her mind, it could have happened only yesterday, not over twenty years ago. The walk of shame from his bed and back home was like hiking up Everest wearing ankle weights. She had never felt so ill in her life. She has tried to block the whole experience from her mind. Yes, she had just lost her mother, only months after losing her father. But still. What she did was wrong in every way imaginable, an outright violation of all her moral codes.

'Discovering your husband has lied to you is one thing.

Finding out his betrayal involved sex... well, multiply that by a million. Add your best friend into the equation, and...' April knocks back her drink. 'It's off the scale.' She thrusts her empty glass across the table. It smashes into Lori's glass. 'I think I need another of those, don't you?'

The dogs sit up. Misty whines, sensing her mistress's upset. 'April, it meant nothing.' Even after all these years, Lori still can't find words to explain what happened. 'You weren't even together at the time.' This is the truth. April and Paul had been apart for some weeks. April's decision, not his. He was gutted. He'd asked her to marry him. She got the jitters. They had only been together a few months. They were so young; shouldn't they be travelling the world and trying new adventures? Meeting different people? What if he wasn't the one? April had only dated one other guy, who she had never slept with. Lori heard it all. Night after night, they spoke on the phone – sometimes for hours. One-way repetitive conversations that Lori grew tired of after three weeks. April ended up telling Paul she needed a break. Not that it lasted long. Within a month, they were back together. 'Honestly, it meant nothing at all.'

'Nothing at all!' April screams, then quietly says, 'Funny, that's exactly what Paul said.' She mimics her husband's low voice. '"It was a stupid mistake, darling. I can't even remember how it happened."' She jabs her forefinger at Lori, stammering and mumbling. 'So, I want you to tell me, *best friend*. How did it happen?'

'No, April, please.'

'Go on, give me all the s-s-sordid details, you traitor!'

Lori drops her elbows on the table and slams her head into her hands, forgetting her abrasions. It hurts, but it's nothing less than she deserves. She exhales a deep breath as she slides her fingers down her face. 'I wish I could tell you.' She shakes her sorry head. 'But the truth is, I don't know how it happened. I came home from uni that summer to pack my parents' house up, but I couldn't face it. The first evening back, I went to the pub to meet the old crowd. Paul was there, but you were working on that set in Cumbria. Everyone got crazy drunk. Like we did in those days.' Lori's shoulders hunch in shame. Sweating and nauseous, humiliation shoots through her. 'The next thing I knew, I woke up next to him.'

'Say it. Go on, say the words. *I woke up in your husband's bed.*'

Lori looks to the ceiling, biting her lip. She closes her eyes.

'Say it.'

Lori opens her eyes and stares at her friend. She doesn't know what to say to have a chance of salvaging this situation. 'But he wasn't your husband then, or even your boyfriend. You weren't together at the time. But that's no excuse, I know.'

'How many times did it happen?'

Lori smacks the table, recoiling with the pain. 'April, you must believe me. It was only once. I promise you.'

'*Only* once. That's OK, then?' April runs her hands through her hair, releasing the strands of blonde stuck to her forehead.

'No, it isn't. It was one time too many.' It's Lori's turn to stare into her glass. Perhaps she will have a refill after all.

'How can I believe a word you say?'

'Because I'm telling you the truth.'

'Why did you lie to me all these years?'

'I never lied to you.'

April scoffs. 'Paul's exact words. You just never told me you fucked my husband.' She gets up, snatches her glass from Lori's hand and goes to the kitchen, mumbling something about never being able to trust anyone ever again. Lori hears liquid splashing into a glass and slurping as April guzzles another drink. Lori's head drops to her chest.

She wants this night to end.

Now.

Misty whines. Reaching over to her dogs sitting upright on the loveseat, she strokes their fur to reassure them. Shadow places his head on Misty's back.

More liquid sloshes into a glass. April returns to the dining area, bangs her drink on the table and slumps into the chair.

'Why did he tell you?' Lori asks.

'He didn't.'

'How do you know then?'

'I got a letter through the post telling me to ask you both about what went on between you.'

Lori frowns. Who would do such a thing? Who could do such a thing? No one else knows. Unless Paul told someone. But she knows he'd never admit to that. 'Who-ever from?'

April shrugs. 'They didn't sign it. When I showed it to Paul, he broke down and confessed.'

The fresh injection of whisky is taking hold. April's eyelids are heavy, her words even more slurred. How much did she have before she got here?

'I always wondered why I never saw you that summer. You didn't even wait a day until I returned from Cumbria to see me. Now I know why. I thought that odd at the time. I hadn't seen you for weeks. But it's all making sense.' She lifts her glass but misses her mouth. A driblet of whisky sullies the front of her dress. 'Who would've thought, hey? The two people I loved and trusted the most in my life have destroyed everything I ever believed in.'

The tears start. They come in waves, splashing down April's face in torrid outbursts. She drops her head in her hands. Her whole body is shuddering. Lori lets her be. It's got to be for the best. Let her cry herself dry. April peers sideways at Lori. 'You've made a fool out of me. And you've destroyed my marriage. I'll never forgive you.'

Lori shuffles her chair up against her friend's and grabs her wrists, wincing with pain as she shakes them. 'April, listen to me. You can't let one stupid mistake ruin what you and Paul have. He adores you – totally adores you. You've got four wonderful kids together. You've always been happy. Don't let one drunken moment that happened years ago ruin all that. We were young! Just kids! Your marriage is as solid as a rock. You can get through this. We can get through this. Come on, let's get to bed. We can talk more in the morning. Everything is better after a good night's sleep.'

April pulls her wrists from Lori's grip. She cackles like a witch. Such a contrast to the ladylike April. It's the whisky. It's sucked up all her gracefulness and replaced it with a drunken inelegance. April would be horrified to see herself like this. 'You think I'm spending the night under the same roof as you? Never again will that happen.'

8

April hauls herself up and sways towards the kitchen, pausing to steady her step on the wooden beam. 'Where are you going?' Lori asks. April ignores the question and continues staggering. Lori follows her, leaning against the kitchen and dining area partitioning as her friend opens the stable door. Lori rushes over to her. She has to stop her. 'April, it's dark out there. You don't know the roads. You'll hurt yourself.' She repeats, 'Where are you going?'

Tripping over her drunken words, April expels expletives as she aggressively jabs a finger at Lori. Her nail digs into Lori's chest. It damn well hurts. Lori can smell her friend's pungent breath, even though they have drunk the same spirit. 'Tell me, Lori, how many lives have you ruined? Precious, righteous, no-nonsense Lori Mortimer?'

April isn't being fair. During her career as an investigative journalist, Lori may have ruined lives. But they were lives that deserved to be ruined. The many drug and people traffickers spring to mind. As do the child abusers.

'Always out to get the bad guys. Look at you. You even manage to screw up those who love you.' She scoffs and delivers her parting words. 'Never thought I was on the list of your fuck-ups, though. How incredibly naive of me.' April grabs the snakeskin strap of her handbag, slings it over her shoulder, and exits the stable door.

Her words sting. Partly because of the venom with which they were delivered. But mostly because they are untrue. Lori hates injustice of any type. Always has. It's partly what led her into a career in journalism, where she went above and beyond to seek out the bad guys.

Lori locates her battered garden shoes and goes in pursuit of her friend. Her queasiness has subsided, but her pestering aches and pains remind her of her injuries. 'April, it's late. Don't tell me you intend to drive. Please stay here.'

April lifts a hand in dismissal as she wobbles along the path. 'You've crossed the wrong person this time, Lori Mortimer.'

Lori returns to the cottage, races upstairs and throws on some clothes. She grabs the dogs' leads and beckons Misty and Shadow. She isn't about to go out into the dark night without her loyal companions, especially having been spooked already this evening. She wants to know where April is heading, and, more importantly, that her friend isn't going to be stupid enough to get back in her car. If something happened to her, Lori would never forgive herself.

The moonlight helps the two women to navigate the uneven lane, traversing the potholes, and stumbling over the mounds tyre tracks have formed during the years of inclement weather. The pain in Lori's knee hinders her attempt to keep up with her friend, along with the dogs regularly stopping to pee, leaving their scent. It makes progress difficult. The direness of the situation doesn't make the scene any less creepy. Shadows are cast by the moonlight. The hedgerow rustles with wildlife. An owl hoots in the distance. Though relatively close to the village, the remoteness is stark.

Ignoring the throbbing in her knee, Lori picks up her pace and manages to catch up with April. They have left the lane and are now walking along the single-track road, where visitors to the nature reserve and falls park. Darkness still shrouds them, save a single ineffectual streetlight some distance off. 'Answer me, April. Where are you staying tonight?' But either her friend can't hear her or she is ignoring her, because she continues towards the village.

Lori lets April be, but remains several steps behind her, wondering where she is going. Does she know someone else around here? It's possible. She only lives a forty-minute drive away, but Lori can't recall her mentioning anyone. At the entrance to the village, April answers Lori's question as she turns into the lodge to the side of a small garage, which has rooms to rent in chalet-type units. April lurches towards her black VW Golf. Only one of two cars parked there. She opens her bag and removes a set of keys.

'Oh no you don't,' Lori says, steering her away from the car, assuming her friend's intention is to get behind the wheel.

April shrugs Lori off. 'Leave me alone. I need to get my

44

stuff.' It's a feeble attempt, and Lori has to help her locate a small holdall from the footwell behind the driver's seat. A security light clicks into action as April stumbles towards a picnic bench in front of the chalet and plonks herself down. Lori straddles the seat opposite and sits on the dogs' leads to stop them roaming off. She strokes their heads. They sense all is not well and sit obediently by her side.

April looks ghostly and, usually, Lori would tell her so – that's the kind of friendship they share – but tonight, she curbs her usual truthfulness and says, 'Don't throw away what you have. It's history. It happened so long ago. Paul adores you. You know he does. And you weren't even together at the time,' she repeats.

April unclasps her handbag and removes a packet of cigarettes and a lighter. She lights up and sucks her first puff as if trying to make a point. Lori inwardly sighs. She hates to see April with a cigarette, and April knows this. They both used to smoke heavily but gave up at the same time. One of the many things they have done together over the years. It was when Lori found out she was pregnant with Molly. A month later, April found out she was pregnant with her and Paul's second son, Nathan. He entered the world early, so Molly and Nathan were born only two weeks apart and virtually grew up together. It was only when Howie disappeared that they seemed to drift apart. Molly lost her way in so many ways. It hurt Lori deeply to see them lose touch. Lori tried everything to keep their friendship alive, but the only ball Molly was playing was bouncing between relationships with people Lori definitely wouldn't class as true friends.

'Frankie Evans has been released from prison.' Lori doesn't know why she blurts this out. Perhaps it's because she hopes it will evoke some sympathy.

April's gasp of surprise echoes around them. 'You're kidding me.' She takes another puff of her cigarette. 'When?'

'Six days ago. I only found out tonight.'

'How?'

'I saw it on the news.'

'How the fuck did that happen?'

Lori is taken aback. April rarely swears. 'A technicality.'

'That's the most bonkers thing I've ever heard,' April scoffs. 'Well, it would've been before today. Finding out my husband slept with my best friend kinda tops it.'

Lori ignores her friend's sarcasm. 'I know. I'm still trying to process it.'

They sit in silence while April puffs away on her cigarette. Halfway through, she drops it onto the gravel and extinguishes it with the sole of her sandal. Grabbing her bunch of keys from the table, she stands and heads towards the end chalet. Lori follows her. The keys clink as April attempts to insert one of them into the lock. She must have checked in earlier. Her hand slips and she misses. She tries again but her legs give way and she falls against the door. Lori prises the keys from her friend's fingers and opens up for her.

The room is small but pleasant and comfortable, with an archway leading to a small ensuite. Lori guides April to one of two single beds, where her friend drops onto the mattress. Lori perches on the edge of the other bed. 'I'm so sorry this has all come out. If I could turn back the clock, believe me, I would.'

'I always said you needed to be careful who you upset, what enemies you make,' April says. A series of hiccups interrupt her words. Lori feels as if another person is sitting opposite her. Someone she has never met before. April continues. 'One day, it'll all catch up with you. But you never listened to me. No! When has my opinion ever counted? All I ever got was your flippant response. What was it? "I'm on the side of good. Goodness will prevail".'

In the thirty or so years they have been best friends, Lori has never seen April like this.

Hell hath no fury like a woman scorned.

'Well, let me tell you. Revenge, Lori Mortimer. Revenge is sweet.'

9

Given what she has been through the past seven years, it takes a lot to make Lori cry. This comes close. Her eyes are burning, and she stifles several sharp intakes of breath to prevent herself from breaking down. She has always cherished her relationship with April. Through the years, as their husbands chased their dreams and built their production company, April and Lori have remained firm friends, as close as sisters. They've shared the highs and lows of living through their twenties, thirties and half of their forties and always laughed at how they imagined themselves in their seventies, sipping prosecco in floral bikinis on the beaches of the South of France and not giving a damn.

Years of shame and regret knot in Lori's stomach as she traipses home, as do thoughts of Frankie Evans. Misty and Shadow sense something is up. They know her so well. They follow her like her silhouette in the moonlight; their heads hung low. She ups her tempo, eager to get home and down that glass of whisky. The night she's had, she needs it. Nearing the bottom of the lane leading to her cottage, she hears a car approaching. Strange. No one ever ventures down here at this time of night. In fact, no one comes down here much at all. They won't see her in the dark. Spooked, she pulls the dogs away from the road and onto the side of the footpath, wincing from the pain as Misty's lead scrapes across her knee. The painkillers she took earlier are wearing off. If she's not mistaken, the distinct sound of the chugging engine tells her it's Ray's Defender. It must be getting on for eleven o'clock. The passing car tells her she is right. Oblivious of her presence, he turns into the lane leading to her house. What's he doing turning up at this time of night?

She hurries as best she can up the lane, which is treacherous in the dark with the crevices and potholes. When she reaches her cottage, Ray's car is parked outside. But there is no sign of him. Yanking on their leads, Misty and Shadow sense her trepidation. Her fingers aren't strong enough to restrain them. They free themselves from her hold and bolt to the back of the house, barking loudly.

Lori rushes after them to find Ray at the stable door, bending over, stroking their heads as he peers towards the end of her garden and the small, hexagonal-shaped room she calls her writing den about fifty metres away. She likes to work down there sometimes. Masked by a row of hawthorn bushes, the den is hidden away and would be hard to find unless you knew it was there. Just the way Lori likes it.

'Hey, you scared me. What're you doing here?' Lori asks.

Ray straightens up. 'Sorry, I was just on my way home and wasn't sure you'd be up for a walk in the morning.' He picks up a carton of milk from the ground and waves it in Lori's direction. 'So I thought I'd drop this off for you.'

'You're out late.'

'So are you!' Ray rolls his big brown eyes that are edged with wrinkles.

Or smile lines, as Howie used to call them. "Smile lines make people more sincere", she remembers him once telling her. "Bet you didn't know that?"

Ray laughs at himself. 'Stupid me for having a second coffee while I was putting all the shopping away. I was wide awake. So I ended up prepping for the morning.' He hands her the milk and digs his hand into his back pocket. She reaches out to take the carton of milk from him, circling her forefinger around the handle. 'Don't mind, do you?' he asks, producing two dog treats. Misty and Shadow are wagging their tails like there's no tomorrow. Lori shakes her head, squatting to remove their leads. Ray drops a gravy bone into each of Misty and Shadow's gaping mouths. 'There we go. Couldn't leave you two out, could I?' He strokes their heads as they chomp on their treats.

She should ask him in, but she's exhausted after the night she's had. She was just on her way to bed, she could say. But that sounds so lame, given she has been out.

'Thanks for the milk. That was kind of you.'

'How're your hands?'

'I'll live.'

He reaches down and grabs another package, handing her a small plastic box with two chocolate croissants inside. 'In case you can't get out in the morning. I know how much you love these.'

She hesitates before securing the milk under her arm and taking the box. Now she feels obliged to invite him in. Awkwardness clogs the air as much as the heavy heat. Lori holds the plastic box close to her chest as if trying to protect herself from the threat of the second person of the evening entering her space. The kindness police are poking her in the back. Ray has shown her nothing but friendliness and generosity since she first ventured into his café as the snowdrops arrived. And he couldn't have been more hospitable. He is always inviting her into the café to sample his latest coffee creation. He's one of the good guys. Or so she thinks. One thing she learnt from her days of reporting and journalism: not everyone is who they seem.

His tall, broad frame towers over her five-foot-four figure. He jangles his car keys. 'I'll be seeing you, then. Look after those wounds.' Is that disappointment she can see in his lowered eyebrows and the slight downward turn of his mouth?

She can't stand it. Her mouth spills the words before her head can stop them. 'Would you like to come in?' Her voice croaks with apprehension. 'My coffee-making skills are nowhere near your standards, but I make a mean cocoa if you fancy a cup.'

He smiles. 'Sounds good.' He's a very attractive man in a weathered kind of way. Mid-fifties, he's ten years older than Lori, who should be celebrating her forty-fifth birthday in December. April has been on at her to organise something because April is a party girl at heart; any opportunity for a celebration, she is the one who shows up with the balloons and party poppers. And April has never let her forget that Lori never had a party for her fortieth. Many emails from April crowd Lori's inbox asking if she has thought about what she wants to do. Does Lori want to come to Chester and stay? April would love to plan a party for her. She'd put a marquee up in the garden. The old gang would love to see her. Paul has agreed to help. Or they could always come to Wales if Lori prefers. Or how about they meet up in a fancy restaurant? But any enthusiasm Lori tries to muster is trapped in the forthcoming seventh anniversary of her husband's disappearance, and she has yet to reply to any of April's messages.

She unlocks the door and holds it open for him. He cautiously enters, nodding at his feet. 'Want me to take my boots off?'

'You're OK.'

They stand on the doormat like a couple of embarrassed teenagers. They both go to speak at once, and laugh. 'You first,' she says.

'No you, please.'

'Let me put some milk on.'

He places a hand on her shoulder. She glances at his touch and shudders. 'You're injured. I can do it,' he says, his tone as gentle as his breath on her face.

Lori pulls away from his touch. 'Don't be so silly. I've got a few cuts and scratches, that's all. I haven't lost a hand.

Besides, how many hundreds of cups of coffee have you made me since I moved here?' She takes a small saucepan from the hook above the stove and pours some milk inside to heat up.

'Fancy another walk this evening, did you?' he asks, smiling down at Misty and Shadow, who are loitering by his feet in the hope of a further show of his generosity.

'Don't ask. I had an unexpected visitor. She's staying at the B&B, so the dogs and I walked her back.' She places the whisky tumblers in the sink and remarks on the weather to cut the conversation dead. She doesn't want to talk about April.

He looks around. 'I didn't know this house was so nice inside, now. I came here when I first opened the café. An older woman used to live here, and I delivered her meals when she had a hip replacement. Old Parsons must've redecorated before you moved in.' He runs his hand along the worktop. 'And put in some new units.'

Silence descends as Lori makes their drinks. She knows he is looking at the vast array of framed photos that adorn most of the walls – photos of Howie and Molly, some alone and some of them together. Some have Lori in them. But mostly, they are of Howie. Ray wants to ask her questions, she can tell. It's the way he bites his lower lip. Just like everyone she hasn't seen for a while over the past seven years. Her special shot catches his eye. The one of her and Howie on Padstow beach, the year he was last with them. She had it enlarged to A3-size and it takes pride of place, dominating the wall leading from the kitchen into the dining area, so it's hard to miss. It was late winter, the

February half-term, and Howie had made them take their shoes and socks off and paddle in the Atlantic. It was bitterly cold, but they didn't care. The contentment radiating from their smiling faces and effortless laughter is proof of that. Ray's eyes are transfixed. He can't help himself. She knows because she often is as well when she looks at that photo.

'Here we go.' Lori hands him a cup of cocoa. She has not made it as hot as she likes. She needs to be alone.

He sips his drink, nodding towards the gallery of pictures. 'Very nice.' He takes another sip, pointing at the area above the sink. 'You've got some beautiful photos here.'

'That's my husband, Howie, and my daughter, Molly,' she says, unusually feeling the need to explain.

'Can I ask where they are?'

'Molly lives in Birmingham. And I haven't seen Howie for almost seven years.'

'Oh,' he says. It's the phrase she often hears on the rare occasions she imparts this information.

'He went to work one day and never came home.' Her voice trembles. 'And I haven't seen him since.'

10

'He just disappeared.' It's more of a statement than a question, but there's no doubt Ray wants confirmation of his assumption.

Lori clicks her fingers. 'Just like that.' The snapping sound reverberates in the quietness.

'Wow. I'm sorry. That must've been difficult for you and your daughter,' Ray says.

She nods. He wants more, she can tell, but he's too polite to ask. 'He was caught on CCTV at a petrol station before he drove to work. I saw the footage. He was acting normal. He filled the car up with diesel. Paid by credit card. All as he usually would. And that's it. There were a couple of sightings of him on roadside cameras going to the studios, but after work, nothing.'

'That's tough. I'm so sorry.'

'No one – his work, friends, family – can come up with any reason why he would've just left like that. Or where he might have gone.'

'You must all be so devastated.'

'His parents are dead, but he has a sister, Barbara. Since they were kids, they've always been as thick as thieves. If there was anyone he was going to spill his troubles to – apart from me, I like to hope – it was her. But she met him for lunch a few weeks before, and she said there was nothing out of the ordinary about his behaviour.' Lori takes a sip of her drink. 'And, before you ask, we were very happy.'

Ray's eyes scan the room. 'I don't doubt that.'

Misty appears at Lori's feet and lies down. As if she can sense her mistress needs her support. 'The police didn't take it seriously at first. That's how I felt, anyway. He wasn't high risk, they said. Nearly two hundred thousand people are reported missing in the UK every year. Can you believe that?'

'I've heard similar statistics.'

'Most people turn up within twenty-four hours or are found within a few days or weeks, so they don't start looking straight away unless the person is vulnerable. You know, disabled people, or those with a history of mental illness. And, of course, minors.' Lori exhales a long breath. 'I've gone over every possibility, but nothing adds up. Everyone says the same. We'd just planned a holiday of a lifetime. A two-week trip to Dubai and Mauritius with our friends and their kids. It never went ahead.'

'What did he do for a job?'

'He ran a video and film production company, mostly corporate work, with Paul, who is my best friend April's husband. He has no explanation either. Nothing.'

'I don't know what to say.'

'Paul's been a pillar of support, despite how badly it's affected him. Howie and he met with a new client that day and were positive they were going to sign with them. Which they did end up doing. They were planning a meal out with April and me that weekend. The three of us have done everything to try to find out what happened to him. A few months after he disappeared, when we felt the police case started to go cold, Paul hired a private detective. The guy is still looking for him. Not that we've had any updates for ages. Nothing transpired, apart from a few snippets of CCTV and the few sightings that led nowhere. They turned out not to be Howie. That's what we had to go on in the beginning. And that's all we have to go on now.'

Lori shakes her head. 'The thing is, people don't just vanish into thin air. Everybody knows that. I ask myself every day, when will it all end? The uncertainty is torture. All I know is, as hard as it is, I have to keep the hope alive.'

'Crikey, Lori. What a nightmare to live through.'

'It's coming up for seven years next month.'

Seven years since Lori was plunged into a storm in the middle of the ocean she has had to learn to survive. Every day is a challenge. Some more so than others. Some days the waves are fierce and overpowering, and she knows she just has to ride them. On other days, they are not as harsh but engulf her broken heart nonetheless.

They stand against the work surface, drinking their cocoa. She should invite him into the dining area to sit down, but if the kitchen is a testament to her missing husband, then the dining area is a shrine.

'At first, we thought he'd been in an accident. April and Paul helped me scour all the local hospitals. Paul drove us around them all.' She shakes her head, her lips twisted. 'I remember it so vividly. The three of us were trying to act composed for each other, but there was no mistaking the desperation we all felt. When it was evident that he wasn't in any of the hospitals, Paul said to let the police do their work.'

'And the police got nowhere?'

'Don't get me wrong. They did what they could. They eventually carried out a widespread search. They say it's still going on, but,' Lori shrugs, 'I guess there's only so many times you can go through CCTV and follow up on dwindling leads. The media got their teeth into it for a while. I pulled some strings and called in some favours, and it got bigger coverage than a lot of missing persons cases. I mean, as I said, lots of people go missing every day. Most cases don't make it to the media.'

'You know what, I think I vaguely remember it now,' says Ray.

'There were three reports of sightings of him with another woman in London. I didn't know what was worse. Potentially finding out that it was actually him, or finding out it was just another false alarm like the other erroneous "sightings" of him that nothing came of.'

'I guess it wasn't him then.'

She shakes her head. 'They interviewed everyone Howie had been in contact with. Family and friends, everyone he worked with. Inside and outside the company – he was popular. But everyone said the same thing. He was a happy man; a regular guy going about his business. The police concluded there was nothing wrong with his state of mind. From the outset they worked on the hypothesis that he went abroad, even though his passport was at home. It's not easy, but it's not impossible to get a fake passport, apparently.'

'Easier than it should be, so I've heard.'

'They thought it could be amnesia but soon ruled that out. He would've been seen. His car would've been found. Foul play was considered for a while, but there was nothing to back that up. They had nothing to go on. Not a single person witnessed anything untoward. Even the petrol station attendant said Howie seemed happy. He remembered him because Howie commented on the weather and wished him a happy day, and no one does that any more, he said. It's a case that has baffled the police and everyone who knows him. Howie Mortimer simply vanished into thin air.'

11

_____

Ray shakes his head. 'It seems unbelievable that someone can disappear like that with so many surveillance cameras about these days. I don't know what to say.'

'There's nothing you can say. Every morning when I wake up, it's the first thought I have. Is this the day I'm going to find out what happened to him? Is he living on a beach somewhere in Thailand, working in a bar, remarried with children? Or is he, as many people speculate...' Her voice falters. 'Is he dead?'

'It must be so tough.'

'Sometimes, I don't know which would be worse. That he is out there somewhere living his best life with someone else, or that he's dead. If I'm honest, I fear the latter. He just wasn't the type of guy to go off with someone else.' Lori sighs heavily. 'And he would never have left Molly.'

'You've been through hell.'

Lori raises her eyebrows. 'I've tried to live with it. What choice do I have? I'm not a quitter.'

She never gives up. Never. She's not that kind of person. Inexplicably her mind wanders. "Don't be so stupid. You're one of the most strong-minded people I've ever met," she recalls Howie telling her all those years ago when she was going for her dream journalist job for one of the big tabloids and having doubts about whether she was good enough. They had stopped outside the newspaper's plush headquarters. "There are no flies on you, my darling." He kissed the top of her nose. "They won't even bother to interview anyone else once they've met my wife," he said with the confidence of a tiger and pushed her towards the entrance. "I'll be waiting for you in that wine bar on the corner." An hour or so later, she met him with a smile so big, Howie immediately nodded towards the barman who appeared with two glasses of champagne. "Cheers to my extraordinarily clever wife," Howie said, raising his glass. "I knew you'd nail it."

'I refuse to believe he's dead. But then, on the other hand, I can't believe he can be on that beach living another life with someone else.'

'How has Molly coped?'

'She hasn't. She was a daddy's girl. She rebelled big time and has spent the last seven years falling in with the wrong crowds. The poor girl, or woman I should say. She's twenty-three now. It's been heart-wrenching to watch.' Lori puts her cup on the side and holds her hands in the air, her fingers crossed. 'But she seems to be getting herself together, and I'm hoping she's over the worst.'

'I guess it's hard to move on with your life.'

Lori nods. 'Closure, that's all I want. I've been living in limbo for the past seven years. One way or another, I want a body, dead or alive.'

'Do you believe he'll be found?' Ray asks.

'It's a crucial time coming up. When someone has been missing for seven years, you can make a declaration claim for presumed death.'

'I didn't know that.'

'It's not a piece of information many people need to know. There's a process to go through with the courts.' Lori swallows hard. 'But I can't give up on him.'

'I can understand that.'

'Some people are saying I should. You know, prepare to go through the process, but it's not quite that simple. I...' She shrugs, unable to bring herself to tell him the real reason.

That it would mean they could invoke Howie's will, which would see Molly come into a sum of money that Howie left for her. Money Lori doesn't want her daughter to have because her father's disappearance turned her from the sweetest child into a drug addict. And trying to help her only pushed her further away.

'I overheard you say you were married once, but I've never liked to pry,' Lori says, to shift the focus away from her. Despite the numerous cups of coffee they've shared over recent months in Ray's café, neither of them have discussed their private lives. It's as if they have both sensed it was a subject off limits.

'My wife died twelve years ago, two days before her fortieth birthday.'

'Goodness, I'm sorry. What happened?'

'Food poisoning, would you believe.'

'I didn't think people died from food poisoning these days.'

'It's rare, but it does happen. She developed complications.'

'What did she eat?'

He scrunches his eyes up as he answers her question. 'A seafood risotto she had in a restaurant. She developed an infection. Which in itself she could've coped with, but it led to a condition called Guillain-Barré syndrome.'

'I've not heard of it.'

'Not many people have. In simple terms, it's an autoimmune disease, where the immune system attacks the body's nervous system. It's a rare disease to catch, especially at her age. And even rarer to die from it. She was just incredibly unlucky.'

'She was so young.'

Ray nods. 'We were living in London at the time. After I lost her, I couldn't stay in the house. So I sold up, handed in my notice, and moved up here. I've been here nearly ten years now.'

'I know what you mean. Too many memories. Howie and I have a house in Chester. I couldn't bear to stay there, either. It was so tough on Molly. Shortly after Howie went, I rented it out and have moved around the country ever since.'

'You still speak of him in the present tense.'

'I have to believe he's still alive. If I give up on him, what hope does he have of ever being found? My friends, Paul and April, are the same. They refuse to give up on him. I was an investigative journalist before he disappeared.'

'You never told me that.'

'What did you do before you moved here?'

'I was a finance manager for a shipping company. So, what was your biggest story as a journalist?'

'I was in Lebanon for a while. And then, probably, it was Betty Tailor's murder. It was on the news for days.'

'The writer?'

'That's right. I was the one who helped nail the bastard who did that to her. A guy called Frankie Evans. Shortly before he was arrested, I met with him. He told me he knew what had happened to Howie. Something he later denied saying. I reckon he was toying with me. Tonight, I found out he has been released from prison. He is that guy we saw on the TV in the café.'

'The guy looking for revenge?'

'That's him.'

'How come he has been released?'

'A technicality. I've wondered all this time if he does know what happened.' The grandfather clock in the corner of the dining area, that belongs to the landlord, strikes the hour. A signal for Lori to change the subject. She has revealed enough of herself for one night. 'So you never had children?'

He looks down at his brown, worn, walking boots. 'We'd been trying for years, with no success – been through all the checks – doctors prodding and poking, but they found nothing wrong. It was exhausting, to be honest. She became obsessed with it all, understandably. They put it down to the stress of her job. We even got third opinions, but they all said the same. Her job was stopping her chances of falling pregnant. She was an anaesthetist, worked stupid hours. So, she quit. She was seven weeks pregnant when she died. She never knew. Otherwise we'd never have chosen to eat seafood.'

'I'm so sorry, Ray.'

There's no mistaking the pain still lurking inside him. It's in his furrowed brows, and in his lined face. 'The worst thing is, she didn't want to go out that night. A new restaurant had opened up nearby, and being a bit of a foodie, I was eager to go. She loved fish, so I'd made us a reservation for her birthday. But when it came to going, she said she was tired. Little did we know she was pregnant. I persuaded her to go. It was her birthday, after all. I said we'd skip starters and come home for pudding. She agreed. I should've just cancelled the booking. Then she would still be with me now, and I'd have a daughter.'

'You've really been through the mill as well.'

'We both have. But you know how it is. You have to learn to live with what you've got.' He looks up to the ceiling. His Adam's apple bobs up and down. 'She's somewhere waiting on the other side. I'll see her again one day.' His gaze falls to Lori. He gives a tight-lipped smile. 'Nothing in life is guaranteed. Not even the next breath. We need to be grateful for what we've got, I guess.'

'That's a very positive way to look at life.'

'It's what has got me through the past twelve years.' He gives a small laugh. 'Well, the past nine anyway. I was a wreck for the first three years after she died. I lost my wife and child on the same day. It doesn't get much shittier than that.'

'I know,' Lori says. 'Believe me, I know.'

Filling the uncomfortable silence, Rays says, 'Is your friend not staying with you, then?'

'She's staying at the B&B. Long story.' Lori picks up her cup and places it in the sink, suddenly uncomfortable with his presence in her space. 'I'm afraid I need to get some sleep.'

Ray steps over to the sink and rinses out the two cups. 'I'm sorry for your loss.'

'With all the technology around, it's unimaginable that someone can vanish without a trace, isn't it? I just can't get over the fact that someone must know something.'

12

After Ray leaves, Lori feels uneasy. She double checks the stable door is locked, the patio doors too, before settling the dogs. Before she makes her way upstairs, she checks the front door. All is secure.

The night is still warm, but she closes the bedroom window. When she gets into bed, she picks up her phone to check on April. She dials her number. Hardly surprising, the call diverts to voicemail. Lori pings her a text.

> We need to talk. I'll stop by in the morning. Don't let this ruin what you and Paul have. Or what we have. You know how much I love you. L x

She notices three missed calls from a number she doesn't recognise. Who could that be? She finds Paul's number. She wants to know how this has happened. After so long, how has it come out now? Her call goes to his voicemail without ringing. She is about to leave a message when the unknown number calls again. She answers it.

'Lori, it's Paul. I've been trying to get hold of you. Have you seen April?'

'You've got a new number.'

'No, my phone's broken. April threw it at me. Something dreadful has happened.'

'I know. She turned up here and confronted me.'

He breathes a deep sigh of relief into the phone. 'I'm glad she's safe. What did you say?'

'I couldn't lie. She was drunk before she arrived and downed a load of whisky while she was here.'

'Get her on the line, please. She's not answering my calls.'

'She's not here. She checked into a chalet in the village.'

'Why?'

'I offered, but she refused to stay with me. She'd already checked in before she got here.'

'Where's the chalet? I'm on my way.'

'Seriously, Paul. Leave it to me. She needs time alone to process this. I'll go down there first thing in the morning.'

'I can't believe this has happened.'

'Who sent the letter?'

Paul's words are filled with anguish. 'I don't know. It arrived in the post. She showed it to me. It said you're not the friend she thinks you are, and I'm not the perfect husband she thinks I am, and she should ask us both why.'

'Whoever sent that?'

'I don't know. I've never told anyone about that night.'

'Neither have I,' says Lori.

'Are you sure?'

'I can't believe you're asking me that. Do you really think it's something I'd admit to?'

'Ditto,' he says.

'I'll go and see her as soon as I wake up.'

'Please call me as soon as you've seen her. And, Lori...'

'What?'

'I'm sorry. We've never talked about it, so I've never had a chance to say it before. But I'm truly sorry for what happened that night.'

Lori feels uncomfortable. A shiver creeps down her spine. She doesn't want to be reminded of their mistake.

'It was pure drunken stupidity.' Paul takes a deep breath. 'You're meant to be staying here this weekend.'

'That's not going to happen now. I'll have to find a hotel or an Airbnb. I'll call you in the morning.'

Lori puts down her phone. She turns to the empty space beside her and whispers, 'Sweet dreams, darling,' as she has every night for the past seven years. It's what Howie used to say to her before they turned the lights out. She thinks about what she omitted to tell Ray that she told the police seven years ago.

She and Howie had argued before he left home for work on the day he vanished. Nothing big. A stupid bicker about whose turn it was to empty the dishwasher. It was out-of-character for Howie. A smooth operator, little riled him. But something had that day. He'd been out with Molly the night before. Lori had been working late. As she had been for weeks, working on the Frankie Evans case.

Even she would admit, it became an obsession. When she asked Howie what was up, he'd snapped at her. Molly said he'd been fine at dinner the night before. Work colleagues reported him acting normally and Paul said he didn't notice anything unusual about his mood, so Lori has always put it down to them working so many hours. That they'd argued the last time they saw each other is the ultimate twist of the knife plunged deep in her heart.

Sleep is a long-lost friend Lori is desperate to meet but can't locate, however much she tries. She counts her breaths – closing her eyes for three counts, opening them and staring at the faint light of the moon beaming through the window for another three counts. Nothing is working. After an hour, she gives up, snaps the light on and descends the dark, narrow staircase. If she works for an hour, she might be able to get something together to give to Hector when they meet on Friday. She used to do this in the early days after Howie's disappearance, work for a couple of hours until the fatigue drove her back to bed.

But instead of opening her work in progress, she can't resist googling Frankie Evans again. She knows it's not a good idea. It's a dark place she shouldn't go. Reading more about that monster is not going to fix her insomnia. But it's like her fingers have taken control of her rationality. She pauses. They tap the air above the return key. 'Don't do it, Lori. Don't do it,' she mutters to herself. Returning to her novel would be the most sensible thing to do. She envisages the scowling look Hector will throw her way if she doesn't have at least a synopsis to give him. But it's not enough to stop her forefinger from hitting the return key.

She berates herself for the control that man still has over her. When he was put inside, she thought she'd rid herself of him from her life. He was no longer of consequence. She felt like she could breathe again. But now he is out, it has unsettled her. No. It has angered her.

She squints at the screen, her nose scrunched up like a rabbit's, as an article about spiritual balancing tops the search. Frankie Evans' name appears in the headline which captures her attention. He was featured on this week's *God's Way* podcast posted last night, titled: *Loving thy Neighbour. Even when they are not worth loving.* Why hadn't she seen this when she'd googled him earlier?

She reads the opening paragraph about relationships and values that merges into Frankie's story. The man who found God while serving a life sentence for a murder he claims he played no part in. It was God who saved him. God who showed him the light. The Lord paved the way to his freedom.

Is this some kind of joke? An invite to press play and listen to Frankie's full story flashes on the screen. And, just as she couldn't help herself googling his name, she can't resist pressing play. Lori gasps. It's Frankie, for sure. Lori will never forget that voice until her dying day. What she hears is quite incredible. If it is to be believed. Frankie claims there were no flashing lights, visions, or spiritual encounters; his journey towards his faith was pragmatic, rational.

Quite simply, he developed a love of reading while he

was inside, and one day while in the prison library he unearthed a book of bible stories. Laughing, he jests that they were rather good and claims he devoured the book in less than twenty-four hours, staying up late into the night to finish it. The following day, he obtained a copy of the *King James Bible*. A book he never would have dreamt of opening. Intrigued, he couldn't put it down, either.

Approaching his reading with an open mind, he started to discard personal feelings of hate and envy. These notions were replaced with questions. Frankie says he had a stack of them. He started to attend mass regularly, bombarding the chaplain with questions as he reflected upon his rogue way of living. Before long, after much soul-searching, he was hooked, he says. He welcomed his new spiritual existence. It was gratifying, refreshing, life changing. His new understanding gave him peace and solace, especially at a time when his mother was seriously ill. Frankie Evans was ready to repent and surrender his life to the Lord.

Furthermore, he now wants to seek out those who had wronged him and offer his forgiveness.

Can this possibly be the same man? Is he to be trusted? Did he make this all up to increase his chances of an early parole? Maybe, but he certainly sounds convincing.

Lori listens intently, staring at the sound waves flicking up and down on the screen of her iMac. Towards the end, she notices there is unquestionably something different about his voice. The anger seems to have dissipated. He is full of praise for the Lord and explains how God has rebalanced his life and given it value. He commits to spending the rest of his life doing the Lord's work.

Seven years ago, Lori would have understood how this could happen to someone. How God could help them in their time of need. When she was a child, there was a Sunday morning tradition in Lori's family. Even then, she never slept in. Why sleep when you could be reading? She would set an alarm to wake her up earlier than on school days. Any opportunity to start a new book. Even though she was often tired from staying up late on a Saturday night to finish her last one. She would listen to her parents get out of bed and her mother slip outside to take the dogs for a walk while her father cooked breakfast. She can almost smell the sizzling bacon as she recalls those days. After breakfast, she would put on a dress and accompany her parents to church. Even when she left home for university, she often attended a Sunday service. And she always said a prayer before she went to sleep at night. Always.

Until her husband was taken away from her, and her faith abandoned her too.

She licks her dry lips. This is a farce. Frankie Evans is the man who starts fires and kills elderly women, not the polished man talking here about how he has found forgiveness for those responsible for putting him away. Her, he means. She knows it. And how he would like nothing more than to meet up with those who wronged him.

Stunned, she continues listening. It's clear he's referring to Lori. He has something important to tell her, after all. Something that she'll want to hear. And he is confident that God will find a way to make that happen.

Lori screams at the screen. 'No, he bloody won't!' She shuts the tab. A wave of nausea gushes through her as the memories come flooding back of the day she met Frankie in that grubby, rundown café that smelled of cheap coffee. It was shortly before he was arrested for the part he played in Betty Tailor's horrifying death. She was apprehensive about going to meet him on her own at first but decided he wouldn't do anything to harm her. Not in such a public place. When it came to it, she wasn't scared. And she refuses to be scared of him now.

13

Lori grabs her phone and finds April's number. She needs to talk to someone who understands. And April is that person. Paul as well. They are the two people who have supported her the most since Howie vanished into a thick cloud of mystery, and Molly strayed from the rails of a promising future into a hopeless place where, whatever Lori did, she could no longer reach her. In fact, the whole of the Bennett family were there to hold up Lori the best they could, despite the grief they were all bearing. April and Paul's second son, Nathan, tried his hardest to help Molly. They were best friends. But he was only sixteen at the time, and too immature to fully cope with Molly's decline.

It was such a traumatic time. Howie's disappearance affected so many people in so many ways. But April was the one to stay with Lori, night after night. The one who accompanied Lori to the police station when she was called in for questioning, because at one point Lori felt she was a suspect. The investigating officer never said it outright, but she could detect it in his tone and endless questions. She, a culprit in her husband's disappearance? How could they possibly think that? Then came Paul and April's turn. As business partners and close friends, they also had to face questions, but it was clear to anybody how much they had been affected too.

She can't call April. Not in the state she was in. She calls Paul. He picks up on the first ring. 'Have you heard from her?' he asks.

'Something has happened.'

'What?' Paul gasps. 'Oh no. Please don't say something has happened to her.'

'No, it's not April.' Lori pauses, knowing how much this is going to affect Paul. Desperate to know what had happened to his best friend and business partner, Paul had tried to meet with Frankie too, but he'd refused. 'I'm not sure if you've seen it on the news, but Frankie Evans has been released from prison.'

There is silence while Paul digests this information. 'You *are* kidding me.'

'I wish I was. His legal team got him off on a technicality, apparently. He wants to meet with me.'

'How do you know?'

'I saw it on the news, and I've just listened to a podcast.'

'What podcast?'

'*God's Way.*'

'That's insane.'

Lori continues. 'I know this sounds crazy, but he has found God, apparently.'

'Found God? Where?'

'In prison. He spoke about it on the podcast. He has forgiven me for what I did to him, and it sounds as if he is trying to reach out to me.'

'And you believe that, do you? The God thing?'

'He sounded convincing.'

'He did it to get out of prison early. I'd bet my bottom dollar on it.'

'He knows what happened to Howie, Paul. You have to believe me. I just know it.'

Paul's voice is stern. He and April know more than anyone what Frankie Evans put her through. 'Lori, stay away from that man. He's playing with your head again.'

'But what if he really does know what happened to Howie?'

'Forget him. That man is scum. I promised you, didn't I?'

'I know.'

Lori lets it drop. Since the day Howie vanished, Paul has vowed he will find out what happened to the man who left such a dent in all their lives. Paul has followed up on every lead, searched every avenue when Lori was too broken to carry on, and kept her hopes alive with his determination to seek out the truth.

They end the call and Lori goes to the kitchen to fetch a cup of coffee. A stupid idea, she knows, but there's no way she'll be able to sleep now, so she might as well get on with some writing.

When she returns to her computer, she checks her emails. Only to wish she hadn't. It's the title of the email that registers first because she doesn't recognise the address: evansandthelight@soundsmail.com.

She rereads the title: *Hello, Lori. PLEASE read this.*

The body of the email is concise. Frankie Evans has something to tell her. Something serious that she will want to hear. He won't tell her over email because, like sometimes things are best left unsaid, equally some messages are best delivered in person. He wants to meet her. She mustn't be afraid. Have faith in the Lord, and he will provide the courage she needs to take this next step. Below his signature is his mobile number in case she'd rather speak to arrange the meeting.

She shuts down the computer. There's no way she'll be able to work now.

She returns to bed, clutching her mobile phone to her chest. She can't believe this turn of events. Is this it? After all this time, is she finally going to find out what happened to Howie?

Or is he bluffing? Does he just want to entice her to meet him, so he can gloat about his release? He sounded so genuine on the podcast. She lifts her phone and retrieves Frankie's email. She can't help herself. How can she let this opportunity slip by? What if he really does have some information that will lead to Howie? She knows speaking to him is the only way to answer that question. Only then will she be able to gauge whether he is playing with her, tormenting her as he did all those years ago. Or if he is a changed man, as sincere and genuine as he sounded on that podcast and his email would have her believe?

She rereads his email and in a moment of spontaneity, or madness, she fires off a text to the mobile number he left beneath his name.

Let's talk. Call me tomorrow on this number. Lori

This isn't a moment of temporary madness, she tells herself. She can't live like this any more. The not knowing is torturing her. Stress is fatal. It's tormenting her, killing her, day by day gnawing away at her like a deadly disease and edging her towards an early grave.

Frankie Evans could be the key to end her suffering.

14

After a scarce few hours' sleep, interrupted by a dream of seeing Howie again, Lori awakes exhausted. It's the dream she has had numerous times over the years. The one that leaves her drenched in sweat. Howie is standing within shouting distance. Lori is running towards him, her arms flung open wide, but however fast she runs, however damn hard she tries, she can never reach him.

She checks her phone. There's nothing from April or Frankie. She tries to call April, only to get her voicemail. Lori swears. She is desperate to speak to her.

Normally, she would stay in bed on a morning like this, but with the UK in the middle of a heatwave, the dogs need their morning walk before it gets too hot. Temperatures are expected to reach thirty-eight degrees in the valley today. And she needs to prepare for Molly coming to stay for the weekend to dog sit while Lori goes away. Lori can't wait to see her daughter, and Molly has said she'll stay for a couple of days when Lori gets back.

She discards the white cotton cover she pulled off the duvet in the early hours when the heat became unbearable and slips into the T-shirt and denim shorts hanging off the bedpost. Howie loved her wearing shorts. He was always telling her she had the shapely pins of a model. She scrunches her shoulder-length blonde locks, now flecked with strands of grey, into a high ponytail on the crown of her head. Howie used to love it when she wore her hair like this. He called her a pineapple.

'I'm coming, my darlings. I'm coming,' she calls out to Misty and Shadow, both whimpering from downstairs as they do every morning when she stirs. If they could talk, she knows they would be telling her to get a bloody move on.

As Lori fills the dogs' bowls with food, her phone buzzes. 'Molly? What's up?'

'Mum, I need to ask you something.'

Her daughter sounds... spritely. It throws Lori. 'What's happened this time?'

'Why does something need to have happened?'

There's silence.

Molly continues. 'Can Albie come and stay this weekend with me? He has client meetings in Chester today but can meet me at the station tonight.'

Lori pauses. Albert is Molly's new boyfriend. Lori met him a few months ago at a lavish party Paul threw for April's birthday. Lori wasn't sure of him at first. But after spending the evening with him and Molly, she thought he seemed a decent guy. He treats Molly well, which is much more than she can say for the unsavoury characters Molly has hooked up with over the years.

'Mum, did you hear me? Can Albie come with me this weekend?'

'Of course he can.'

'You sure?'

'He's more than welcome.' Lori means it. She's used to living remotely, but Molly might not feel as comfortable staying here on her own, even though the dogs would protect her as much as they protect Lori. Molly's not been here before. In fact, it's been months since Molly has been to see her at all, which was last summer when Lori lived at the previous house, also desolate, that she'd rented in the Lake District for a year, where she managed to write two books. Apart from last Christmas, which they spent at April and Paul's house, they've only seen each other at April's birthday party and when Lori has visited her in Birmingham. 'Will you be on the same train?'

'Albie will arrive before me, but you know what trains can be like. He can wait for me. If you get there at six-thirty, that'll be great. I'll text you if there are any delays.'

Lori hears her daughter take a deep sniff. The rush of disappointment that Lori has experienced so many times in the last seven years courses through her. It tightens her chest and clenches her stomach. Her voice wavers. 'Molly, please tell me you're not using again.'

'Mum, I told you at April's party. I still smoke ciga-rettes, but I've been clean for a year. And I intend to stay that way.'

'Sorry, I heard you sniff. You can't blame me for worrying.'

'My hay fever is acting up. The pollen count is sky high around here at the moment. Stop stressing. You need to trust me.'

15

Lori stops at the chalets and knocks at April's door. There's no reply. She is about to knock again when a middle-aged woman dressed in jeans and a royal blue sleeveless smock appears, carrying a bucket of cleaning products and dragging a Henry vacuum cleaner behind her. The woman says something in Welsh.

'I'm sorry, I don't speak Welsh,' Lori says. 'I'm looking for my friend who stayed here last night.'

'She checked out.' The woman inserts a key into the door.

Lori swears under her breath. She wanted to catch April before she left. She dials her friend's number and leaves another message. This is breaking her heart. Life is too short for arguments. Haven't she and April always vowed to each other that they will always try to resolve their differences? Not that they've had many of them. Their bond is so strong. They must be able to sort this out.

After a brisk walk around the village, Lori returns

home and tries to scramble together a synopsis of her new book for her meeting with Hector tomorrow. She continually checks her phone. But no one calls apart from Paul asking if she's heard from April. They discuss where she could've gone. April has so many friends, she could be anywhere. 'She just needs time,' Lori tells Paul.

Thoughts of April and Frankie Evans turn her stomach all day. She finds it hard to concentrate but manages to write a rough synopsis and complete another chapter of her new book. Afterwards, she searches for an Airbnb in Chester. There's no way she can stay with April and Paul for the weekend, now. She settles for a studio apartment in the centre of the city, close to April and Paul's house. Not the best accommodation, but it's the cheapest available last minute. It has turned into an expensive weekend she hadn't budgeted for.

She googles Frankie again but learns nothing new. Clicking on the *God's Way* podcast, she presses play and re-listens to the whole section on Frankie. She can't stop herself. When she has finished, her conclusion about him remains the same. He sounds genuine. She checks her phone. Frankie still hasn't replied to her message, but she can see that he has seen it. Why is he keeping her waiting? Is this him playing mind games?

Early evening, she takes the dogs for a walk. It's still hot, so they have to make do with a ten-minute stroll around the village. She drops into the café. Ray is shutting up shop but tells her she must sample his latest coffee. 'You look tired, if you don't mind me saying.'

'I'm nervous about my meeting with my agent tomorrow,' Lori says as she sips the drink he pours for her. This isn't true, but she doesn't want to tell him the real reason for her not looking her best.

'This one is infused with cardamon. Apparently it's rich in antioxidants and helps to lower inflammation. The Healer, I've called it,' Ray says. 'Ideal for your injuries. And don't be nervous. You've got this.'

She briefly smiles. She wishes she shared his confidence.

Turning into the lane leading to the cottage, Lori swears at the familiar vehicle parked behind her car. The dogs bark and yank on their leads. Various pieces of gardening equipment fill the rear of the open-back truck: an old lawnmower, a hedge trimmer and a large chainsaw. Although she adores this house, it's a shame about the landlord. He's one of those people who could be aged anywhere between forty and sixty, and he never looks at her when he speaks. Is it any wonder he creeps her out? She wants him to go, this man who often turns up unannounced in his tatty boilersuit and boots with holes in the toes.

What is he doing here anyway? Doesn't he know it's against the terms of her lease for him to show up without her permission? Of course he knows. But it's partly her fault. When she first moved there, he came to the property at regular intervals every day for the first two weeks. It was the thick of winter, and he was repairing a section of the old quarry stone brick wall that edges the right-hand side of the garden. Not that it needed fixing, as far as she could make out. She should have told him back then that he must call or text her first. Also – she didn't realise this at first – her lease doesn't include her use of the detached garage to the right of the property, or the large shed beside it. He lives in a small bungalow on the outskirts of the opposite side of the village but uses the rundown garage for storage. The next lease she signs, she will read more carefully.

Lori tames Misty and Shadow with a small treat from her pocket, telling them what good dogs they are as they sit submissively at her feet. Her landlord isn't the type you want to upset.

Mr Parsons hands her a stack of post, sending a whiff of old clothes her way. 'I came to fix this,' he says in a strong Welsh accent.

He fiddles with the latch of the large letter box by the iron gate that leads to the side of her house. Damn annoying thing; she hates it. The lock is broken, and the door, which has an annoying rooster painted on the front cartoon-style, is always coming unlatched and bangs in the wind.

Lori takes a deep breath. 'Perhaps you could give me notice next time you're coming. It freaks me out a bit when people turn up unannounced.'

'I did message you.'

Did he? 'Oh, I'm sorry.'

'It looks like I'll have to come back.' He drops a screwdriver in his toolbox. It clangs against the other tools. 'I don't appear to have the right screws.'

Lori stops listening. She is more interested in the red envelope wedged in the middle of the letters he has just handed her. Her stomach turns three-sixty. *Not another one.* What is that man trying to prove? The man she rightly called out all those years ago for physically abusing his daughter. Claims he vehemently denied.

'Is that OK, then?' Mr Parsons asks, staring at the letter box.

'Sorry?'

'I said I'll get the right screws and come back to fix it at the weekend.'

'Sure.'

Rushing around to the back of the house to the table and chairs by the kitchen window, Lori opens the envelope, although she knows she shouldn't. She should just tear it up and throw it in the bin. That's been the advice. But every time David Grove has sent her one of these letters over the years – this must be coming on for the tenth or so now – she always has to read it. Even though the typed message has never changed. She pulls out the red piece of paper and unfolds it.

Hello Loretta.

It's me.

What do I keep telling you?

You can run.

But you can't hide.

However hard you try.

The time has come.

Payback time.

True to his style, it's monosyllabic, and the postmark displays Manchester. How does David Grove always manage to find her? Every county, every village, every house, she has lived in these past seven years, he has managed to track her down. Lori would admire his ingenuity if it wasn't so bloody sick. Especially after the past twenty-four hours. Perfect timing. As if she hasn't got enough to contend with at the moment. She stuffs the letter into the back pocket of her shorts. She's got bigger fish to fry. The Frankie Evans sharks of this world, not plankton like David Grove. She has to admit, though. He has left her wondering. How the hell did he find her again?

16

Before leaving for the station, Lori straightens the spare room and changes the bed covers. She clears the family photos on the bedside tables and puts them in a plastic box. There's at least a dozen of them. On nights she can't sleep, she often comes in here and lies on the bed, staring at happier days. They'll upset Molly; she knows they will.

The summer influx of tourists busy the roads, and the journey to the station takes longer than Lori anticipated. Perspiration dampens her forehead. She should have got the air conditioning fixed when it first started blowing warm at five-minute intervals last summer. But with money tight, it's never made its way to the top of her list of priorities. A screeching of brakes returns her attention to the road. The driver in front has stopped abruptly for a young cyclist who has pulled out of a side street without paying attention.

She arrives at the railway station agitated. Molly is waiting for her, sitting on the edge of the pavement to the side of the entrance, smoking a cigarette. At least, Lori hopes it's a cigarette. Molly is leaning against a backpack, so big it looks as if she is making a stop on an around-the-world tour, not visiting her mum for a long weekend.

Molly waves and extinguishes her cigarette. Very little clothing covers her body: a pair of shorts that shows off her shapely legs and a leopard print crop top that stops under her small breasts. Or is that just a bra? Patent pink Dr Martens, the colour of which matches her bobbed-style hair, complete the alternative appearance she adopted soon after her dad disappeared.

A train pulls out of the station as she follows her daughter's gaze towards the entrance. Albert appears carrying two cans of drink, a smaller backpack slung over his shoulder. He is taller than Lori remembers – more than six feet – and if he were a character in one of her books, she would describe him as clean-looking. His skin is as smooth as a baby's, and his eyes a deep blue. It's not the colour of them that is entrancing, Lori thinks, it's their upturned shape. Like cats' eyes, they tilt upwards as if he has had an eye lift. At April's party, he had gone out of his way to make conversation with Lori. She was flattered. He is the first boyfriend of Molly's that she can admit to liking.

He hauls Molly's large backpack over his other shoulder and takes her hand to help her up. They stroll over to Lori, chatting and giggling as if they haven't a care in the world. Lori sighs. What it would be like to be young and feel that way again. She gets out of the car and opens the boot for Albert to discard their luggage. He smells of deodorant trying to disguise the sweat of a busy day. The backpacks drop with a thud against the folded dog cage. Molly kisses Lori's cheek. 'It's so good to see you, Mum. I've missed you so much.'

Lori throws her arms around her daughter and squeezes her tightly. 'Same here, darling. Sorry I'm late. The traffic was horrendous.' She pushes Molly away. 'Let me look at you.' Lori smiles at her daughter's button nose, which is almost exactly the same as Lori's. Apart from this, she looks just like her dad. 'It's good to see you. It's been too long. You're looking well.' She nods at Albert. 'Welcome to Wales. It's nice to see you again.'

'I've been busy,' Molly says. 'I've got lots to tell you.' Molly has the enthusiasm she used to possess in abundance. It's refreshing. She gets in the car. There's an excitement about her that tugs at Lori's heart. Radiance shines from her, her large brown eyes smiling as much as her thick lips. Molly looks so much like Howie when she smiles.

'Where're the dogs?' asks Molly.

Whatever Molly has or hasn't done the past seven years, there's no denying her unquestionable love for Misty and Shadow. Misty is her dog after all. In the months following Howie's disappearance, when Molly fell further and further into a well of depression and destruction that nothing Lori did or said could pull her out of, Lori suggested a new addition to their family. Dogs are meant to be the glue that holds a family together, she had read somewhere. Lori used it as a bartering tool. If Molly stopped skiving her sixth-form lessons, Lori would buy her a dog. It worked. At first. Throughout her childhood,

Molly had never asked for much. She had been the easiest, the sweetest, of kids to raise. The child who had a thirst for life, a love of nature, an affectionate laugh. But all those endearing attributes slowly started to disappear the same day as her dad. In fact, while growing up, a dog was the one thing Molly had begged her parents for. But Lori had her career. A career that didn't have the time or the space for a canine friend. Until the Frankie Evans case and her husband's disappearance.

'Why didn't you bring them with you?'

Lori checks her phone. She grits her teeth. There is still nothing from Frankie. 'I left them at home.'

Molly cries in dismay, 'Why?' A younger Molly flashes before her eyes, as she recalls the day she drove her to collect Misty. Lori had exhaustively researched the breeder. It took a while. And as soon as the breeder opened the toddler gate to her kitchen, Lori knew they wouldn't be leaving with just one new pet. They were there to pick up the last puppy from the litter of eight, but two remained. The person who was meant to take one of the remaining two had changed their mind last minute. Molly was immediately attracted to the liver and white one, instantly naming her Misty. The black and white one, who they later named Shadow, positioned himself at Lori's feet, his eyes speaking words Lori could understand, "Please don't leave me here alone". At the time, Lori wondered whether it would have been better to have sought larger dogs to provide greater security, but there's no denying how protective her springer spaniels have proved over the years.

'The air conditioning is up the spout, and it's too hot for them in here.'

'This car has had it, Mum.'

'I know. It's a pig to start sometimes as well.'

'Albert will look at it for you.' Molly turns to her boyfriend in the back seat, tapping away on his phone. 'You're good with anything mechanical, aren't you, darling?'

Darling! Lori's eyes widen. When has Molly ever called anyone *darling*? She must really like this new man of hers. Lori looks at Albert in the rear-view mirror. Clean-shaven, he wears his blonde hair high and tight with tapered sides and longer on top like they do in the army. He clocks Molly who has turned around to look at him and nods. 'I'll sure take a look, babe. It may need some new spark plugs.' He looks at Lori. 'Air conditioning is a bit beyond me, though. You probably need to get a garage to regas it.'

'He's so good at fixing things.' Molly's smile lights up her freckly face. 'Are you OK, Mum? You seem on edge.'

Is it that apparent? 'I've a lot going on.'

'Like what?'

'Deadlines.'

They make small talk about the heatwave and Lori's reason for moving yet again to a house out in the sticks. 'Cute place,' Molly says, when they arrive back at the cottage. 'How you can live so isolated, though, I'll never understand. It'd give me the right willies.'

Lori laughs. 'I like it this way. And the dogs would never let anything happen to me.'

'True. True. I can't wait to see them.'

'I've taken a carbonara sauce out of the freezer,' Lori says. 'Are you hungry?'

'I told you she would,' Molly says to Albert, laughing. They retrieve their backpacks from the boot, and she hooks her arm through his. 'Albert wanted to pop along to Domino's when he arrived at the station, but I told him you'd want to eat dinner with us.'

Molly continues chatting, but Lori isn't listening. Her phone is ringing.

Frankie Evans is calling her.

17

Lori's pulse races.

'You OK, Mum?' Molly asks.

'I need to take this call. Here're the keys. I've sorted the spare room for you. Take your bags up, and I'll start cooking when I'm done.'

'Who is it?'

'Only another author I need to talk to.' Lori hates lying. More so, she hates that it's Frankie Evans who is making her lie.

Lori walks around the side of the house. Molly mustn't overhear this. Accepting the call, she gingerly lifts the phone to her ear. She can't believe this is happening. She's about to speak to Frankie Evans. By the end of the call, she might learn what has happened to Howie. Never would she have imagined finding herself in this situation.

'Hello, Lori, how are you?'

'Frankie.' She pauses, unprepared.

'I've been waiting for your call.' It's definitely him, still confident, but not as arrogant, and his voice has a calm lilt that never used to be present. Molly and the dogs' excited reunion emanates from inside the house. 'I'm sorry I didn't phone earlier. It's been one of those days.'

Neither of them says anything – awkwardness pushed to the extreme – until Frankie continues. 'Look, I know this is not the most pleasant of conversations, and I fully appreciate how difficult this must be for you. I admire your bravery in contacting me.' He is coming across so differently. It's as if that ghastly encounter she had with him seven years ago happened with someone else. He sounds older, wiser, his voice void of the menace it once projected. It's as if discovering God has emptied him of all his spite and anger and filled him up with gratitude.

'You have information about my husband.'

'I do.'

'Please tell me…' Her voice falters. She doesn't want to sound desperate, in case he is bluffing, although hearing him speak, she doesn't think he is. 'Please.'

'I know this must be hard for you. I'm not being diffi-cult, but I can't discuss it over the phone, and I don't want to put anything in writing. I know you may not want to, but would you be up for meeting me?'

Her heart misses a beat. 'How do I know you're the changed man I've heard about?'

Frankie gives a gentle chuckle. 'Where from?'

Lori can't return the humour. 'The *God's Way* podcast.'

'You've listened to it?' He sounds surprised.

'I have.' She omits to tell him how many times.

'Then you must know I've forgiven all the injustices. I'm a man of God now. You've nothing to fear from me.'

He seems sincere. If she didn't know the previous incarnation of this man, she would say he sounds like a decent enough guy. But she does know what he was once like. And she's finding it hard to forget. 'Where?'

'Are you still living in Chester?'

She hesitates. She doesn't want to give anything away. 'I'd rather come to you.'

'Sure. What about coming to my church in Tattenford? I'm sure you'll agree a house of God is as safe a place as any.'

The desperation for the truth drives the words out of her mouth with little thought. 'I could meet tomorrow evening.' She is shocked at herself. After everything that has happened, how can she have agreed to this? But it's a silly question. She knows why. She doesn't want to lose this chance. Frankie could lead her to Howie. Besides, she can always change her mind.

Frankie clears his throat. 'That could work.'

'What's the address?'

'I'll send it to you. It'll be in your interests, I assure you. I can arrange for the vicar or warden to be there, if you want. Of course, they won't disturb us. But no police. I've seen enough of them to last me forever. What time can you be there?'

She makes a quick calculation. 'Eight-thirty.'

'That suits me. I really want to help you find peace. Just one thing.'

'What?'

'I need to have your reassurance.'

'What do you mean?'

'I need to protect my family. I want your word that what I'm going to tell you hasn't come from me. I have my kid to think about. I'm sure you understand.'

She softens her tone. There's something about the way he is talking that tells her he is telling the truth. 'Frankie, tell me. Is my husband still alive?'

'Bye, Lori. I'll see you tomorrow.'

She goes back inside. Molly and Albert have gone upstairs. She throws her phone on the side and leans against the kitchen worktop, taking short, sharp breaths. Within a minute, her phones beeps. It's Frankie with the directions to a church on the outskirts of Tattenford village. She checks a map. It's approximately a forty-minute drive from where she has booked the Airbnb in Chester. Her stomach turns as she glances at her watch. In less than twenty-four hours, she is going to finally learn what happened to her husband.

18

Molly bursts into the kitchen, snapping Lori out of her trance. 'Mum, I've been calling you. Didn't you hear me?' She is carrying a present, beautifully wrapped in green shiny paper with a flamingo print and tied with a pink bow.

How thoughtful she is. Lori loves flamingos. She loves their stilt-like legs. And the pinkness of their feathers changing, depending on the country they come from, she finds fascinating. Molly hands her the gift. Lori unwraps it. Inside, she finds a white summer dressing gown covered in flamingos. She rubs the silky material between her fingers. 'It's beautiful. Thank you, darling.'

'I knew as soon as I saw it you'd love it.' She pauses. 'What's wrong, Mum? You look troubled.'

Lori fakes a smile. Her daughter is home, and there's a contentment about her that Lori hasn't seen for such a long time. Seven years, almost. This is an evening to be happy. Not one to drag up the past that she has wallowed in for so long. She nods at her phone. 'Nothing's wrong, darling. I was just checking to see if Hector had emailed me details of our meeting tomorrow.'

'Albert's going to look at your car.' Molly wrestles playfully with the dogs, while Lori throws together the quick meal she had planned. All she needs to do is boil the pasta and warm the carbonara sauce. She watches Molly testing the dogs' memories of tricks she taught them when they were puppies. They shake her hand and roll to order, playing dead on her command. There's definitely something different about her. She looks healthy, her cheeks not so hollow. Perhaps it's that. Lori swallows the lump of hope that she might be getting her old daughter back. She can't bear to be disappointed again.

Her old daughter – wouldn't that be a relief after all these years? The girl who loved life. The sweet one. The caring one. The likeable one. Lori has always loved her daughter with a passion, but wouldn't it be good to *like* her again?

Molly gets up from the floor, brushing dog hairs from her shorts. A healthy, negligible, roll of flesh protrudes over the waistband of the shorts. Something Lori hasn't seen since Molly was a toddler.

'I have some news for you.'

Lori slides a lid on the pan of penne and looks at her daughter, praying she's not going to say she is pregnant.

'I'm going to uni.'

Lori stops stirring the pasta sauce. 'Wow! That's great news. When? How? Where? What are you going to study?'

The flurry of excited words is too much. 'Steady on

with all the questions,' Molly laughs. A laugh of the Molly before her dad disappeared. 'I've got a place at Liverpool to study English. I start next month.'

'Next month! Why didn't you tell me before?'

'I applied last year and got a place, but I wasn't ready. I am now.'

Overcome with excitement and relief at the news that her daughter finally seems to be getting her life together, Lori hurries to the fridge and produces a bottle of champagne. 'This has been in here all year waiting for a day like today. Pop the cork, and I'll fetch some glasses.' She goes to the sideboard in the dining area to find some flutes.

The cork pops with a bang. Molly fills the flutes, and they clink glasses. 'Big congratulations. I'm so proud of you.'

'Thanks, Mum.' They sip their drinks while Molly relays the details of her course, and her living arrangements. 'I wasn't sure about mixing with all the freshers, so I've rented a flat.' She smiles coyly. 'Well, actually, we've rented a flat. Albert and I are moving in together. Next week, in fact.'

Lori is taken aback. 'That seems... quick.'

'It feels so right.'

'What about his job?'

'He's quit his job.'

'That's a bit drastic, isn't it?'

'Not really. He's been planning to for a while. He worked from home for months during the pandemic and proved you don't need to go into the office every day to get your work done. Do you remember me telling you at

April's party that during lockdown, he set up his own business in his spare time? He's been building his client base
ever since. He has six solid clients now and is about to sign
contracts with another one that he had a meeting with
today. That's why we travelled separately. He took the train
this morning to Chester to meet with some clients.'

'He's keen then,' says Lori.

'He sure is. He's saved up enough to support himself
for a year. That's the beauty of being an IT geek, he can
work from anywhere. All he needs is a computer. He says
he doesn't even need a desk, although I tell him he does.
It's not good for your back to sit in bed, or on the sofa,
working.' Molly shrugs her slender shoulders. 'If it doesn't
work out, then he can always find another job. The new
flat we've found has two bedrooms. We're going to put two
desks in the smaller one and use it as an office.'

Lori gapes at her. She seems so grown up all of a
sudden. 'It's all working out for you. You seem really
happy. Happier than I've seen you for a long, long time.'

Molly smiles. 'I am, Mum. I'm finally getting my act
together.'

'So what're your plans for the next month before you
start?'

'I've got two weeks left at the company I've been
temping at for the past six months, then Albert and I
thought we'd go on holiday.' A wide beam spreads across
her face. 'I can't wait. This job is so boring, but at least I
can work from home and the money is good. I've been able
to save up to pay my half of the deposit. Mum, are you OK?
You seem a little distant.'

Is she not wearing her worries well? Lori reaches out to hug her daughter. 'All's good. I'm so pleased for you.' She feels a warmth in Molly's embrace that has been absent for too long. She draws away, fighting back the tears in her eyes with a wide smile. 'Dinner's nearly ready. Set the table, would you? Knives and forks are in the drawer next to the sink.'

After dinner, Albert says he has work to do and disappears upstairs. Lori isn't sure if he really has or is trying to give her and Molly some mother and daughter time. 'Cocoa?' Molly asks.

'Coffee for me.'

'At this time of night?'

'I've got work to do.'

Molly glances at the kitchen clock. 'It's twenty past ten, Mum.'

'I know, but I have a deadline to meet and bills to pay.'

Molly rolls her eyes. 'Coffee it is.' Molly makes the drinks as she chats away.

It's just like old times. Before Howie disappeared, Molly would always make an evening cup of cocoa for the three of them. The familiar feeling creeps upon her. It's haunting. She can't help it. Molly should be making three drinks. Howie should be here with them. It should be the three of them, laughing together like they used to.

'Mum, are you listening to me?'

Lori returns to the moment. 'Sorry, I was miles away.'

'I didn't want to ask you.'

'Ask me what?'

Molly twists her lips. 'I need some money. I've been saving for the past year, and taken out a loan for my uni fees, but I was thinking.'

Lori knows what's coming. Her heart meets her stomach as the memories squeeze her insides. The time she gave Molly twelve hundred pounds for the month's rent in advance on the flat she wanted to move into with her then new boyfriend. The flat that never transpired because the so-called boyfriend vanished with the funds before they even reached the landlord's bank account. Then there was the money Molly needed for a new phone because hers had disappeared into the hands of a mugger. And the two thousand pounds to contribute to a new car only to find it went up her nose instead. It left Lori questioning whether the boyfriend Molly was meant to be moving in with ever existed. And if a mugging had ever taken place. It destroyed her to see her daughter suffer so badly. All Lori wanted to do was to help her. But when someone won't accept your help, there's little you can do other than keep reminding them you're there whenever they need you.

Molly takes the drinks into the dining area, her eyes roaming around the pictures of Howie. She sits down. 'I never wanted to ask you for another penny. Not after last time. And I'm not technically asking you now. I know it's something you don't like discussing, but I think we need to have this conversation.' Molly clears her throat. Lori knows her daughter well enough to sense she is not finding this conversation easy. 'It's seven years next month since Dad went.' She pauses, cupping her hands around her flushed cheeks. 'There's no easy way to say this, but we can apply to the courts to officially declare him dead. Then we can invoke his will and release the money he wanted me to have. And you can sell the house and make life easier for yourself.'

Lori bites her bottom lip, frowning at the sadness etched in every crevice of her daughter's face as she talks about her dad.

'Come on, Mum. It's time to face up to it. Dad's not coming back. You've got to move on with your life. We've got to move on. We've been struggling all these years. Let's make things easy for ourselves.'

'But we don't know he's dead.'

Molly sighs loudly. 'Mum, come on. It's time.'

'I feel like I'm giving up on him, and I can't tell you how painful that feeling is.'

'But we need to be realistic. And pragmatic. I need money. You need money. Come on, look at you. You don't need to be struggling.'

Lori finds it vulgar. Money doesn't interest her. It never has. Even when she was a teenager and her friends were competing for who had the best designer gear, her only desire was for signed hardcopies of her favourite authors' latest releases. 'Money isn't everything,' she says, leaving the table and walking through to the kitchen and over to the stable door. Leaning on the bottom half, she takes in large gulps of air. She's not ready to have this conversation. She'll never be ready. Not until a body is found, or Howie tells her to her face that their marriage is over. Only then will she be able to move on. What kind of wife would she be otherwise?

Lori doesn't hear Molly approach, but she feels her comforting hand on her shoulder. 'Dad's not coming back, Mum.'

19

'There's a fish pie in the freezer, and I've left you some money under the fruit bowl to get some food in. I'm sorry, I didn't know what Albert likes, so I thought I'd let you sort your own food.' Lori feels dreadful. Her mind has been so distracted, she forgot to go shopping.

Molly yawns, running her hands through her bed-messy hair. 'Mum, I've lived on my own for how many years? I think I'm capable of feeding me Albie and myself for the weekend. I'm more interested in this.' Molly flaps a red piece of paper in the air. 'I found it on the floor when you went to bed last night. Who's it from?'

Lori swipes a tea towel from the oven door handle, folds it and unfolds it. Damn. With everything else going on, the letter from David Grove had moved from centre stage to the back of her mind. It must have fallen out of her pocket at some point last night.

'Is someone threatening you?'

Lori stammers. 'There's... a story... behind this.'

Molly glances from Lori to the letter and back to Lori. 'There's always a story with you, Mum. And I think this is one you need to tell me. Loretta? I didn't know anyone even called you by that name. So enlighten me. Who the hell sent this?'

Lori places the tea towel back over the handle of the oven. 'The dogs must get walked twice a day. And not when it's too hot. I'll be back Sunday lunchtime. We can spend some time together then.'

Molly, dressed in a skimpy nightie that bares her slim arms and shoulders, raises her eyebrows. 'Mum!'

'The food at the café is great as well. Ray – the guy I told you about – will look after you. He does a mean breakfast and makes the best coffees, so make sure you visit. I told him you'd be in at some point over the weekend.'

'What's got into you? Why are you so stressed? Who sent this letter?'

'I don't have time now. I'll tell you when I get back.'

Molly places a hand on Lori's shoulder. 'Mum, I'm worried about you.'

Lori smiles at her daughter. This is the old Molly. The caring Molly. 'I'm fine.'

She's not fine.

Not at all.

Her best friend has gone AWOL. She has to meet her agent for lunch, and she is behind schedule with her latest book. She knows what to expect, though. The resulting pressures, forthcoming deadlines, thinly veiled threats of the repercussions of failure, tempered only by Hector's enthusiasm, will exhaust her. And seldom does she walk away from a meeting with Hector when her workload has not at least doubled. Then there's the birthday celebration tomorrow night. She could really do without that, but she can't let her friends down. They haven't seen her for ages. There's the letter from the guy she pissed off years ago, as well. And to top it all, she is meeting Frankie Evans tonight. She dare not tell her daughter any of this.

No, she's far from fine.

Her fifteen-year-old Honda is on its way out. Lori really shouldn't be using it for long journeys. It can survive pottering around town, running errands and fetching daughters and their boyfriends from the station, but it's not cut out for motorway driving now it has reached its twilight years. She prays it survives the eighty-odd mile trip to Manchester, then Chester and back again. It's sucking up petrol worse than ever, and it's leaking oil. Not a huge amount, but lately she has noticed penny-sized splodges where she parks. And sometimes a hot, rubbery smell wafts into the car when she turns the engine off. She's sure there's something wrong with the engine's cooling system. It could be something as simple as a leaky hose, but she must get it checked out.

Or, as Molly so bluntly put it last night, with extra funds, a new car is within reach. If she so chooses.

Lori reflects on their conversation. She resigned herself a few years ago to the idea that Howie would most likely never come back to them, and she knows she can't put off the inevitable indefinitely. Both she and Molly need to move on with their lives. But every time she has tried to give the subject serious consideration, she ends up spinning in circles of what-ifs. What if Howie walks in through the door one day with a perfectly good excuse as to where he has been?

A call from Paul distracts her from her thoughts. 'Any news?' she asks.

'Nothing. I'm seriously worried.' He sounds short of breath.

'She'll turn up.' Lori tries to sound upbeat. April has been gone for twenty-four hours. 'Have you checked with her brother? She might have gone to stay with him.'

'I casually called him last night. He doesn't know what's happened. Not that he let on, anyway. But he was a bit off with me, which made me think he was lying. I still can't work out who could've sent that letter to her.'

'Me neither,' Lori says.

'Are you sure you've never told anyone what happened that night?'

'Positive.'

'Are you driving?'

'Yep. I'm heading to Manchester to see my agent, and then I'm coming to Chester for the weekend, remember? Martha's birthday celebration. Not that I'm in the mood for going to that now.'

'Of course. You're still more than welcome to stay.'

Is he mad? If April shows up and finds Lori staying in her house, any ounce of hope Lori has of repairing their friendship will be annihilated. 'I've booked an Airbnb a couple of streets from you.'

'I guess it's for the best.'

'When April turns up, I'd like to see her. If she'll agree to it. And I'd like to meet with you.'

Paul continues talking, but the signal is intermittent, and she can't understand what he is saying. When it cuts out, she tries to phone him back, but the call clicks to his voicemail. She leaves a message relaying her plans. After meeting Hector, she's heading to the Airbnb. Can she and Paul meet tomorrow morning?

She stops at the next service station and waits in line with yawning commuters and bored kids for a cup of coffee. Smelling the freshly baked pastries, she opts for a pain au chocolat. Not her usual go-to, but she needs the energy. And it might provide some comfort for her cranky mood. When she goes to pay, she realises how out of touch she is with the real world. Since when did a drink and a snack cost close to a tenner?

It's only when she pulls out a chair from under a table cluttered with empty cups and dirty napkins that she realises a strange but familiar feeling is taunting her. A bald tanned guy dressed in a black suit, his tie hanging loose around his neck, is sitting diagonally opposite her at the adjacent table. Frankie was bald and was fond of holidays in the sun. Lori places her purchases on the table and tidies the mess from the previous customers onto a plastic tray. Frankie Evans worked as a bouncer for a nightclub before he was charged with Betty Tailor's murder. In person, on the TV, she has only ever seen him in a black suit. She switches position, so she doesn't need to look at the man sitting at the next table.

Connecting with Frankie Evans has unnerved her. She goes to take a bite of the pastry only to slap it back in the bag, pick up her coffee and hurry back to her car.

As Lori rejoins the motorway, her phone rings from its cradle. It's Paul again. 'April messaged me. She *is* at her brother's. I thought he was lying to me when I asked him if she was there.'

Lori breathes a big sigh of relief. 'Thank goodness for that.'

'She needs some space to think and doesn't want me contacting her.'

'Don't then. Let her be.'

'What are you up to this evening? Nathan has just called and sprung it on me that he's coming over in the morning.'

Lori pulls into the middle lane to overtake the driver doing no more than fifty in the inside lane. 'That's kids for you. Molly asked if Albert could come and stay with less than a day's notice.'

'Apparently he arranged it with April last weekend. I don't want to miss him, so can we meet up for an hour this evening? I've got that paperwork for you, and those documents for you to sign that I told you about last week. Usual stuff, nothing major.'

She considers telling him about Frankie, but she knows he won't be happy. Seven years ago, he was nearly as frustrated as she was at the way Frankie Evans toyed with her about knowing what happened to Howie. 'I can't make tonight.' The words shoot out of her mouth before she can stop them. 'I'm meeting Frankie Evans.'

Paul laughs. 'Did you just say what I think you said?'

'Yes.'

'Frankie Evans. You're meeting...with... Frankie Evans?' Paul stammers. 'No, Lori! There's no way you're meeting that man.' He continues, 'April would forbid it. Hell! Howie would forbid it!'

'Did you listen to that podcast I told you about? He has changed.'

'I did listen to it. He faked the whole God thing for parole.'

Lori clenches her jaw, and her fingers grip the steering wheel so tightly her knuckles whiten. 'He knows what happened to Howie. I know he does.'

'Hell, Lori. He's playing you. Can't you see?'

Paul's emphatic response disturbs her but, deep down, she knows he is only trying to protect her. Or is he echoing the subconscious thoughts she banished long ago for the sake of her husband? 'I need to do this, Paul. I need to know. We need to know.'

'I don't understand.' Paul's voice beats around the car. 'You're going to willingly put yourself in grave danger.'

'But what if he has information for us? By the end of the day, we might know what happened to Howie.'

'Lori! Has it slipped your mind how dangerous that man is?'

20

_____

Paul apologises. Lori understands how he feels. Anger and frustration consumed her for so long after Howie's disappearance. Until she realised such feelings would kill her if she didn't find a way to conquer them.

She hears Paul take a sharp intake of breath. 'At least let me come with you.'

'Would you?'

'Howie will never forgive me if he finds out I let you go on your own.' Paul always speaks about Howie in the present tense. Recently Lori has wondered if he still truly believes Howie is going to magically appear one day, or if denial is his way of dealing with his grief.

A welcoming wave of relief ripples through her. She hadn't realised how uneasy she had been about seeing Frankie again. Not that she's scared of him. Not at all. He wouldn't chance hurting her. He has got his kid to think about. He knows he'd be straight back inside if anything happened to her. She is more apprehensive about hearing the news he has for her.

'Where are you meeting and what time?'

Lori explains the location of the church. 'It's about forty minutes from you. I'm going to go back to the Airbnb after I've met with Hector, and we can head off from there.'

'Seems a bit strange, don't you think?'

'What do you mean?'

'Why there?'

'He lives there now. His wife moved to Tattenford when he was inside. Her parents are from there, and I guess she wanted to be closer to them.'

'I can't help feeling this isn't a good idea.'

'I need to know, Paul. I need to hear what he has to say. I thought you would too.'

'Of course I do. Should we involve the police? Get them to go with us? I'm sure they'd be interested.'

'He said no police. He doesn't want them involved. He said he has his son to think about now.'

'But if he's found God, surely he'll forgive you?' Paul says. His tone is full of sarcasm.

'I'm not scared of him, Paul.'

'I'll pick you up, and we can go together.'

'Thanks. I have to say, I'm a bit nervous. Well, a lot, actually.'

'No shit.'

Lori meets Hector at a tapas restaurant in the city centre where he has promised her ox cheek to die for. He is already seated at a table for two when she arrives and stands to greet her. 'How are you, darling?' he says, air-kissing her as he flicks the end of his summer light-weight scarf over his shoulder. He has aged since she last saw him, which was pre-lockdown. His blonde hair is thinning and his sideburns have tufts of grey at the edges she's sure she hasn't spotted before. They've conducted all their meetings via Zoom since the pandemic, so it's good to see him again in person. There's nothing like lunch with Hector to lighten your mood.

'You're not yourself,' he says as the casually dressed waiter uncorks a bottle of white wine Hector has already ordered. 'What's stressing my favourite author?'

Lori laughs. 'I bet you say that to all your authors.'

Hector laughs too. 'Most of them.'

Lori is fond of larger-than-life Hector. He may be small and trim, but his personality fills the room. She prefers to keep their relationship professional. He's a good agent. Partly because he owns his own agency and works far longer hours than is healthy. And partly because he is a natural at what he does. Possessing a sound understanding of the publishing industry, he has made his way onto the Christmas card list of everyone who matters. He tried to recruit other agents into the business before the pandemic hit, but each time it never worked out, so he has settled for employing an assistant, who is super efficient.

The waiter fills their glasses as Hector tells her about his recent wild trip to Amsterdam – "a city where hedonism wears the crown" – and the birth of his nephew who is the spitting image of him – before knuckling down to business. 'Sales of your latest novel are starting to pick up.'

That's financial music to Lori's ears. Perhaps she can get the air conditioning in her car fixed when she receives her next royalty payment. But then she remembers she has only just received one, so she'll have to wait another six months.

'I feel we're about to enter uncharted waters of success for you, Lori. You need to ride that wave.' Hector raises his glass of wine. 'Cheers, darling.'

Lori takes a sip, forcing herself to tuck into the selection of dishes he has ordered. Her appetite is lost in thoughts of what's in store in the evening ahead, but she knows she must eat. She'll skip the ox cheeks, thank you very much, but the truffled goat's cheese with almonds and honey looks worth a try. 'Ride that wave? By hitting my deadline, you mean. I've already told you I'm on track.' She can't believe the bullshit coming out of her mouth. 'I feel invigorated. You're going to love this next one.'

He taps his hand on the table. A smile of delight reaches his raised eyebrows. 'Hit me with it.'

Lori explains the plot of her new story. The one that came to her the night she discovered Frankie Evans had been released from prison.

'Love it. Love it!' Hector butts in as she is halfway through. He takes a swig of wine. 'Don't keep an excited man waiting. Carry on.'

She continues, entertained by his genuine interest. He's like a kid at Christmas.

'So, how does it end?' he asks when she stops talking.

'I'm not sure. I have a few ideas.'

He claps his hands. 'Spill them. Don't keep me in suspense.'

Lori laughs. 'You know me. I need to work on my stories before deciding on the ending.'

'What do you have in mind?'

She explains how she envisages the various endings for her story.

'Write them all out. That's the best way. I'm thrilled with the way it's all going for you. It's a numbers game. You know that, Lori. I'm not talking about your latest master-piece. Hold the back page. I've got some exciting news for you!'

A cheeky smile crosses Lori's face. On an empty stomach and a nervous system on the highest alert, the wine has been quick to react. She must stop at one glass. She holds up her hand. 'Don't tell me. Netflix is buying the rights to all my books and is going to make a mini-series for each of them starring Meryl Streep, Reese Wither-spoon and Anya Taylor-Joy, with Cher performing the music accompanied by the Muppets.'

Hector's blank expression says it all. 'Lori.'

'I'm right, aren't I?' she mocks.

He laughs. 'Not quite, but I have another two-book deal for you. I'm finalising the contract as we speak.'

Lori sits back in her seat. 'Wow. Where did this come from?'

'I wanted to discuss it with you today. See, it's a bit of a challenge. We're shooting for two publications in the next twelve months.'

'A year to write two books, plus finish the current one? You're mad.'

Hector winks at her. 'You know me, darling.' He picks up the bottle of wine from the cooler and goes to refill her empty glass, but her hand dives in to stop him.

'That's it for me,' she says. 'I'm driving.'

Hector's eyes open as wide as his brazen grin. 'All the more for me. Now come on, try these ox cheeks. I insist. They're cooked to perfection. Simply divine.' He pops one onto her plate.

'So, are *we* shooting for two novels, or am *I* ?' Lori says, enjoying the effect of the wine calming her nerves.

'Well, technically you, of course.'

'Hector. I'm going to burn out. I've still got to finish this current one.' She doesn't add she has only just started it. She takes a bite of the ox cheek and wants to spit it out, but her manners force her to swallow the piece of beef.

He reminds her about needing to ride the exciting wave of success coming her way. 'You're popular, current, and your readers buy your books without even reading the blurb. Hell, they don't even read the title!'

'Stop yanking my chain.'

'But it's true. Seize the day.' He downs what's left in his glass. 'Carpe diem. Blah, blah, blah.'

After a brief visit to Hector's swanky offices, Lori walks to her car in a daze, her shoulders slumped with the weight of having been beaten into submitting to a tumultuous twelve-month slog. She could've done without that today.

Why didn't she just say no? Thankfully, the contract is not yet ready for her to sign. Hector is still negotiating a couple of the finer details. He'll email it over to her when it's ready. There's still plenty of time for her to say no.

Lori thinks about what Molly said last night. She could make life so much easier for herself. Remove the need to scrimp and scrape and slog her way through life. And now that Molly has got herself together, Lori, although still wary, wants to help her daughter.

She can't make a decision yet.

Not until she finds out what Frankie Evans has to say.

21

_____

The Airbnb experience doesn't start well. The benefit of advertised private parking doesn't transpire because all the slots are taken, and Lori has to search the adjacent streets for a space. All the way up the five flights of steep stairs to reach the attic studio, the garish wallpaper and the smell of stale socks makes her apprehensive about what's in store behind the door at the top. When she reaches the top, she is breathless.

The smell continues into the apartment, where the décor is just as dated. She should've paid more attention to the reviews. No wonder it had availability at such short notice, despite being ridiculously expensive. With the sharp rise in petrol costs, plus the food she'll have to buy, this weekend will end up costing a fortune. Disposable income she doesn't have. Not with the shortfall on the mortgage of the Chester property. The year before Howie vanished, they'd had an extension built on the back of their house and had an expensive new kitchen fitted. A project they'd been planning for years. But the rental income doesn't cover the cost of the mortgage and the hefty ten-year loan, which Lori is still paying off. Then there's the cost of tomorrow night with the girls. With their leaning towards consuming far too many cocktails, their evenings together never come cheap. It'll be even more expensive tomorrow as they are celebrating Martha's birthday.

At least two nights is all she has to suffer in this dive. Such a shame she can't stay with April and Paul. She adores the nights she stays with them. She always sleeps deeply. Anyone would. Their spare room is like a five-star hotel with its comfy mattress and crisp Egyptian bed linen that makes you feel as if you're cocooned in cotton wool. And if there were an award for the perfect hostess, April would be a contender for the first prize.

Lori takes a quick shower, ignoring the mildew infesting the grout between the tiles, and changes into a pair of jeans and a fresh T-shirt. That's the right thing to wear, isn't it? Or should she stay in the white summer dress she met Hector in? Her nerves are getting the better of her. Who gives a monkey's about what she is wearing? Sweat dampens the T-shirt. What is she thinking? It's far too warm for jeans. She rips off the clothes and changes back into the dress.

She has an hour to kill before Paul picks her up. She should take a nap. It will do her good. But she knows the knot in her stomach that has refused to loosen ever since she first discovered Frankie had been released from prison won't allow her to sleep. Digging her laptop out of her holdall, she opens her work in progress. It takes ages to load. She really needs to get a new laptop. Her phone rings. It's Paul. He sounds stressed. 'Listen, I'm stuck at work. I won't make it home before going to Tattenford. I'll have to meet you there. Text me the address, can you?'

As she walks to her car, her nerves overwhelm her. She didn't realise how much she had been counting on Paul driving her to the church. The tapas meal she shared with Hector has given her indigestion. She knew she shouldn't have bowed to his insistence of sampling the ox cheeks.

She tries to find comfort in music as she drives west towards Tattenford, but not even Guns N' Roses can help her. Taking the suggested junction from her phone's Maps app, she drives along a busy road that dissects a dense forest. Turning right down a winding lane, she hesitates. The track can barely accommodate her Honda, let alone the cars travelling in the opposite direction. Trees form a thick tunnel, lending an eerie effect. Thankfully, due to consideration from oncoming drivers, she can navigate the track until she comes upon an open area where a prominent hotel sits in state upon a large green surrounded by fencing. It looks like the kind of place where she and her girlfriends could enjoy a spa weekend.

The navigation leads Lori another half a mile until she reaches her destination – a medieval church that must date back to the Norman times. Dusk is falling, and she couldn't be more grateful that Paul is coming to meet her. Lori wonders what April would say if she knew where she was going. She would tell her not to do it. Lori knows she would. She would tell her to go to the police. But Lori's gut tells her that's not the right thing to do. She needs to meet with Frankie face to face first. Reaching for her phone, she dials Paul's number. She needs some reassurance here. The call goes to his voicemail. She swears. He'd better be on his way.

Surrounded by dense forest, the church is partly camouflaged by several large oak trees and a single yew within its grounds. It looks foreboding in such a remote location. Some people would say the same about her cottage. The ancient graveyard with headstones at odd angles defying gravity completes the nocturnal gothic scene. Lori questions her sanity for agreeing to meet Frankie here without studying its whereabouts in more detail. She thinks back to her investigative journalism days. Such surroundings would never have got the better of her. Her assignments led her to far darker places. She needs to find her big girl pants and wear them with bravery.

The place appears deserted. It's ten to eight. She has arrived much sooner than anticipated. Her heart is beating in her ears. Grabbing her phone to call Paul, now she sees there's no signal. She looks around. There's not another soul in sight. Not wanting to wait alone, she drives back along the track, checking for a bar on her phone, but there's none.

A small lane leads her to the main village. It's like something out of *Midsummer Murders*. There are no street-lights. She has heard of this before, where local residents refuse to have them installed to protect the character of the village. Not a wise view, if you ask her. Especially this evening. She doesn't like it. She should have insisted that she meet Frankie in town. Not a church in the middle of nowhere. She contemplates driving away, back to the Airbnb, but she knows she can't. The news she has been waiting to hear for nearly seven years is only minutes away.

Frankie Evans has the power to end her suffering.

She gasps. At last, a signal appears on her phone. She dials Paul's number. He answers instantly. Trying her best to keep the anguish out of her voice, she calmly says, 'I'm here. Are you far away?' Lori hears the beep of a horn.

'I've been trying to call you. I'm having a bloody nightmare. There's been an accident, and I'm stuck in traffic. I'm not moving.' He sounds as stressed out as she feels.

'Get here as soon as you can. The church is stuck in the middle of a forest. It's like a scene from a bloody *Scream* movie.'

'Don't you dare go in there without me.' Paul's voice is high-pitched; his nerves have got the better of him. 'I mean it. I'll get there as soon as I can.'

Lori sits for ten minutes, trying to calm herself, before heading back to the church. As she negotiates the multitude of craters denting the road, the suspension bottoms out. Lori winces. What a racket. When she pulls up outside the church for the second time, she switches off the engine and waits. A flicker of candles glimmers through one of the stained-glass windows. Someone is definitely in there. Perhaps more than one person. The churchwarden? The vicar? She should have thought this through. What was she thinking? She should have had a backup plan in place.

It's so hot in the car, the night air draining. She opens the window, tapping her fingers on the ledge. The night is drawing in, and within the shroud of the forest, it's even more pronounced, the eerie dusk making it difficult to comprehend the scene that moments earlier was clear. Lori sits listening to the evening chorus of birds and rustling animals in search of their dinner.

Sighing, she checks her phone. It's jumping in and out of signal. It's now gone eight-thirty. She can't stand this any longer. Where the hell is Paul? When one bar shows, she tries his number again, only to reach his voicemail. She swears. Paul's the type of person who is glued to his phone. He usually picks up immediately, as if constantly waiting for a call. Why isn't he answering now?

Lori glances towards the large wooden church door. If it looked foreboding before, it is close to terrifying in the late summer evening gloom. She wipes a layer of sweat from her forehead. Is Paul going to make it? If she waits any longer, Frankie might leave. And she can't let that happen.

Drumming her fingertips on the steering wheel, she tries hard to think under what other circumstances she would commit to such an ordeal. In her distant past, yes, no problem. But now she can't think of one, other than if it involved Molly. In frustration, she thumps the steering wheel with such force pain vibrates through the palm of her hand. She checks she hasn't opened the wound that was healing nicely.

Damn this. She can't wait any longer.

She gets out of the car only to quickly get back in. Her hands are trembling. She grabs the steering wheel, her rigid arms as straight as rods, and propels her head backwards, ramming it into the headrest. She needs to find the courage to do this. Frankie can't leave without her speaking to him.

Summoning her inner strength, she casts her mind back to 2006. The Lebanon war when she was highly respected by all in her field for the badass reporter she was. Back then, nothing fazed Lori Mortimer. It was the most exhilarating, yet formidable, stint of her whole career. Thirty-four days of conflict when media facilities were targeted with what seemed like an endless barrage of missiles, and one of her fellow reporters lost his life. She was asked to return to Lebanon in subsequent years, her knowledge invaluable in capturing the plight of those innocently embroiled in the conflict. And while the opportunity excited her, she refused, turning to investigative journalism. Not because she was scared. Far from it. But because she owed it to Molly and Howie not to put herself in such precarious positions again. It wasn't fair to those who loved her so much. Molly and Howie missed her when she left for long periods, and fretted. They belonged together, Howie used to say. The three of them.

Relaxing her arms, she looks at the church again. 'Come on, Lori, you're dithering. Get on with it!' she says out loud. Meeting Frankie, a converted man of the Lord, in a remote church is a walk in the park compared to many of the experiences she has faced in her past.

Or should she wait for Paul? She opens the car door and gets out once more. With purposeful strides, she scrunches up the gravel path to the church. Halfway, she stops. A fox crosses her path, startling her. A flock of birds take flight from the surrounding trees, their warning cries alerting others of the approaching danger. She stands still, not wanting to aggravate the predator, and it immediately skulks into the bushes.

Grasping the iron handle on the heavy oak door, she twists and pulls. The door freely opens, with no sinister creaks or screeches. She hesitates, taking stock and allowing her eyes to adjust to the inner gloom. Within minutes, she is going to find out what happened to Howie. Attempts to control her breathing prove fruitless. How she has longed for this moment.

A waft of dampness tinged with a woody incense hits her as she steps inside the eerily noiseless building. Her legs are going to give way at any moment. Standing in the entrance, Lori instinctively crosses herself, the same as her mother always did when she took Lori to church as a child. Her pulse thumps in her ears as she looks down the rows of rickety wooden pews. Her line of sight leads up to the altar, and some lit candles which provide the only illumination. Save, that is, for the final shards of daylight filtering through the magnificent stained-glass window depicting Jesus on the cross.

Her teeth chatter. A shiver runs through her. It's chilly, despite the intensity of the outside heat. What was that noise? She can barely make out a figure in the front pew kneeling to pray. 'Frankie?' Lori isn't quite sure why she is whispering. 'Frankie,' she calls, a little louder. 'Is that you?'

Silence.

Is he so deep in prayer that he can't hear her? She steps down the nave, her virginal white dress shimmering against her bare thighs. Sweat, despite the chill in the air, trickles down her temple. A few feet from him, she stops and repeats his name.

He doesn't reply.

Her senses roar into overdrive.

Something isn't right.

22

Intuition, a sixth sense, call it what you like, but Lori knows something is terribly wrong.

The figure before her is motionless. She gingerly takes another step towards him. 'Frankie?' She is within touching distance now. It is him, all right. Seven years in prison haven't altered his stocky frame. She looks from side to side and up and down the aisle but can't see anyone else around. Not that she can make out. A cry of disbelief escapes her as, suddenly, Frankie rocks to one side from what appeared to be a position of prayer and slumps from the pew onto his back and into the nave with a thud.

He stares up at Lori, his eyes teeming with impassioned fear. But it's not the look of terror that makes Lori jump back in shock. It's the blood. So much blood oozing from a wound at the side of his stomach. Has he been shot? She feels like she is in a dream, a nightmare of the worst kind. 'Fuck! Frankie! What's happened?'

'Gun,' comes the faintest of murmurs from Frankie's

lips. He splutters as he tries to talk. Blood trickles from the side of his mouth.

His words spur her into action. 'Help!' Her screams echo around the stone building. 'Help! Someone, help me!' she continues, despite knowing they are alone. Or are they? Is someone hiding between the pews or behind the lectern, ready to shoot her as well? She looks around. The building suddenly feels so vast, and she so small. She sinks to her knees and grabs Frankie's arm. She doesn't know what to do. Who would? She isn't trained to deal with such catastrophes. She places both hands on the wound and tries to stem the flow. But her efforts prove fruitless. Blood oozes between her fingers. She screams again at the life draining from Frankie's body.

Releasing one hand from his stomach, she fumbles in the pocket of her dress to locate her phone, only to cry out in despair when she sees there is no signal. She drops her phone and repositions her hand on the wound. His eyes are rolling. 'Frankie, stay with me.' She reaches over to grab a cushion from the pew and presses it onto his stomach.

'Too... late.'

'No. No, it's not.'

'Going to... Him.'

'Who?'

Frankie's eyes roll back in his head. Lori slaps him. 'Stay with me.' His eyes return to fix on her. 'Who did this to you, Frankie?' She feels faint. This is a catastrophe. Frankie Evans can't die. She has hated this man for so long. Loathed every part of him with such venom that she wouldn't have cared if he died. She even put him into one of her books. A character who faced his end in the vilest of ways. But she doesn't wish this on Frankie. Not now. It's not right.

Blood seeps through the cushion. 'I... forgive you.' A wry smile flickers over his ashen face.

Lori presses harder onto the wound. 'My husband. You said you had information about Howie. Please, Frankie. Please tell me,' she begs him, any smidgeon of dignity forsaken.

'Sorry. Ask...' And with these words, Frankie Evans exhales what she fears is his dying breath.

Lori shakes him. 'No...!' she wails. 'Frankie, no!' She shakes him harder. Should she give him CPR? She needs help. She grabs her phone, desperately hoping for a signal, but there's none. She snatches another pew cushion and, placing it on the other one, presses down with all her might. 'Hold on, Frankie,' she cries, but fears her efforts are in vain. He is unconscious. He is not breathing. Is he dead? She places the heel of her hand in the centre of his chest and her other hand on top. Interlocking her fingers, she begins compressions. Blood has seeped through his T-shirt and pooled on the floor beneath his body. She cries out loudly. This isn't real. But it is. And she has to face it. He's not going to make it. Leaning over him, sobbing, she draws him to her chest.

No one should die alone. No one.

She comes to her senses. She needs to get out of there. What would it look like if she is caught covered in blood – Frankie Evans' blood? Would she get blamed? She feels sick. Her head is spinning. She needs to get a grip. Placing her hands on the ground, she pushes herself up to stand. 'I'm going for help, Frankie. Hang on in there.'

She wipes her hands on her dress. Grabbing her phone from the floor, she runs as fast as her sandal-covered feet will allow. As she approaches the heavy oak door, she trips over an iron rod that looks like a bar lock for the door. It slices into her toenail. She stumbles, swearing at the pain, so intense she fears she's going to throw up. But there's no time to stop. She hobbles out of the church and rushes back to her car.

That hotel she passed earlier must be the nearest place to get help. For a moment, she considers returning to the Airbnb, grabbing her belongings and driving home. No one would ever know she had been there. She could feign a temperature and say she has all the signs of Covid so, sorry, she won't make it to her friend's birthday celebration. But these thoughts come and go in a haze of shock and confusion. Of course she could never walk away from this situation.

Lori drives to the hotel on autopilot, constantly checking her phone for a signal. She needs to get help for Frankie. He can't die. People survive worse, don't they? She doesn't bother trying to find a parking space when she arrives. The car screeches to a halt in front of the revolving doors, where she abandons it and rushes into the foyer.

'Ambulance! Get an ambulance!' she cries out to the startled pair of receptionists sitting behind a marble desk. A middle-aged couple checking in gasp and step aside. The blonde woman trips over her cabin bag in her haste to get out of the way. 'Church,' Lori cries, breathless. 'A man has been shot.' She looks down at her dress, now more red than white. 'They need to be quick,' she whimpers, realising that was a stupid thing to say. Of course they need to be quick.

One receptionist is on the phone; the other is staring at Lori. The couple disappear as if they can't be seen to be a part of this. Blood is leaking from Lori's foot. 'So much blood.' Lori collapses to her knees, shaking with fear and repeatedly whimpering, 'It wasn't me.'

23

Someone calls out, 'Whatever's happened?!' Lori recognises the voice, but she can't place it. She feels like she is in another world. As if she is a character in one of her books, and she is making all this up to ensure the story is as twisty as possible. It can't possibly be real, can it? She shakes her head. It is. It's as real as the strong arms embracing her. 'Are you hurt?' the comforting voice says.

Lori lifts her head, relieved to see Paul's muscular frame kneeling beside her. He looks as pale and panicked as her, but it's hardly surprising. If anyone came face to face with a close friend soaked in blood, they wouldn't look their best. 'No,' she cries, collapsing into his arms.

'I need some help here,' Paul shouts to the receptionists.

'How did you know I was here?' Lori says, confused.

'I was on my way to meet you, and I saw you pull in here. What the hell has happened?'

A tall, black-suited young man appears. A gold badge

with *Manager* embossed in black is pinned to his lapel. He is remarkably calm for his age, and for the chaos that has invaded his reception area. 'Please, ladies and gentlemen, could we allow these people some space,' he says authoritatively to the rubberneckers who are already busying themselves with conspiracy theories. Hushed tones of, 'Have you ever seen so much blood in your life?' to, 'She looks like she has murdered someone,' flitter around. Lori wants to scream at them. They could never understand what she has experienced this evening.

The manager politely tells his guests to follow his colleague to the bar area. He hooks an arm through Lori's, nods at Paul, and they raise her to a standing position. 'Let us get you somewhere a little more private,' he says, his tone kind and comforting.

She doesn't want to go somewhere more private. She wants to go back to the church to see Frankie. He could still be alive. He might speak to her. 'You need to get an ambulance to Frankie.' Her words come urgently. She is breathless, hyperventilating with shock. She wrenches her body from their hold. 'You have to take me back there. I need to save him. He can't die.'

'Please stay calm. It's all arranged. Come with me.' With Paul and the manager each shouldering half her weight, they escort her along a corridor. The manager calls over his shoulder to one of his receptionists, 'Bring a couple of blankets and some sweet tea to conference room A, please.'

A table large enough to comfortably seat a dozen people dominates the modern air-conditioned room. The manager pulls out a chair. Paul guides Lori to sit down and takes the chair beside her, continuing to embrace her. Her head falls onto his shoulder. 'Blood. So much blood.' Lori shakes uncontrollably. The air conditioning is making it feel like a winter's day in there. The door opens, and one of the receptionists hands the manager two blankets. He drapes one around Lori's shoulders and offers the second one to Paul.

He takes it and thanks the manager. 'Have this one too, Lori.' He places the second blanket around her.

'I think Frankie Evans is dead,' Lori says through chattering teeth. 'I tried to save him. I really did.'

'Where is he?'

'Church. He's in the church.'

'I told you not to go inside.'

'Someone shot him.'

'What? Who?'

Lori hunches her shoulders. 'I didn't see anyone else there. It'd already happened before I arrived. There was so much blood. I've never seen so much blood.'

'You should've waited for me.'

'It wasn't me. I promise. I'd never do such a thing.'

Paul hugs her into him. 'What? Of course you wouldn't.'

Lori shakes her head. 'Blood. So much blood.'

A waiter arrives. He places a tray holding two cups of tea and a sugar bowl on the table. 'Would you like something stronger?' the manager asks his two uninvited guests. Lori shakes her head, as does Paul, and the waiter disappears as quickly as he arrived. The manager scoops three spoons of sugar into each cup and slides them across to Lori and Paul.

Taking deep breaths, Lori describes what has happened. A knock at the door stops her mid-sentence, and two police officers enter the room. PS Hammond, an incredibly tall woman who looks as if she needs a good night's sleep, introduces herself and her colleague, PC Conners. They have seemingly been briefed on the situation. 'Are you injured?' PS Hammond asks Lori.

Lori shakes her head. 'Not physically.' Apart from her toe that she stubbed on the way out of the church, she is fine. But mentally, no, she's far from fine. The events of the past hours will terrorise her and leave painful scars in her head for the rest of her life.

PS Hammond pulls out two chairs, and the officers sit opposite Lori and Paul. PC Conners unfolds the screen protector from a tablet, places it on the table, and begins typing. PS Hammond coughs and clears her throat. She asks Lori and Paul for their full names and addresses. After they have given them, PS Hammond says, 'OK. Let's start at the beginning, shall we? Please tell me what has happened.'

'You need...' Lori stops. There's a terrible taste in her mouth. She takes a sip of tea. 'You need to get down to the church. You might be able to save him.'

'Who?' asks PS Hammond.

'Frankie Evans.'

'My colleagues are taking care of that as we speak.' PS Hammond points at something on PC Conner's tablet. He looks up at her and she nods before turning to Lori. 'I'd like you to tell me what has happened. Then we can get you out of those clothes. But first, can I get you anything?'

'Yes. You can get us out of here,' Paul mutters. He runs his hand through his hair flopping in front of his face, sweeping it out of his grey eyes.

PS Hammond ignores him. 'Medical teams have been deployed to the church. I've called for assistance here, but, as you're probably aware, resources are extremely stretched in the area. Now, let's get to the bottom of what has happened this evening. Frankie Evans. How do you know him?'

24

Between gasps, splutters and stuttering, Lori relays how her life has become entwined with Frankie's over the years. Paul helps in places when her explanations require more clarity.

'Why did you go to the church to meet him tonight?'

'It was his idea to meet there. He lives around here somewhere. I don't know where. I was only going along with his suggestion. He was going to tell me what happened to my husband.'

PS Hammond frowns, her eyes narrow as if she is deep in thought. 'I recall this case. I'm sorry you still don't have closure. It must be extremely difficult for you.' Her frown deepens as she leans forwards, places her elbows on the table and rests her chin on the ledge her hands have formed. 'Why would you agree to meet a man like him in such a remote place?'

'To be honest, when I first agreed to it, I didn't realise how remote it was. But, even so, I wasn't scared of him. He had just been released from prison.' Lori's voice quivers. 'This was my chance to find out the truth.'

'Do you believe Frankie played a part in your husband's disappearance?'

'Who knows? He said he forgave me.'

'Forgave you for what?'

'The investigation I carried out into him. And then he said to ask.'

'Ask who?' says PS Hammond.

'He didn't finish his sentence.'

'Who do you think he meant?'

'I have no clue.'

PS Hammond stretches her shoulders back and repositions herself. 'So you came all the way from Wales to meet Frankie tonight.'

'No. I was coming to Chester this weekend anyway. I had a meeting earlier with my agent, and I was going to a friend's fiftieth birthday tomorrow night with...' Lori nods her head sideways, 'Paul's wife, April, but...' She stops when Paul steps on her injured toe. Is he trying to stop her talking about the reason why she has checked into an Airbnb and is not staying with them? He is right. The police don't need to hear about that. 'But... I won't be going now.'

'So you never heard a gunshot?'

Lori shakes her head. For the first time all evening, anger sets in. The last gleam of hope of ever learning what happened to Howie has possibly slipped through her fingers. It isn't fair. After all this time, surely she deserves closure.

'And why were you here tonight?' PS Hammond asks Paul.

Paul sits up straight. Lori and he exchange glances. Even in her current state, Lori can detect a note of accusation in the police officer's question. Paul explains. Lori hears the pain in his voice. The choking heaviness that hinders the flow of his words that has been there since they last saw Howie. She often sees it in the sadness and bitterness that darken his grey eyes, especially on the occasions she visits him at the studios, where Paul has insisted on keeping Howie's desk in their office as it was when he disappeared. When he comes back, Paul has said from day one, he wants Howie to know they never gave up on him.

Paul explains how he ended up playing a part in the evening's drama. 'I didn't want Lori to go on her own. I was going to meet her, and we were going to go together, but there has been a dreadful accident on the A483, and I got stuck in the aftermath.'

PC Conners stops typing and looks up from his tablet. 'I heard about that accident. They had to call in an air ambulance.'

'That's right.' Paul stares at PS Hammond. 'You don't think I was involved, do you?'

'What makes you ask that?' PS Hammond asks, pursing her lips.

'Nothing.' Paul blinks. 'Sorry, it's all so odd.'

PS Hammond's radio crackles. 'Excuse me.' She steps outside the door. PC Conners continues tapping away on the tablet. There's an uncomfortable silence. Lori places her forearms on the table, clasping her hands tightly. After what feels like an eternity, but is only moments later, the door opens, and PS Hammond beckons PC Connors outside.

Paul and Lori exchange alarmed glances. Lori lowers her voice to a whisper. 'I can't believe this has happened. I know the guy could be dead, but this was our one chance.' Lori can see the despair on Paul's face. She shivers. 'It's freezing in here.'

Paul places his arm around her and rubs her shoulder.

'I want to get out of this dress.'

'I don't know how these things work.'

Lori frowns. 'What do you mean?'

'Will they want it for evidence?'

With all the reading and research she has ploughed through on police procedure for her novels, she knows the answer to his question. 'Only if they suspect me.'

'Ask them when they come back in.'

'You don't think they think it was me, do you?'

Paul squints at her, shaking his head. 'What kind of question is that? I'm worried they think I'm involved. Did you see the way that woman looked at me? She's scary.'

'You'll be on CCTV somewhere in the traffic accident.'

'Good point. It'll probably be one of the first things they check out.'

PS Hammond returns to the room and sits down. 'I'm sorry to inform you that Frankie Evans was pronounced dead at the scene.'

A moan escapes Lori.

Paul shuffles in his chair. 'That's dreadful news. What

now?' he asks. 'Can I take Lori to get cleaned up somewhere?'

'I understand you want to get out of those clothes and freshen up, but I'll need you both to come to the station to make formal statements.'

Paul grabs the side of the table and jumps up. 'You can't think we're responsible for this.'

PS Hammond lifts her chin, frowning at Paul. 'It's standard practice.'

'I'm sorry.' Paul looks as if he is about to cry. 'It's all a bit overwhelming.'

PC Conners enters the room carrying two plastic bags. 'The hotel manager is arranging a room for you to take a shower.' He hands the bags over to Lori. One contains a white towelling robe with the hotel's crest, the other a white towel. 'You can change into this.'

'I simply want you to come to the station and make a statement. Is that OK?' says PS Hammond to them both.

Lori looks at Paul, and then at the two officers and nods in compliance. She knows she has no choice.

PS Hammond stands up. 'Lori is, after all, a key witness in a murder enquiry.'

25

It's a little after midnight when Lori finishes making her statement. Paul is waiting for her, sitting on a wooden bench in the reception area of the police station. It's busy in there, and noisy. A drunk with a messed-up, bloody face is shouting out expletives at no one in particular and a youth is provoking him by telling him to put a sock in it. Paul springs up when he sees Lori, offering his arms as if he needs to catch her from falling.

She feels a mess in the grey clothes that were given to her when she arrived. They are at odds with her open-toe sandals. They gave her a plaster for her toe while she was waiting for the detective leading the case to speak to her. At least it has stopped the bleeding. She tries to talk, but Paul hushes her with a squeeze of her arm and whispers in her ear, 'Let's get out of here.'

Paul leads her to his car parked in the adjacent street. He appears on edge, but who can blame him? 'What the hell!' He clicks his car fob. The flashing lights of his Audi startle Lori. 'How did we find ourselves messed up in this?'

'Hell knows.'

'Did they make you feel guilty?'

'No,' Lori says. 'I don't think they did. They just wanted to get the facts down.'

Paul helps her into the front seat of his car before getting into the driver's side. 'It took them long enough.'

'Tell me about it. They've taken pictures of my car.'

'Why?'

She shrugs. 'Routine, they said. I've got the keys back. You look dreadful.'

'You don't look too great yourself.' They reciprocate lame smiles. He switches on the engine. 'I guess it's not every week you think you're going to find out what happened to your best friend who disappeared seven years ago, and that best friend's wife could end up a suspect in a murder enquiry. Oh, yes, and your wife leaves you because you slept with her best friend.' He glances at Lori with raised eyebrows. 'Many moons ago, I might add.' He flips the indicator and pulls into the road. 'Not a good week, eh? I'm not surprised we both look like hell.'

The heat defeats her. She opens the car window. 'They'll see I tried to save him. They'll know it wasn't me, won't they?'

'Of course,' Paul says in his usual confident manner. 'How could someone your size overcome a man like Frankie Evans? It's like putting Tyson in the ring with Kylie Minogue.'

Lori can't find it in herself to laugh.

'Forensics will prove you didn't do it,' Paul says.

'How?'

'They just will.'

'I guess so.'

'And you saw no one?'

'Nothing. That sergeant told me officers will be looking at CCTV over the coming days. It's pretty desolate out there, but surely someone saw something.'

'I made a statement as well,' says Paul. 'It didn't take as long as yours. But that's understandable.'

They go over the events of the evening, Lori answering all of Paul's questions. 'Have you heard any more from April?'

Paul sighs deeply, shaking his head.

'At least we know where she is now. She'll be home soon.'

'Do you want to come home with me?'

'Best not,' says Lori. 'Not without April being there.'

'She'll understand, in the circumstances.'

'You're only saying that because you're a bloke.'

'What does that mean?'

'Believe me. It won't do either of us any favours for April to find me staying at your house. Drop me off at the hotel to get my car, would you?'

'Did they offer you a solicitor?'

'It was mentioned, but I didn't need one. I was only making a statement. Why?'

Paul turns into the hotel grounds. 'I just want to make sure you're protected.' He parks next to Lori's battered

Honda that has been moved to a parking spot in front of the hotel.

'Paul.' She touches his arm.

'What?' he says with an expression that conveys he isn't going to like what she is about to say.

'Howie is dead.'

His hands grip the steering wheel. 'Stop it. You don't know that.'

'I think I do. I think that's what Frankie was going to tell me.'

'And you believe he'd tell you the truth?'

She slaps her hand on her chest. 'I feel it.'

'Stop it. You don't know for sure.' His voice wanes. 'Not until they find a body. Please don't lose hope.'

'Why? Seven years, Paul. We need to face it. If he was still alive, something would have come out of the wood-work by now.'

'Stop it. He screwed with you. Right until the bitter end, Frankie Evans screwed with your head.'

'We're both tired. Let's talk about this in the morning. Let's meet for coffee before I go home. I'm not sure when I'll be back in Chester, so we can get that paperwork out of the way too.'

'You sure you're up for that? It can wait.'

'I'd rather get it sorted.'

'You're not staying for Martha's birthday do, then?'

Lori shakes her head. 'Unless April still wants me to go, which I'm sure she doesn't, I just want to get home.'

'I don't blame you. Nathan is coming over. Do you want

to see him? He was asking about Molly when I spoke to him.'

'Does he know what has happened this week with April?'

'No. April wouldn't want him to know. I don't, either. Have you told Molly?'

Lori shakes her head. 'I think it's something we best keep to ourselves. I still can't work out who could've sent that letter.'

'Me neither.' He pauses. 'Are you OK to drive? You could leave the car here, and I'll bring you back to collect it in the morning.'

Lori opens the car door. 'I'm fine.'

'I'll follow you to the Airbnb and make sure you get there OK.'

'Let's meet at that coffee shop at the top of your road before Nathan gets to you. I need to check out by ten.'

'Gluttons, you mean?'

'That's the one. I'll head back to Wales afterwards. Unless, of course, April turns up and agrees to see me. But I'm not holding my breath.'

'Are you sure you'll be OK on your own?'

There's not one person she wants to be with right now. Unless, of course, Howie miraculously appeared. 'I'll call April and leave her a message – brief her on what has happened. If you hear from her, please tell her I'm desperate to speak to her.'

Paul reaches into the footwell behind his seat and produces a plastic bag from which he takes a packet of baby wipes. 'I popped to the shop while I was waiting for you. This was all I could find. Open up, and I'll clean the car for you.'

'Wouldn't the police have cleaned it?'

Paul shrugs. 'You stay here. Probably, but just in case.'

Lori couldn't be more grateful. She squeezes his arm. 'Thanks. You always come up trumps.' She hadn't even considered that this would need doing. This is typical of Paul, always so thoughtful.

'It's what friends are for. You'd do the same for me.'

She unlocks her Honda, waiting as he cleans any traces of Frankie Evans' blood from the seat, steering wheel and hand brake and wherever else he can see it has landed. When he has finished, he says, 'See you tomorrow. And, Lori?'

'What?'

'Don't give up hope. There's still no actual proof Howie is dead.'

Paul drives off. He has always been fiercely loyal to Howie's plight – always there to pick her up every time she has fallen to her knees when the grief has become too much to bear. He's right. Of course he's right. She never was a quitter. It's not time to give up on her husband. Not yet.

26

Lori suppresses the anger threatening to overcome her the entire way up the stairs to the Airbnb studio. It takes all her effort. Her toe is throbbing. When she gets inside, she kicks the door with her good foot. Such outbursts are unlike her, but she can't help herself. She rips off her grey clothes and takes another shower. Even though she took one at the hotel, she still feels filthy.

She suffers another sleepless night. Thoughts of Frankie won't leave her mind, and the people in the flat below play hip-hop music so loudly she could sing along if she knew the words. And the mattress has so much give she feels like she is sinking for what's left of the night. Just like she is sinking in real life; further and further into a pit of depression. Or is her mood playing with her mind, already overcrowded with thoughts about how to move on with her life? She's tired. Years of hoping Howie will walk through the door have taken their toll. She knows Paul wants to believe Howie is still alive, but he never witnessed

Frankie's dying words. Not that he said Howie was dead. It was more what was left *un*said.

Her thoughts are all over the place, but by the time dawn breaks, she has made a decision. The events of the past few days seem to have crystallised the past seven years in her mind. She is beginning to see things so much clearer. She can't carry on like this. If Howie does come back, she'll welcome him with open arms full of love, of course she will, but for now, for the sake of her daughter and her sanity, when she has tackled the hurdle of yesterday's trauma, she needs to find a way to move on with her life.

At seven o'clock, she ventures out in search of coffee. The streets are slowly beginning to wake up, but it's Saturday and few people have surfaced yet. She loved this time of day on the weekends when she lived in the city. Most Saturday mornings, she used to leave Howie and Molly in bed and stroll around the local park or along the high street. Just her with her jumbled thoughts from the week. She would use the time to methodically sort them into orderly piles and discard the unimportant ones, clearing her mind for the week ahead. She would always return home refreshed, via their local deli, with three frothy cappuccinos and a selection of pastries. Howie was fond of a cinnamon roll and Molly loved the Danish pastries with a dollop of custard in the middle. She swallows hard at the memory. It was a ritual that got broken, like so many things, the day he disappeared.

She finds a Starbucks, orders a flat white and plonks herself in one of their comfy armchairs, where she tries to call April again. There's still no answer. She leaves a voice-mail asking her to read her email. She then composes a lengthy message to her friend, relaying what has happened and repeating her desire for April to get in touch. As soon as she presses send, her phone pings. Her hopes rise, thinking it's April. But it's Ray. He has sent a video of a miniature milk bottle filled with what looks like a White Russian cocktail. He is stirring the liquid with a black and white striped straw. Ice cubes clink against the glass. She smiles for the first time in a long time, as she reads his text.

Another scorcher here in sunny North Wales. I hope all is going well in Chester. I missed you and the dogs stopping by for coffee this morning, so I thought I'd send you this. An iced number to start such a sunny day. I reckon 'Summer Vibes' suits this one. What do you think? Ray

She types a reply, unable to comprehend the two tears that roll down her face.

Sounds perfect. I wish I was there. Lori

. . .

After returning to collect her belongings, Lori locks the owner's keys in the Airbnb's key safe, and heads out to meet Paul. He is already waiting for her when she arrives at Gluttons, a small family-owned café she and April always visit when Lori comes to stay with them. It reminds her of Ray's café, but this one is far bigger and busier. It's run by Pablo, with his second wife, Sofia, and their three sons. One from each of their previous marriages and the third from theirs. A motley crew, if ever there was one, but they make it work.

Pictures of flamenco dancers line the walls – the women in red ruffled skirts, the men in tight-fitting trousers and Cordovan hats. The pungent smell of churros frying is intoxicating. April always insists on sharing a portion when they come here, but today Lori is thankful Paul only has a coffee waiting for her at the corner table for two. She hasn't eaten since the tapas with Hector yesterday but still can't face food. She feels as murky as the cloudy glass of lemonade Paul is drinking.

'April called,' he says. 'I missed her, but she left a message. She's not going to Martha's birthday bash.'

'I sent her an email and told her what happened with Frankie. I hope she'll call when she reads it.'

Paul slides a file towards her and digs a pen out of his shirt pocket, vigorously clicking it on and off. 'You don't need to sign now. Take them all away with you. You can always put them in the post. Once you sign off on them, I'll sort the electronic side out for the accountants.' He starts talking about turnover and profit margins.

Lori's eyes glass over. 'I need to talk to you about something.' The owner appears with two bacon sandwiches. Lori grits her teeth. The smell of grease is nauseating. She orders a Diet Coke.

'Go ahead.' Paul tucks into the sandwich. Drops of grease drizzle out of the side.

Lori has to look away. 'I've decided. I'm going to make a claim for Howie's presumed death when the time comes next month.'

Paul slowly places his sandwich on the plate. He whips a napkin from the holder at the side of the table and wipes the grease smearing his chin.

'Life has become too much of a struggle, and it's only going to get harder. I haven't even produced one book this year. Hector says my latest book is starting to pick up. Even so, you know I only see a fraction of that. And have you heard about interest rates? They're set to double by the end of the year. That's going to cripple me with the Chester mortgage. It crucified me when the Chen family moved out last year, and those new tenants messed me around. Remember? The house ended up empty for three months. It put a real dent in what little savings I have, trying to cover all the bills. Let alone the cost of living crisis and fuel costs.' She momentarily closes her eyes. 'If I don't do something, I'll end up penniless.'

'So you need money?' Paul thumps his palms against his temples. 'I can see if we can get you an increase from the company.'

'It's not going to cut it.' She knows how the company has also struggled these past seven years. When you lose a workaholic from your management team, it's only a matter of time before the cracks appear. Paul had to employ an assistant to soak up some of the tasks Howie used to carry out. And what with the pandemic and now the recession, new business has been hard to come across. 'The Honda is about to conk out too. I'm constantly scrimping and scraping and under pressure to work all hours. I'm wrung out.'

He pushes his plate away. 'Times are hard for us all. But I understand, especially for you.'

A waitress brings Lori the Diet Coke. 'Meeting with Hector yesterday made me realise I don't want to be beholden to tight deadlines. It's too stressful. I've lost the joy of writing... and the joy of life, if I'm honest. And there's Molly to consider.' Lori takes a sip of her drink. She knows this isn't going down well, but she needs to be honest with him. It's not like these thoughts have come overnight. She's been battling them for months. 'I know this isn't the right time to say this, but I've been thinking.' She finds it hard to say. 'That I could possibly sell our shares in the company.'

'I thought you might say that.'

Her voice wavers. 'I need to move on with my life, Paul. I don't want to sell Chester. If Howie does come back, at least his home is still there. But who knows what state he'll be in if he returns? He won't be able to just step back into his old life.'

'If... if... Lori.' The hurt on Paul's face is torturing her. 'When did you start replacing "when" with "if"?'

'Now that Molly has got herself together, I want to help her. Howie left her a sum in his will, and if we can find the right buyer – and I won't do anything without your blessing – the money I can release from the company will see her through uni.'

'I understand, but...'

'What?' Lori's phone buzzes. No Caller ID flashes on the screen. She dithers. She wants Paul to finish what he was going to say but given everything that's going on, she should answer the call. It buzzes again. She picks it up to hear PS Hammond's voice. She scowls, staring at Paul.

'Following on from a couple of leads, I'd like you to come back into the station to answer a few more questions,' says PS Hammond.

'What about?'

'We can discuss that when you come in. When can you get here?'

Lori looks at her watch. 'I could be...' She pauses to regain control of the high-pitched tone her voice has adopted. 'I could be there in half an hour.'

'Thank you.' PS Hammond ends the call.

'Who was that?' Paul asks.

'That sergeant from last night. There have been some new leads. She's got more questions for me.'

27

Lori sits alone in a sparse, hot, and sticky interview room. Is anyone going to bring her some water? She picks at her fingernails, looking around, wondering whether there are officers in an adjacent room spying on her, gauging her movements, looking for signs of guilt. The interview room door opens abruptly, and a tall man enters carrying two plastic cups of water. 'Good morning.' He slides one of the cups across the table to Lori. 'I'm DI Bradford. Thank you for coming in at short notice.'

Guarded, Lori says, 'Where's Sergeant Hammond?'

'I've taken over here. You don't mind if I call you Lori, do you?'

'Not at all.'

'OK, good. Let's get going.'

'I'm confused. I made a statement last night and reported everything I know. Several times, in fact.'

DI Bradford is wearing a suit that hangs emptily from his skinny frame. He speaks clearly and concisely with the authority his rank commands. 'That may be so, but we've been following up on a couple of leads, and I need you to corroborate a few points. This must be a terribly unsettling time for you, but I'm sure you understand we must build an accurate picture.'

Lori nods. It rarely happens, but she's too scared to speak. Terrified she'll say the wrong thing.

'You're not under caution, but you have a right to legal representation, if you wish.'

She knows how these things work. If she asks for a solicitor, she could be here all day and late into the evening. She can't spend all day holed up in here. The solace of the mountains is calling; all she wants to do is get home to her daughter and the safety of her dogs. She shakes her head. She's innocent here. She has the emails from Frankie she showed them last night asking to meet with her. He asked her, not the other way around.

'Let's crack on, then. Unfortunately, seeing as the area where Frankie was murdered is so remote, the CCTV coverage is rather sketchy. So we're relying on eyewitness accounts.' DI Bradford appears to be watching her intently as he speaks. 'Your statement said you arrived at the church just before eight-thirty pm. Is that correct?'

Lori wonders where this is leading; she can't help thinking it will be down a deep, dark hole. Maybe she *should* get a solicitor. 'Yes, that's correct.'

The DI raises his eyes from the folder he brought into the room with him, fixing on Lori's concerned gaze. 'It's just that this morning one of my officers had a conversation with a gentleman who lives in Tattenford, who said he was walking his dog around the area last night, and at approximately seven forty-five pm – give or take a few minutes – he saw a car matching your car's description parked outside the church.' He leaves a pregnant pause, allowing Lori to digest his words.

Lori is baffled. 'I don't understand.' Then it clicks. He is right, of course. She went there first but arrived early, so she left to find a signal on her phone. She slaps her forehead, reprimanding herself. 'You're right.'

'Carry on.'

'Yes, I did go there beforehand, briefly. I was early and wanted to speak to Paul to see where he was because he said he would meet me there. I couldn't get any reception on my phone, so I drove into the village, thinking I'd get a signal there.'

'You're changing your statement, then?'

'Sorry. I was mistaken. I apologise.'

DI Bradford looks at her for a second longer than is comfortable. Or is that her imagination? 'You previously stated that you arrived at the crime scene just before eight-thirty pm. Now you're saying you actually went there twice. Once at seven forty-five pm and again just before eight-thirty pm. Is that right?'

'I'm sorry. It was a crazy night.' This is insane. She was the one who tried to save Frankie's life. She raised the alarm. So why is she sitting here as if she was the one who pulled the trigger? 'You don't think I'm wrapped up in all this, do you?' He can't do. If he was going to arrest her, he would've told her she needed a solicitor. She knows this for sure. It's not in his interest to try to trap her.

'As I said, it's paramount that we build an accurate picture of the course of events that occurred last night, with specific facts. We can't leave anything out. Now, is there anything else that may have slipped your mind?'

'No.' Lori stares at her fingers.

'How about I get us some more water, and you take another read of your statement.'

'Of course.'

He places some papers in front of her. 'Take your time.'

When he leaves the room, Lori studies the words she put her signature to last night, combing through her tangled thoughts for any piece of information she could have omitted that could prove valuable. She is rereading it, trying to reconcile her recollection of what actually happened last night to the words she put her name to, when he returns to the room and hands her a cup of water. 'I think everything is included,' she says.

'Wait here, please, and I'll get an amended version for you to sign.'

He is gone for what seems like hours. What is he up to? Is he doing this on purpose to make her sweat? All she wants to do is get out of here and go home. She bites her thumbnails, deeply regretting coming to Chester this weekend. She should've stayed at home, and then none of this would have happened. She could have spent an enjoyable few days with Molly and Albert.

DI Bradford returns and takes the papers. 'Thank you for coming in, Lori. I appreciate your co-operation. While you're here, do you recall seeing any other vehicles last night? Only, I've just caught up with one of my team, and there has been a sighting of another car in the area at the time in question. A dark VW Golf.'

Her mind immediately wanders to April. She owns a black VW Golf. Lori dismisses the thought as quickly as it enters her head. 'There were a couple of cars on the lane approaching the hotel. Not that I'd be able to tell you the make and model. But I didn't see any around the church. No.'

'Are you certain?'

'I'm sure I would've noticed as I was looking out for Paul.' She pauses before adding. 'I'm not a suspect, am I? You don't think I'm involved in what happened to Frankie Evans, do you?' Lori feels as if she is repeating herself, hoping to gain reassurance from the DI.

He is giving nothing away. 'Why? Should I?'

'No!' The word comes out louder than Lori intends, as does the sound of her hands striking the table.

DI Bradford raises an eyebrow. 'OK. Let's leave it there. Thanks again for coming in. I'll be in touch.'

28

Thankfully there are friendly exchanges as the detective leads Lori out of the room. DI Bradford comments on how rancid the coffee is, and Lori tells him he must visit Ray's café if he ever finds himself in North Wales. But still, she feels like a naughty schoolchild who has failed to complete her homework to the required standard. Leaving the building as quickly as she thinks appears acceptable, she rushes to her waiting Honda. She sits for a minute to compose herself and mull over the cacophony of thoughts screaming around her head. They are deafening. She's thoroughly washed out.

As soon as she navigates her way onto the main road, nagging thoughts continue to pester her. Is she connected to Frankie's murder? Did the murderer know she was going to meet him last night? Did Frankie have information about Howie that the murderer didn't want her to have? Who knew she was going to meet him? She'd only told Paul and

April. Who did Frankie tell? Could April have come to the church? DI Bradford mentioned the sighting of a VW Golf. Lori laughs. That's the most absurd thought. Why would April have been there? Besides, there are millions of VW Golfs on the road, and thousands of them must be black, or a dark grey. Frankie *must* have told someone, but who? Or was his demise unrelated to their meeting, payback from before he got put away? A honking car horn startles her. She has veered onto the other side of the road.

'Mum!' Molly is waving enthusiastically, waiting by the gate with the dogs when Lori pulls into the lane. They strain on their leads at the sight of Lori's car. Molly lets them go. The gratifying homecoming sends a lump to Lori's throat. Molly looks so well, so healthy, so happy. Seeing her like this reminds Lori of when she was younger and didn't have a care in her perfect little world. What Lori would do to return to those days. She climbs out of the car, dropping to her knees as Misty and Shadow come bounding towards her. She nestles her head between theirs. She wants to cry. It hasn't felt so good to be home in such a long time. But she doesn't want to worry Molly. When she stands up, Molly hugs her. The dogs continue to jump up, jeopardising their balance, nearly pushing Molly over.

Molly retrieves Lori's holdall from the car, chatting away about the past twenty-four hours, as Lori follows her nearest and dearest around to the back of the house. Lori breathes in the relief of the mountain air and the comfort of familiar surroundings.

'I've got dinner ready for you,' Molly says when they enter the kitchen. She points to a serving plate of chicken skewers on the worktop waiting to be cooked alongside a large bowl of freshly prepared salad. Hunger pains grind in Lori's stomach, reminding her she has eaten very little since she left here. 'I just need to finish making a dressing for the salad.' Molly picks up an old jam jar and sloshes some olive oil into it, along with a grind of salt and pepper. 'You look exhausted, Mum. Want to tell me what's happened? Your message this morning didn't make sense. Why have you come home early?'

Lori leans against the kitchen sink, looking at her daughter. When Molly was growing up, she adored cooking. She took after Howie. He taught her how to make all his favourite dishes, Lori's too, until Molly was as much a connoisseur in the kitchen as him. But she can't remember Molly cooking anything since Howie was no longer around to champion her efforts. Lori slips a hairband from her wrist and scoops her hair up into a pineapple, blowing her fringe off her face. Despite all the windows and the stable door being open, it's still stifling, even though it's early evening. She goes to the fridge and pulls out a bottle of wine.

'Why didn't you go to Martha's birthday party?' Molly adds a spoonful of mustard to the jam jar and shakes the ingredients for her salad dressing.

'I don't know where to begin. Where's Albert?'

'He's working at your desk in the snug. I hope you don't

mind. Our bedroom is like an oven. We've taken over the snug while you've been gone.'

Lori does mind. She doesn't like the thought of anyone using her desk. It's her space. But she hasn't the energy to say so. She grabs three glasses from the cupboard and pours the wine into two of them. She was ready to blurt out everything to her daughter about Frankie Evans. Now she's not so sure. She can't face it at the moment. Besides, Molly looks so content. Nothing like the hollow-cheeked girl of the past seven years.

'Mum!'

Lori jumps. 'What?'

'Did you hear what I just said? Come on, spill the beans. You said before you left you would tell me. I've been worried.'

'Tell you what?'

'What's the deal with that threatening letter? Who calls you Loretta?'

29

Lori is silent. Drained of energy, she could do without the third degree. 'He's just some saddo who is best ignored.'

'Not if he's sending you that kind of shit. Who is he?'

'Language, please.' Lori goes over to the door leading to the lounge and closes it. 'I'll tell you quickly. But it's not something I want anyone else knowing.' Lori drinks her wine. It goes down smoothly. Too smoothly.

'Why not?'

'I just don't.'

'I don't like the sound of this.'

Lori takes a big gulp of air as if she is about to dive into deep water. 'When you were a toddler, do you remember that nursery you went to with Nathan? You probably don't.'

Molly chuckles. 'The one with all that Brio stuff? We used to either fight over it or build all those train tracks and demand that the helpers judge whose was best, but they never would.'

'That's the one.' Lori manages a brief smile at the memory. 'You both used to stay for the morning sessions, then April would pick you up and look after you until I finished work.'

'I remember.'

'There was another kid who went there called Stacy. Stacy Grove. Do you remember her?'

Molly shakes her head.

'They lived out of town in one of the villages. You had a couple of playdates with her, and I used to bump into her dad, David, each morning when I dropped you off. At first, I thought he was a nice guy.'

'But he wasn't, I'm guessing?'

Lori nods. 'One Saturday afternoon, I took you to their house for Stacy's fourth birthday party. There was no answer from the front door, so I took you around the back. We were the first to arrive. David was in the garden with Stacy, and I thought I saw him hit her. I couldn't be sure, and she seemed unfazed, so I passed it off as my imagination. But it made me uneasy. I had intended on running a few errands while you were there, but after seeing that I didn't want to leave you, so I ended up staying for the party. But I didn't witness anything more. He seemed like a doting dad.'

'I'm trying to remember them, but I can't.'

Lori continues. 'Then, one morning, when I was dropping you off at the nursery, I saw him hit Stacy again. I mean, really thump her. What was most alarming was that she didn't even cry. As if it was an everyday occurrence.'

Molly takes a sip of wine. 'What a brute.'

'I agree. Anyway, in those days I was the type who couldn't stay quiet about that kind of thing. And still wouldn't. I'd seen it in my job – read stories about abused kids. So I told the nursery manager. She said she hadn't observed any untoward behaviour. I argued with her and demanded she do something about it. She said she'd been trained in such matters and hadn't noticed any signs of abuse but would keep an eye out. I thought she was in the wrong. She should've reported my concerns without delay. So I called social services myself. There was an investigation. Stacy and her brother got taken into foster care. David's wife left him. She got the kids back but refused to let him have anything more to do with them. She moved away, and, as far as I know, he never saw his kids again.'

'Wow, Mum. That was heroic of you.'

Lori thinks back to those days when she was an investigative journalist. She was fearless and bold. She still is. Just not to the extent she was back then. 'David Grove didn't see it that way, of course. He put two and two together and deduced it was me who had reported him. Someone, and the nursery manager denies it was her, let it slip that I was the whistleblower who raised the initial concerns. Anyway, he periodically sends me these letters.'

Molly looks horrified. 'How long has this been going on?'

'A few years.' They started when Howie disappeared, but Lori doesn't mention this. It's best to avoid starting a conversation about Molly's dad.

'Aren't you scared?'

'He's harmless.'

'Are you kidding? Someone who writes shit like that isn't harmless.'

'He just wants to scare me. He wouldn't do anything.'

'What makes you so sure?'

'If he was planning something, he would've done it by now.'

'Have you reported him?'

Lori shakes her head. 'When I got the first few, I didn't have the bandwidth to deal with them.' Lori gives a brief laugh. 'I knew the weasel would only deny it was him.'

'You should've gone to the police, Mum.'

'I couldn't be bothered. As I said, he'd only deny it.'

'Go now.'

'The police have far better things to do than waste time on the David Grove arses of this world.' *Like finding your father*, Lori wants to add.

'How often does he send them?'

Lori shrugs. 'I get a few a year.'

'You should report him. Tomorrow. Go to the police.'

Lori sighs. 'There's really no point.'

'How did he find you here?' Molly scrunches up her nose. 'How does anyone find you in the places you've lived in these past few years?'

'I don't know how he manages it, but he does.'

'Doesn't that creep you out?'

'Not really. I've got the dogs. You know how they can be when they think I'm under threat.' Lori reminds her that when they lived in Cornwall the postman thought they owned a pair of Rottweilers. 'He's just messing with me. His way of getting his own back. He doesn't scare me.'

'How come you've never told me about him?'

Because you've been in another world for the past seven years – a world of white powder and dodgy boyfriends, and I haven't been able to reach you. 'I didn't want to worry you.' Lori finishes another glass of wine. She needs some breathing space. 'Would you mind if I took the dogs for a walk before dinner? I'll only be half an hour.'

Molly doesn't budge. 'Who knows about him?'

'Not many people. April and Paul. If anything happened to me, he'd be the first person the police would look into. So nothing is going to happen. Stop stressing.' Lori wants to add that David Grove is the least of her worries. She changes the subject, commenting on the smell of the chicken. 'What spices did you use?'

'Turmeric and paprika. Have you given any more thought to what we discussed before you went?'

Lori lets out a scream. Molly looks startled. For a split second, Lori stares at the figure she can see in the reflection of the patio doors before spinning around to the kitchen doorway. 'Albert! I didn't hear you open the door. You scared me.'

He holds up his hands. 'Sorry, I didn't mean to.'

Lori hadn't realised how on edge she was. Passing a glass of wine to Albert, she refills Molly's. 'You two enjoy this,' she says. 'I'm off out with the dogs.'

Albert extends his arms around Molly's middle and kisses her neck. 'Smells good, babe. I'm hungry.'

Molly giggles and says to Lori, 'I'll come with you and you can tell me why you didn't go to the birthday party.'

Usually, Lori would love nothing more than for her daughter to accompany her on a walk, but she needs some headspace. She doesn't want to worry Molly with everything that has happened. 'I just didn't fancy it in the end. All that drunken debauchery. You know how much that lot drinks.'

'You're getting old, Mum,' Molly teases.

'You can say that again. Listen, you stay put and cook. I'll be back in half an hour.'

Lori quickly takes her holdall to her desk to recharge her laptop. When she gets there, she clenches her jaw. Her iMac has been moved aside, and Albert's laptop is in its place in the centre of her desk. His screensaver is a picture of the two of them in fancy dress at a party, wearing cop outfits. Molly is brandishing a baton and Albert a gun, both faking stern expressions. It's good to see them having fun, even if they look menacing. She looks around the snug. Molly's rucksack, her closed laptop, and some books are strewn over the small sofa, and several of her belongings clutter the floor. She guesses she has lost this space while they are here. That might not be a bad thing. She'll take her iMac down to her writing den at the bottom of the garden. The change of scenery will do her good.

Lori follows the path that curves through the narrow lanes of the village rather than taking her usual evening route to the mountains. Shadow and Misty are panting as if they have already been on their evening hour-long hike. The humidity has created a fresh layer of perspiration that has seeped through the back of Lori's T-shirt. She tries to distract her mind from the events of the previous few days and from the gravity of the situation she has found herself in, while trying to make mental notes for her new story idea she is working on. How will the plot evolve? How will the story end? But her troubles are too disturbing to concentrate. She tries to find solace in the gardens she passes, each in full summer bloom. But not even the roses of varying colours – tangerine orange, lemon yellow, and blood red – that adorn borders and trellises running up the front of several houses can distract her.

Further in, the houses are stacked on top of each other. From a distance, it looks like a model village. Since moving here, she has always marvelled at the various periods in history represented, separated by centuries and styles, some far more attractive than others. Stone cottages neighbour prefab shingle-covered terraced blocks, tended to in varying levels of pride and care. Be it the time of day she ventures out, or pure luck, she seldom sees many of the inhabitants of the village, which suits her just fine. She is far more likely to come across hikers or tourists walking in the mountains en route to the nature reserve or the falls.

She considers dropping into the café to see Ray, but she doesn't want to burden him with her problems. Besides, she wants to get home, and go to bed. If Molly and Albert weren't here, she'd skip dinner. She can't remember ever feeling so exhausted.

She continues roaming the streets as she compartmentalises her troubles and deals with her disappointments. The weekend has taken her down another dead end in the hunt for her husband. But tomorrow is another day. Isn't that the motto that has got her through the past seven years? She needs to retake control of her life. Her energy levels may be depleted, but the past few days have renewed her resolve. Being still no closer to solving the mystery of what happened to her husband has crushed her, but she *will* find out what happened to him. And she will find out what happened to Frankie Evans. Before the police try to lay the blame at her door.

30

Just as it has been for so long, sleep is a foreign country Lori can't seem to visit. She switches on the light and picks up her latest read. But it's no use. She can't concentrate. The multitude of thoughts racing through her head won't let her. Outside, the wind has picked up since she went to bed. A storm must be brewing. Hardly surprising, given the intense heat of the past few weeks. She discards the book, picks up her phone and scrolls through the media reports on Frankie's murder again. The police are appealing for witnesses and any sightings of the VW Golf seen in the area by a local dog walker. She reads an article about Frankie titled: *From Murder to God: the Journey of an Ex-Prisoner*.

The blood returns to haunt her. She gasps. All that blood – Frankie's blood on her hands, in her hair, his head against her heart as she held him for his final breath. How will she ever get over that?

Stretching over to the bedside cabinet, she opens the

middle drawer and finds the packet of sleeping tablets she succumbs to on nights like these. The doctor first prescribed them shortly after Howie disappeared. They helped at first, but then, like any drug, it wasn't long until she had to up the dose to achieve the same effect. And with Molly to contend with, it wasn't a place she wanted to go, so she stopped taking them regularly. She only takes one now and again when she is desperate. One won't hurt tonight. She reaches for her glass of water but stops. What is that sound? She can hear an intermittent tap-tapping – with no rhythm or regularity, making it more disturbing. She looks towards the bedroom door, irritated. Where is it coming from? She takes a tablet and turns off the bedside lamp. Pulling the duvet over her head, she tries to sleep. But she soon knows, despite taking a sleeping tablet, that any chance of sleep with that creepy noise will be impossible. It's got into her head.

She throws off the duvet and shuffles her feet into her slippers. Sitting on the edge of the bed, she listens again. There it is. It's definitely not her imagination. *Tap, tap, tap.* She grabs the silk dressing gown Molly bought for her and slides her arms into it. The smooth silk feels soft against her skin. *Tap, tap, tap.* What is it?

With the house in darkness, Lori creeps down the staircase, avoiding the areas of each step she knows will creak. She doesn't want to disturb Molly and Albert. At the bottom of the stairs, the wind whistles through the gaps in the front door. Misty opens one eye and gives a cursory glance. Shadow mirrors his sister. Lori bends down to stroke their heads, comforting them as she peers down the dark hallway. With a huff from Misty, the dogs settle back to sleep.

There it is again! The noise is coming from the direction of the kitchen. Lori ties the belt of her dressing gown tighter. As she enters the kitchen, she realises the knocking is coming from outside. She gasps. What was that? Someone is in the kitchen with her. She turns, only to sigh when Misty rubs up against her leg, seemingly unconcerned by the tapping sound. Slowly, Lori shuffles over to the stable door and yanks it open, half-expecting to find a dead bird or Mr Parsons's head dangling from the door knocker, buffering against the door in the breeze. Fortunately, although bizarrely, it is one of the dogs' leads hanging on the door handle, tapping in time with the sporadic wind against the wooden door. Strange. She doesn't remember leaving it there. Lori grabs it and places it in its allocated place on the hook by the door. It's like someone is playing with her head. Confused and tired, Lori locks up and returns to bed, finally surrendering to the peace the sleeping tablet brings.

Lori wakes up later than usual, but it's still early. She's groggy, but at least the sleeping pill worked its magic and led her into a deep sleep. She stares at the ceiling, listening to the birdsong from outside the window as she gathers her thoughts. Frankie Evans remains at the forefront of her mind. Reaching for her phone, she checks her messages, relieved to see her voicemail is empty. At least no one wants anything more from her at the moment. A text from

Ray asks if she is coming into the café today. She replies to tell him yes, she'll be in this evening. She rubs the sleep from her eyes and yawns, looking at the window. The sun stretches into the room, enticing her out of bed.

Her mind is made up. It's time to regain control of her life.

And it all starts by speaking to Frankie's wife.

But first, she needs to find her.

The dogs are with Molly and Albert who are working in the snug. Albert is wearing a pair of headphones with a speaker attached and appears to be on a work call, talking about something to do with graphic user interfaces. He acknowledges Lori with a brief smile.

'What time do you call this?' Molly laughs, pointing at the clock on the wall above Lori's desk. 'Shout if you want us to move.' Molly returns to her keyboard.

Although it irritates Lori to see her little office space taken over, she knows that to move on, a change of scenery is a must. 'You're fine,' she replies, well aware how hot the spare bedroom gets. It usually doubles as her laundry room, as it is next to the cupboard that houses the boiler. 'You're good. I'll work in the den.'

'Do you get wifi down there?' Molly asks.

'Yes, it's surprisingly good.' Lori throws her handbag over her shoulder and bends down to unplug her iMac as Albert ends his call.

'Can I help you there?' he asks. He throws out a hand and stops her picking up the computer. 'Let me.'

Lori steps away. 'Would you take this down to the den and put it on the desk, please? The key is on the hook next to the stable door in the kitchen. The one beside the dogs' leads.' She's about to mention the lead she found in the night, but Molly speaks.

'Would you prefer it if we worked down there, Mum?' Molly raises her eyebrows at Albert. 'We wouldn't mind, would we?'

'Of course not,' Albert says. 'I can work anywhere.'

'No, it's fine,' Lori says.

When Albert leaves the room with Lori's iMac, Molly's phone rings. 'It's work. I need to take this.'

Lori powers up her iMac and opens the four small casement windows of the den. It makes little difference. It's another scorcher of a day, and the air remains still. A good downpour is desperately needed. The dogs are lying on their cushion under the desk.

Facebook is her starting point. That's her plan. Be bold – be brave – like she once was. It came to her when she couldn't sleep last night before she took the sleeping pill. She is going to find Niamh's telephone number, call, and ask to meet her. She will probably refuse. Let's be fair; her husband has just been murdered, and Lori was the person who found him. But Niamh may be persuaded when she hears what Lori has to say.

But when she clicks on Niamh's Facebook page, Lori finds it has been made private. She bangs her palm on the desk. Of course, it could never have been that easy. Nothing ever is.

Lori googles businesses in Tattenford, where Niamh lives. Where Lori witnessed Frankie take his last breath. She finds TE Fitness and clicks on the website. It's definitely the right one. She recognises a picture of Niamh. A telephone number appears at the top of the page, but there's no address. She calls the number, only to be put through to a recorded message reporting that the business is closed for the foreseeable future. Damn. She spends the next hour searching the Internet, looking for a way to get hold of Frankie's wife, only to be driven around and around another cul-de-sac. There's only one thing for it. Although it's the last place she ever wants to go to again, she has to return to Tattenford.

First, she needs to let the effects of the sleeping tablet she took last night completely wear off before she gets behind the wheel of her car. After steeling herself, Lori becomes absorbed in her writing, managing to get down a good chunk of words, despite still feeling a little hazy. At this stage, completing a rough first draft is the priority, so she doesn't obsess over the prose. That will come later in the editing stage. For now, she is only interested in developing her characters and bringing the plot together. She loves this part of the process – draining her brain of her thoughts to unmask the villain of the story. Sometimes she starts with a concise plot. She knows who's who. And she knows which part all her characters play in her story. And sometimes, she makes it up as she goes along.

But who is the villain of this story? She doesn't know yet.

It's early afternoon by the time she enters Tattenford. The village she hoped she would never have to visit again. The church's steeple seems in constant view, following her through the narrow lanes. There is no escaping the reminder of that horrendous ordeal.

Fortunately, she doesn't need to dig too deeply into her toolkit of journalistic techniques to locate Niamh. A bell chimes when Lori, in her sunglasses and a large straw hat, enters the small convenience store next to the entrance of a caravan park. She picks up a carton of orange juice and a packet of crisps and takes them to the till. 'Another beautiful day,' Lori says to the grey-haired woman dressed in a fleece fully zipped despite the weather, who is standing behind a counter displaying copies of the local newspaper and various reduced-priced perishables.

'It is indeed. Chilly in here, though. It's the air conditioning. I told my son it wasn't for me. Fifty-two years I've been here. And have I needed it before? No, I told him. But he insisted.'

Lori holds her purchases in the air and hands over a five-pound note.

'Ah, cash,' says the woman, with a wide grin. 'Don't see much of that around these days.'

'You most certainly don't.'

'I blame Covid. People just want to pay by card now.'

'I guess it's easier. Could I ask you something?'

'Sure.' The woman rings the goods into her cash register. The till pings open. 'Go ahead.'

'I'm trying to locate a friend of mine, Niamh Evans. Do you know her?'

'I sure do.' The shopkeeper stoops and leans forwards. 'Have you heard...' she says, lowering her voice as if the shop is full, 'the terrible news?'

'I have. I want to go and see her, but I can't remember which number she lives at.'

'I don't know the number, dear, but it's the house next to the one with the red telephone box outside it. On Carlton Way. Not that it has a telephone in it any more. Not with all this modern technology these days. It's full of books.' She holds an arm out, pointing a veiny hand towards the door. 'Turn right at the end of this road, then second left. Carlton Way is the next left. You can't miss it.'

'That's right, I remember now,' Lori says, hating herself for the lie. She's lying a lot these days. It's so unlike her.

'Poor woman. She waited all those years for her husband. He gets justice, gets out of prison, and then he gets murdered. Such a lovely woman as well. Thankfully she has her parents. Good people they are.' The woman shakes her head, her lips in a straight line. 'Made his peace with God as well. He was in here only last weekend. Tragic. Tragic. Now where was I?' The shopkeeper returns her attention to the till and counts out Lori's change. Lori keeps the conversation going. It's a handy trick of the trade. You never know what you might unearth. 'Do they have any suspects?'

'The police have been in here asking questions. They

went through my CCTV.' The woman shakes her head. The bell chimes. A young lad enters the shop. 'The last I heard they were looking for a car seen at the church on Friday evening. Black, I think they said.'

Lori takes her change. 'Thank you.' She slots the coins into the charity box on the counter, which is collecting for a local children's hospice, and leaves the shop in search of a telephone box.

31

Lori sits in her car, drinking her orange juice as she recalls her brief encounter with Niamh Evans during the trial. Niamh was heavily pregnant with Frankie's son at the time. It wasn't a pleasant exchange, which is hardly surprising given the circumstances. She checks her phone for any media updates. There's nothing she doesn't already know. Lori crunches the empty carton, drops it in the footwell of the passenger seat to dispose of later and starts the engine. Now to find Niamh.

The Honda chugs along the tree-lined main road through the village, following the shopkeeper's directions until Lori finds herself parked outside a detached, double-fronted Georgian house in the partial shade of a sycamore tree. She refuses to dwell on how much the house reminds her of her family home in Chester. As she gets out of the car, she comes face to face with Niamh exiting the drive, ponytail swinging, as if she is on a mission. The newly widowed woman is wearing gym kit and a troubled face. She stops when she sees Lori. 'Hello, Niamh,' Lori says.

She squints. 'Sorry, do I know you?'

Lori removes her hat and sunglasses, the sun bright on her eyes.

Niamh folds her toned arms across her chest. This woman sure keeps herself in shape. There's not an inch of fat on her. Her thighs are solid muscle, and her crop top displays well-defined abs Lori would be proud to own. 'What the hell are you doing here, Lori?'

'Can we talk… please?'

'I have nothing to say to you.'

'I'm truly sorry for your loss, but I need to speak to you.'

Niamh turns and stomps off. 'Go away. Leave me alone.'

'Please, Niamh. Did you know I went to meet Frankie the night he was murdered?' Lori knows she is probably overstepping the mark. She is being bold; too bold, perhaps. But she knows from her journalism days it's a ploy that often works.

Niamh stops in her tracks. She slowly turns her head. Her shocked expression tells Lori she had no clue about Lori's involvement. 'It was you. The police said he'd planned to meet someone.'

'I met him because he contacted me. Not the other way around.'

Niamh scowls. 'Why?'

'He told me he had information about my husband's disappearance.'

Niamh spins her body around to fully face Lori. 'The police said they had someone helping them with their enquiries.'

'By the time I arrived at the church, he'd already been shot.'

'That's what the police said.'

'It wasn't me, if that's what you're thinking.'

'What do you mean?'

'I didn't kill him.'

'Go away, Lori. Leave me alone. I've nothing to say to you.' Niamh dismisses Lori with a thrust of her hand towards Lori's car and turns on her heel, calling out, 'Don't you think you've done enough damage around here?'

'Stop, please, Niamh. Hear me out.'

Niamh carries on stomping up the road. Lori runs after her, swearing at the pain from her toe. At least her knee isn't hurting her quite as much any more. 'I'm working on finding out who murdered Frankie.'

Niamh stops and turns around. 'Why?'

'Before he died, Frankie was going to tell me what happened to my husband. I know he was. So, I want to find out who did this to him.'

Niamh laughs. 'Isn't that a job for the police? Or are you still trying to make a name for yourself?'

'That's not my intention and never was. I'm no longer a journalist. I gave it up, but I know I'll remain a person of interest if I don't clear my name. And, if I find out who killed your husband, I might discover what happened to mine.'

Niamh chews her bottom lip. Lori stays silent. Another

journalistic tactic she learnt along the way. Give her time to come around. Niamh drops her arms to her side as she gives a heavy sigh of resignation. 'Follow me.' She heads for the path running up the side of her parents' house, checking over her shoulder to see if Lori is behind her.

Lori takes a deep breath and follows Niamh along a short alleyway, flanked on one side by the neighbour's brick garage and the other by a line of conifers. It leads to a quaint barn conversion, sectioned off from the main Georgian house by tall, glossy-leaved bushes. 'What a beautiful home you have,' Lori says when they enter the door that leads directly into a cosy kitchen/breakfast room. Not because she's trying to butter Niamh up but because she means it. With original beams, exposed brickwork and natural stone flooring, it's the rustic type of place Lori has come to love since living remotely. Beyond the bifolding doors and patio area, open countryside extends down to a forest.

'My parents converted it for me when Frankie went away. Have a seat.' Niamh points to the kitchen table that would fit four at a squeeze. 'Drink?'

Lori sits down. 'Water would be great, thanks.'

Niamh squats to fetch two bottles of water from the under-counter fridge and hands one to Lori. 'So what do you want from me?'

'I want to find out who killed Frankie.'

Niamh has half pulled a chair out from under the table opposite Lori, but she doesn't sit down. Her hands grip the back of the chair.

'Where did he tell you he was going that night?'

'To the church to pray. He didn't mention he was meeting anyone.'

Lori feels a slight release of tension from her shoulders. 'I honestly want to find out what happened to him.'

'You ruined his life. I want you to know that. He missed his son growing up. He didn't kill Betty Tailor, you know. He was there the night she died. He was involved in the burglary, but that's as far as it went. He left when things got nasty with the Bright brothers.'

'I'm sorry if that's the truth.' At the time, Lori had been so convinced by her findings, but now she wants to calm the stormy waters that have flowed between her and this woman, so she adds, 'I truly am. But who would want Frankie dead?'

'The police asked me the same question. I don't have an answer.'

'So, all this about him finding his faith while he was in prison. Is it true?'

Niamh raises her eyebrows. 'Hard to believe, isn't it? Someone like Frankie getting all religious, but it's all true. He was a changed man when he came out.'

'How did you cope with that?'

Two tears suddenly spring out of her eyes. They shock her as much as they surprise Lori. This strong woman is not as tough as she looks. Niamh swipes the tears away. 'It's been traumatic since he was released. I never thought he'd get out. I'd started to move on with my life.' She pauses, wringing her hands. 'I met someone else when he was inside. We'd started to get serious, but I broke it off. I had to give Frankie another chance.'

'That must've been difficult for you.'

'It was. Prison changed Frankie. He wasn't the same man. And coping with him being put away, becoming a mum and moving here changed me. Frankie wanted us to continue as if the last seven years had never happened, but I knew from the first weekend he was back that I wasn't in love with him any more.' Two more tears, two more swipes of her hands. 'I feel like the worst person on earth.'

'You shouldn't.'

'I can't help it.'

Lori's heart goes out to the woman. 'Not a day passes when I don't wonder what my husband would be like now if he was found. I wonder if we would still get on.' Lori pauses to take a sip of water. 'If he's still alive, that is.'

Niamh continues. 'This doesn't mean I don't want to find out who killed him. He was the father of my son. He's become inquisitive, asking about his dad these past few years. He hears other kids talking about their dads. And he sees their dads pick them up from school and take them to football. I've had to tell him the truth... to a certain extent. What choice did I have? People talk, and he'll find out at some point.'

'Honesty is the best policy with kids. In my experience, anyway. However hard it is, they need to know the truth.' Lori feels like a hypocrite having withheld what happened this weekend from Molly.

'Frankie was involved with some shady people before he was put away, so I'd rather I found out who killed him before my son grows up and tries to find out for himself. Who knows what he might get mixed up in? I can't tell you how much that scares me. This is the only reason I'm talking to you now. My son has already been through enough in his short life.'

'I understand. My daughter has as well.' They have a lot more in common than Niamh realises.

'I live for my son. So if you want my help to find out who murdered his father, I'll do all I can.'

'I want to be honest with you. I'm still trying to find out what happened to my husband.'

'How come you stopped looking?'

'I didn't, but there was nowhere left to look.' She tells Niamh how she kept hitting brick wall after brick wall every avenue she went down, despite her investigative skills. 'It's like he vanished into thin air. If I'm honest, I've become a bit of a recluse.'

'How did you come to meet with Frankie that night?'

'He contacted me via my website. He must've found out that I'd left my job and become a writer. He said he wanted to tell me what he knew about Howie's disappearance.' Lori pauses, choosing her words carefully. 'I was sure he was going to tell me Howie was dead. But he didn't get to finish what he was saying. His final word was "Ask". And that's what I need to find out. Ask who?'

Niamh sips her water, processing her thoughts. Lori can't quite read her vacant stare. She wonders if Niamh is deciding how much to divulge, or whether she is genuinely trying to recollect. Niamh knows something for sure.

After an infinite pause, Niamh takes a deep breath. 'Someone was in contact with Frankie before he was put inside. I remember because he was not one of his regular cronies. Frankie was irritated by him. Frankie never told me his name, but he did say this guy had some information about your husband's disappearance that would get so far under your skin you'd drop your investigation into him. Frankie said he could use it as a bartering tool to get you off his back.'

'What information?'

'This guy knew where your husband was. That's all I remember. I'm sorry. A lot was going on at the time. If I knew, I would tell you.' Niamh looks at the clock on the wall. 'I'm sorry, but I have to pick my son up from his friend's.'

'Let's keep in touch.'

'Sure.' There's still a coolness to Niamh's tone, but she's not as icy as she was when Lori first arrived.

Lori drives away, frustrated. As she has always suspected, someone knows what happened to her husband. She just needs to find that person.

32

Molly and Albert are still working when Lori returns late afternoon, hot and sweaty, from her trip to Tattenford. She calms the dogs with cuddles and takes their leads from their hook by the kitchen door. The mountains are calling. She needs some head space.

After a long walk, she stops at the café, letting the dogs have a drink before going inside. Ray is in the kitchen, singing along to a Phil Collins song playing on the radio competing with the cake mixer spinning at full speed. A look passes between them. One that says how genuinely pleased they are to see each other. 'What a nice surprise,' Ray says with his usual sunny smile. 'I wasn't expecting to see you today.' He walks to greet Lori, calling out to his assistant, Teagan, a local single mum of three boisterous boys, who is busy in the kitchen, banging crockery and cutlery as she empties the dishwasher. Ray has a soft spot for Teagan. He says she is the only member of staff who is never late and always cleans the barista machine properly and without being asked. 'We were just saying how much we missed your daily visits, weren't we, Teagan?' He lowers the volume of the radio.

'We sure were,' Teagan calls out, rolling her Rs in her melodic Welsh accent. Her voice is overly loud as if she is used to shouting to be heard. Despite how busy the café becomes at certain times of the day, she works here for a rest, she has often told Lori.

'What brought you back so early?' Ray asks.

'I wasn't feeling my best.'

Ray pulls out a chair at Lori's favourite table, which is messy, with a laptop among papers and files. Lori sometimes sits at this table for a couple of hours after lunch with her notepad or her own laptop for a change of scenery. 'You're in luck. I was just about to shut up shop. What can I get you? I've got a new coffee on the go if you fancy it. My Moroccan Mayhem. I think you'll love this one.'

'Hit me with it.'

'I'll be right back.'

Something about being there makes Lori feel at home and she realises, despite it being only a few days, how much she has missed her visits to Ray's shabby-chic café with its vintage crockery and large dresser displaying locally produced foodstuffs for sale. Relative calmness settles in. The smell of a blend of spices wafts over from where Ray is at work behind the counter, standing tall at his barista machine, calmly spooning coffee beans into the grinder. He only recently purchased this machine because the old one finally conked out on him. She recalls him

HER MISSING HUSBAND

proudly showing her how it worked just after it arrived, telling her he felt like a child with a new toy. Man and machine in perfect harmony. He looks over at her, and she quickly looks away, embarrassed he has caught her staring.

He returns with a tray. 'Here we go.' He hands her a cup that smells more of nutmeg and cinnamon than coffee. 'I'm undecided if this one needs milk.' He moves a couple of files aside, making room for a small jug of milk. 'Try with and without milk and let me know what you think.'

Teagan bids them farewell for the day. 'Take the rest of that chocolate cake for your boys,' Ray tells her. 'Wait up, and I'll get it for you. I'll make another one in the morning.' He wraps the cake in foil. His moves are graceful and with purpose. Something she's never noticed before. He hands the parcel to Teagan, locks the door, and turns the welcome sign from open to closed. 'Your daughter popped in a couple of times with her boyfriend while you were away.'

'She said.'

'She's just like you.'

'Really? People say that, but I can't see how.'

'Her mannerisms.' He grins. 'And her coy smile.'

'Do I have a coy smile?'

He winks at her. 'Sometimes. She seems to have her head screwed on too. She and Albert seem pretty serious.'

'They are. He's following her to uni, and they're moving in together.'

'She said. How do you feel about that?'

Lori twists her lips. 'It's all happened so quickly. In my mind, a little too quickly. I wish they'd got to know each other before making such a commitment. But they seem good together. And Molly is happier than I've seen her in a very long time.'

'He's good for her, then?'

'I think he is. What I can say for sure is that he's in a different league to some of the losers she's hung out with over the years.'

'You look very tired, if you don't mind me saying.' Ray's tone is full of sympathy. 'Tough few days, I take it. Want to talk?'

'You'll wish you'd never asked.'

'Try me.'

There's a different air between them today. As if their heart-to-heart the other night has loosened the bricks in the wall of self-protection they have each built around themselves. Lori surprises herself with how much she opens up about everything that has happened to her. When she has finished, Ray looks to be in utter shock. 'See, I told you you'd wish you'd never asked,' she says.

'Do you think they're related?'

'What do you mean?'

'This guy Frankie's murder and your husband's disappearance.'

'I think they may well be, but I can't work out how. Howie knew of Frankie because of my involvement in Frankie's case, but they didn't know each other personally. Not that I'm aware of. If they did, Howie would've said something to me. I can't think of a reason why he wouldn't have.'

'Do you think Frankie was telling you the truth about knowing what happened to Howie?'

Lori nods. 'I do. Especially after talking to Niamh today, and how Frankie changed in prison. He might be able to fool the world, but he couldn't fool his wife.' Lori shrugs. 'Or maybe he could. One thing I'm sure about, though, is that he knew what happened to Howie.'

'What're you going to do now?'

Lori pauses to sip her drink. 'Goodness knows.'

Ray reaches over and gently squeezes her arm.

Lori pulls away as a spark of electricity ignites feelings she hasn't felt for a long time. A very long time.

'Look,' says Ray. 'If I can do anything to help you, please let me know.' He cups his hands around his cup.

There's an awkward silence before she says, 'Thanks. That's kind of you.'

'And please be careful. It sounds like this Frankie guy was involved with some shifty characters.'

'Anyway, enough about me.' She gestures to his paper-work. 'What're you up to?'

Ray groans loudly, nodding in the direction of his laptop. 'It's that time of year. Annual accounts. I hate it.'

'I thought you were an accountant before you ran this place.'

'I was. Doesn't mean to say I was any good at it.'

Lori laughs. 'Tell me about it. Two plus two equals anything but four in my mind.' She pauses. 'You know what? There *is* something you could help me with.'

He raises his hands. 'Fire away.'

'Paul gave me a set of accounts when I was in Chester. I want to get a valuation of the company so I can get advice on if it's worth selling our shares. I want to cover Molly's uni fees and living costs now she's serious about studying. And I'd like to know how much our shares could fetch.'

'Can't you ask your accountants?'

'It's tricky. I mentioned to Paul that I was considering it sometime in the future. He's got so much going on, I don't want him to know I'm seriously looking into it. Not at the moment.'

'Why?'

She doesn't want to tell Ray about what happened with April. 'It's complicated. Paul adored Howie. And vice versa. All along, he has believed that he's still alive and will turn up at some point. They shared an office, and Paul has left Howie's side untouched. Apart from the police pulling it apart during the initial investigation, it remains as it was the day he went missing. He's done everything to find out what happened to Howie. Paul has always said, if it were the other way around, he'd want us all to keep searching for him.'

'Crikey. It must be so difficult for you all.'

'It is. He's also having problems with his wife at the moment. And I sympathise with him. I can't help thinking if the shoe was on the other foot and something had happened to keep me away... I don't know – kidnapped or taken by a weirdo – how would I feel if I came back and Howie had moved on with his life?'

'I can take a look at the accounts for you. Drop them off in the morning.'

Lori's phone rings. Her face loses colour. 'I need to take this.'

It's Niamh.

33

'Seeing you today got me thinking, and it may be nothing, but I thought it was worth mentioning. You might not even have noticed, but Frankie had a scar above his left eye.'

'I did.'

'I hit him, and my engagement ring caught his face.'

'OK. Want to fill me in?'

'I'm not proud of this, and it shouldn't be used as an excuse, but it is what it is. My hormones were crucifying me at the time. Frankie and I had a misunderstanding. I'd employed someone to run my business while I was on maternity leave and, long story short, they let me down big time. Frankie was speaking to someone on the phone. I remember him being very agitated. When he put the phone down, he said something along the lines of, "Some people should take more care over their recruitment policy. You never know what lowlife you could end up with". He was looking at me at the time, and I thought he was directing the comment at me, and I lost it.'

'Is that it?'

'It just so happened that the comment wasn't directed at me. I think it was possibly to do with you and your husband. And the guy who was churning up dirt on you.'

'What makes you think that?'

'How much he irritated Frankie.'

'What's it got to do with my husband?'

'I wonder if that guy, whoever he was, had something to do with your husband's business. A disgruntled employee, perhaps. Anyway, dismiss it if you want. I just thought I'd let you know.'

Lori thanks her and ends the call. Ray is looking on inquisitively. 'You look even more troubled.'

'That was Frankie's wife, Niamh.' Lori frowns as she retells Niamh's story. 'Bit odd, don't you think?'

'It would've come out at the time of the police investigation, surely?'

'I would've thought so, but you know how tiny details can fall through the net. Maybe Paul knows. I'll speak to him.' Lori stands up. 'I should leave you to get on.'

'You don't have to.'

'I need to get back to Molly.'

Strolling home, Lori stops to sit on the grass verge. It grants her a spectacular view of the surrounding mountains which are sucking up the last of the sun. The raucous squawking of seagulls penetrates the evening sky. She has loved living here. But with everything going on lately, she's not as settled as she was. She needs to speak to Paul. She finds his number. He picks up on the second ring. 'I have something to ask you.'

'Shoot.'

Lori is about to say she went to see Frankie's wife but decides against it. She doesn't need reminding that she is playing with fire. She's already aware she could end up getting burnt. 'Did you know of an employee who had issues with Howie before he disappeared?'

'Where did this come from?'

'Something Frankie said to me on the phone before I went to see him,' she lies. Damn. Another lie.

'What's prompted this? It seems an odd thing to come out with now.'

'Was there?'

'The police asked me the same question. You're never going to have a completely happy workforce, especially in the game we're in. There are some tricky characters with big egos. I was the big bad wolf.' Paul's voice breaks. 'But you know Howie. He got on with everyone.'

As she approaches the lane leading to home, Misty and Shadow yank on their leads, and when she turns the corner, she sees the doors of her Honda wide open, bonnet too. Confused, she quickens her pace to keep up with the dogs, now straining on their leads. 'Hello,' she calls out warily.

Albert appears from behind the front of the car and Molly from the driver's seat. 'I've fitted new spark plugs and an air filter for you. It looks like they were well overdue for a change. Should be as good as new.'

'Oh. Thank you.' She is taken aback. 'Where did you get them from?'

'Your landlord. He was here yesterday sorting some stuff out in there.' Albert points to Parsons's garage at the side of the house. 'I asked him where I could get some parts for your car for you. He's a great chap, isn't he? He said he needed to head into town and would pick up everything I needed. And he lent me some tools.'

Lori doesn't know what to say. She's not used to people helping her. 'How much do I owe you?'

He nods to Molly. 'Molly settled up with him.'

Lori thanks her daughter. 'I'll transfer the money to your account.'

'As I said, you'll need to get a garage to look at the air con. And you should get them to look at your shock absorbers and the brakes. I thought I noticed a very slight screeching sound the other night when you hit the brakes,' Albert says.

'Thanks,' Lori says.

'No worries.'

Molly gives Albert the doting look of love. A woman smitten. She turns to Lori. 'I've made a chilli for us. I just need to cook the rice.' Molly hooks her arm through Lori's, like she used to do when she was a child. She chatters away as they stroll to the house. Lori looks behind her, wondering why she feels like someone has not just walked over her grave, but stood on it and jumped up and down.

. . .

After dinner, the three of them watch a film together. It's a rare occurrence for Lori. Seldom does she spend an evening in front of the TV. Molly signs into her Netflix account and chooses a film about a serial killer. Lori tries to enjoy it, but her wandering thoughts constantly distract her. The flickering and tapping from Albert's laptop as he continues working doesn't help. And Molly is scrolling through her phone, which Lori finds mildly irritating. She feels bad for feeling this way but, to be fair, they haven't visited at the best time of her life. It's why she keeps herself locked up. She used to be a social butterfly. Like April, she was always up for a party; once upon a time, in a very different life. Now she's happier with her own company.

When the film ends and Molly and Albert head to bed, Lori stays downstairs. She is wired. There's no way she'll be able to sleep. She decides to carry on working. Often, her best words come to her at night when the world is dormant. She grabs her bag and the fan from the dining area and heads down to her writing den. Her devoted dogs tail her, snuggling up on their cushion.

Lori clicks on her news app, searching for an update on Frankie's murder. Half an hour later, she is still looking, despite knowing she is reading the same stories over and over again, just being reported by different newspapers.

Misty lays her head on Lori's bare foot. Not wanting to miss out, Shadow lays his head on her other foot, and before long, she's back in her zone of escapism, lost in getting her story onto the page. Word after word flows with ease: sentences morph into paragraphs; paragraphs into chapters. She's unstoppable. After the stress of the relentless writer's block she has suffered for the best part of this year, and the resulting imposter syndrome playing havoc with her creativity, she feels euphoric. That's what she loves so much about her occupation. It's an escape from the ugly world out there. The world of missing husbands and fucked-up daughters. The world of pissed-off besties. The world of dirty rats. Her distracted mind absorbs the tension in her neck that has been troubling her for days. She loves this story idea. Her inspiration delivers into the early hours. Several thousand words have worked their way from her thoughts to the screen when a noise outside disturbs her.

Misty and Shadow dash from their bed to the door. Their low growls turn into loud barking. Lori rushes to the door that she left ajar due to the heat. 'Hush now, you two.' She grabs their collars. It's probably just a wild animal, and she doesn't want to let them loose in case they chase it. Not to say the noise hasn't spooked her. She looks out of the den window, but the light from the fluorescent ceiling LED bulbs reflecting on the window don't allow her to see out. She switches off the light. The dogs quieten. She shoos them back to bed and slips out of the den door. Something moves in her peripheral vision, and she hears a clanging noise that appears to come from the pathway at the side of the house that leads to the lane. As if someone has tripped over an item of junk belonging to her landlord lined up against the wall. She sighs. It's probably just a cat or some nocturnal animal.

Lori returns to her desk, as unsettled as her grumbling

dogs. Fishing out two dog biscuits from the pot on the side of the desk, she hands one to each. 'You're good dogs. You wouldn't let anything happen to your mum, would you?' The dogs' eyes exude their usual look of adoration as they chew on their treats before resuming their nestled position by Lori's feet.

It's no good. The interruption has disturbed her flow. Words stop coming. It was all going so well. She saves the Word document she is working on and digs the file Paul gave her out of her bag. Before she takes these accounts to Ray tomorrow, she should take a look, but as she loosens the papers, she yawns. It's late, but she knows that's not the real reason. It's the figures. She never was a numbers person. Even at school, maths was her least favourite subject. But she knows deep down that it's not that either. It's the contrition she feels for even considering selling her share in the business Howie slaved over for most of his adult life.

The photo she brought down from the sideboard in the dining area yesterday catches her attention. It's another one of her favourites of Howie and her at an awards ceremony about ten years ago. He and Paul had won a prestigious award for best production design of a short film they'd worked flat out on for weeks. April had captured the perfect shot of Lori and Howie. Their faces are half-turned to each other, their foreheads just about touching as if they are about to kiss. The glow in Howie's eyes reflects his love for his wife.

She sighs. The heavy bag of guilt she should have

discarded years ago always manages to open with the same thoughts. Howie would never have left her and Molly. And if it had been her who had vanished into thin air seven years ago, Lori knows he would never have given up on her.

34

The following morning, the dogs are waiting at the bottom of the stairs when Lori surfaces, their claws striking the stone floor excitedly like a pair of tap dancers. 'Down, Shadow,' she commands as his front paws dig into her thighs. They tail her into the kitchen, where she fills their bowls with food and water and leaves them eating while she finds the file Paul gave her, and stuffs it in her rucksack.

Opening the stable door, she shuffles her feet into her walking boots. The dogs bound out after her. It's already hot with no sign of a breeze. Lori absently goes to grab the dogs' leads from their home on the hook to the side of the door. But they aren't there. Puzzled, she looks to see if they have dropped to the floor. They haven't.

She always leaves them there. Is she going mad?

She thinks back to last night. Did she put them away after she returned from Ray's? What happened? Her mind is fuzzy. She replays the sequence of events. Albert had fixed her car. She followed Molly into the house, but she can't recall removing the leads.

She goes outside to search for them, but they are nowhere to be found. 'I'm losing my mind,' she says to her dogs. After fifteen minutes, she gives up and rummages around in the basket in the bottom of the pantry that houses their box of treats and various toys, including their spare leads. The ones she doesn't like using because the clasps sometimes get stuck without her noticing, but they'll have to do for now. Unnerved and irritated, she hooks the clasps onto the dogs' collars and shuffles her wrists through the handles. 'Only a quick one today, you two. It's super hot out there already.'

It's early when she stops by the café. She knows Ray will already be there, busy preparing for the day ahead. A ritual he never wavers from, he told her when she commented that he never takes a day off. Apart from Christmas Day, that is. He maintains he must be there early to get ahead of himself, especially in the summer months, to catch the early-morning footfall of walkers off to the mountains or waterfall. They often order food as well as a drink. The dogs are going nuts around Ray's legs, knowing he always gives them a small treat. She delves into her rucksack. 'I've got the accounts you said you'd take a look at for me.'

'Are you stopping for a coffee?'

She shakes her head. 'Just off to the falls before it gets too hot. I'll stop by on the way back.'

He waves the file at her. 'Teagan's due in soon. I'll take a quick look at these.'

'Thanks. I appreciate your help, but you're busy. There's no rush.'

'Not at all. It's what friends are for.'

Lori meanders up the long, gentle gradient of slate shingle path that curves around the side of the mountain and leads to the falls a little over a mile away. She breathes in the fresh scent of the surroundings. Wild pinkish–purple foxgloves sprinkle the landscape. Triangular fronds of overgrown bracken brush against her bare legs. The dogs pull on their leads, sniffing and leaving their scent at regular intervals. Thankfully, they show no interest in the sheep that look on with concern etched on their skull-like faces. A dog barks in the distance, blocking out the faint hum of the falls further up the mountains. It is deep and loud, nothing like that of a springer spaniel. An English mastiff or German shepherd, perhaps?

Lori has that recurring feeling of how much she loves it here in this part of the world: the seclusion, the anonymity, the beautiful surroundings. She contemplates Howie, as she always does on her morning walk. But today, Ray also dips into her thoughts. She can't deny the feelings she has started to develop for him. They feed hungrily on the ever-present guilt she harbours as she imagines having a relationship with someone else. She steers her thoughts back to her husband until she spots a figure on the mountains about a hundred metres away. She flips her sunglasses to rest them on the top of her head. The person is standing still and seems to be gazing her way. Is it the same person she thought she saw last week? Or is she being paranoid?

An elderly couple are walking towards her, hiking poles supporting their stride. 'Another scorcher,' the lady says with a regal tone.

'You must have been up early,' Lori responds, trying but failing to adopt a cheery air. She doesn't have it in her today.

'Up and at it,' the elderly gentleman says, chuckling. 'All part of getting old. Can't lie in bed. There's too much of life worth living.'

A seagull squawks and croons overhead. 'Good for you,' Lori says, glancing up to where she thought she saw the figure. But she can no longer see it, making her question if it was there in the first place. After she swallows the lump that feels permanently lodged in the back of her throat, Lori carries on to the falls with no further sightings.

When she returns to the café, the dogs have a drink. Their tongues flop from the sides of their mouths as they collapse onto the relative coolness of the tiled floor underneath the corner table where Lori claims her usual spot.

Ray appears from the kitchen and places a flat white in front of her. 'I had a quiet moment, so I took a quick look.' He waves the file she dropped off earlier. 'Do you ever look at the accounts?'

Lori takes a sip of coffee, shaking her head. 'Paul takes care of all that stuff.'

'There are four directors, right? You and your husband, and Paul and his wife.'

'That's right.'

'Annual accounts must be formally approved by a majority of shareholders, so you must sign off on them.'

'Yes, I suppose I do. Paul takes care of it all. He is always sending me stuff, but to be honest...' Lori's face scrunches up into a ball of embarrassment. 'I ignore all his emails that have anything to do with finance.'

'Why?'

'I've already told you I'm rubbish at that kind of thing. I can just about reconcile my own bank account. Money and finances and all that stuff doesn't interest me. It never has. I'm a words person, not a numbers person. Paul always encourages me to keep an eye on things. He gives me hard copies of everything I need to sign and goes through it all with me. Why, what's wrong?'

'I'm not suggesting anything is untoward here. And I'm sure the accountants would have raised any issues if there were any. But if I were a prospective investor or looking to buy the company, I'd make a couple of observations.'

'OK. Shoot. Mr Big Shot Investor,' she adds teasingly.

Ray laughs. 'First of all, I know nothing about the industry or what I would expect to see from the way the business is structured. So, grant me a little poetic licence, please.'

Lori smiles. 'Get on with it. I won't quote you or make you sign your comments in blood.'

He returns her smile. 'Turnover has decreased the past couple of years.'

'Covid. Cost of living crisis. Companies have cut their marketing budgets.'

He nods. 'I thought that. But, looking at the administrative expenses, they appear disproportionately high in relation to the turnover.' He points between different figures in the report, which all seem to merge into one.

Lori frowns. 'You're starting to lose me already.'

'In simple terms, you're spending too much compared to the money you're making.'

'Gotcha. What on?'

'Not sure. I need more than this,' he says, waving the file at her. 'I need to drill down into the accounts to determine that. I don't suppose you have access to the accounting software?'

'I wouldn't have a clue. That's Paul's domain. I don't want him to know I'm looking. It's delicate. If I do decide to sell any shares, he's going to be devastated. He'll think I'm giving up on Howie. He's always said that until a body is found, Howie could walk in through the door any minute.'

'I understand that.'

'I need to tread carefully.'

'Call the accountants. They'll give you access, and I can take a more detailed look.'

'Won't they think it's odd?'

'Just say you're getting your finances in order and need login details for the company accounting system. It's an administrative task. They shouldn't think twice about it.'

Ray appears to detect her unease. He absently reaches across and squeezes her hand. 'All I'm saying is if you are serious about selling at any stage, then you must make sure all the T's are crossed and the I's are dotted. Any prospective purchaser will carry out their own due diligence. If anything is amiss or not as it seems, it may jeopardise the sale or reduce the price.'

Lori withdraws her hand from his. She shivers. She can't place why, but for the first time since they met, she's uncomfortable in his presence. Or is that remorse for spending so much time in his company? She needs to go home. 'Should I be concerned?'

'I don't know until I've taken a closer look.'

35

Lori groans inwardly to see her landlord, Mr Parsons, at her garden gate. The dogs bark. They always do. He must creep them out as much as her. Or are they sensing the paranoia that seems to be a permanent feature in her life these days? 'Just fixing the lock as I promised,' he says, fiddling with a screwdriver.

'Thanks,' she says, as she passes through the gate. Didn't he say he was going to do that at the weekend? Albert said he was here on Saturday fixing stuff. Her arm brushes the sleeve of Mr Parsons's coat. The mildew smell makes her cringe. Then she reminds herself that he helped Albert fix her car. She stops to thank him before heading to the cottage.

'Wait,' he calls out.

She turns to his forceful instruction.

'This fell out when I started work.' He hands her a red envelope.

A chill runs through her. Another one so soon? Never

has he sent them in such quick succession. They usually only come once or twice a year. She rips open the seal. It's all so familiar. A typed few lines on a red piece of folded paper conveys the usual message.

Hello Loretta.
It's me.
What do I keep telling you?
You can run.
But you can't hide.
However hard you try.
The time has come.
Payback time.

She looks around, half expecting to see David Grove lurking in the bushes.

Dashing around to the back of the house, she stuffs the letter into her rucksack. Damn him! She can't be distracted. She's got more important things to deal with. Focus, Lori. She needs to focus. She won't let David Grove get the better of her. The time has come, though. She needs to report him to the police.

The smell of frying wafts from the stable door. Molly must be making breakfast, but she finds Albert in the kitchen. It's not that he is standing at the stove frying eggs in one pan and bacon in another that bothers her, but rather his mostly naked body. All he is wearing is a pair of black satin boxer shorts, the waistband of which sits only an inch or so above his pubic bone.

'Hi, babe.' He turns and slams his hand over his mouth, chuckling when he sees Lori. 'Sorry, I thought you were Molly. She went to buy some bread.' He glances at the kitchen clock. 'She's been gone a while. You didn't see her?'

Lori shakes her head. She's uncomfortable, staring at this man wearing only a pair of boxers in her kitchen. It feels like an invasion of her space.

Albert holds up a spatula. 'Fancy some eggs?' The sunlight shining through the kitchen window catches the blondeness of the hairs on his chest.

Her phone rings. It's Hector. 'No, you're good, thanks,' she replies to Albert. 'I need to get down to some work.' She pretends to answer the phone. She doesn't want to speak to her agent, but it's better than talking to her daughter's near-naked boyfriend. She clicks the delete call button but engages in a fictitious conversation as she walks to the fridge to grab a bottle of water.

The dogs sit by Albert's feet, drooling in the hope of a scrap. He picks up a fork, stabs a piece of bacon and tears away the fatty rind with the spatula. Dropping the rind on the chopping board, he chops it in two and hangs each half over the dogs' heads. Misty raises her front paws. Shadow mirrors his sister's eager stance, pirouetting on his hind legs. Their jaws open in anticipation. Albert dangles the pieces over their mouths, teasing them before letting go and squatting down. 'I'm going to miss you when we go,' he says, engulfing them in his arms as if they were his own.

Albert stands up and stretches his arms above his head, leaving them up for too long as if parading his lean physique. Inexplicably Lori is uncomfortable. This man is hyper-confident. She ends the imaginary call and has to look away only to freeze when she notices hanging up on the hook by the stable door the two dog's leads she couldn't find earlier. But they weren't there. Were they? She would bet her last penny they weren't.

'I'll miss you as well, Lori. Thanks for having us. It's been great to get away for a few days. You sure live in a beautiful part of the world.'

She shivers, feeling as uncomfortable in his presence as she did in Ray's before she left the café. What has got into her today? 'What time are you off?'

'Molly was looking at train times before she went out. She's thinking of catching an early afternoon train if that suits you.'

'Sure.' Lori picks up the leads. 'Did you move these earlier?'

'Sorry?' Albert looks at her as if she has grown another head.

'Nothing.' She turns to her hounds and ushers them outside and across the garden to her writing den.

Unsettled, she searches for the number of the company accountants, Hooper & Watts Financial Services, in her phone. Aston Hooper is an old school friend of Howie's, and after Howie disappeared, he used to call Lori every day. Calls that dwindled to weekly and then monthly, to be replaced by text messages or emails, like they had with so many other friends. There is only so long anyone can suffer the awkward silences that follow the words, "No, no news." To be fair to him, Aston keeps in touch more than some of Howie's other friends, who she would have expected to hear from more often. But then that's probably because of the financial connection.

'Lori. This is a nice surprise.' After the "no news" message is conveyed, they exchange a few further pleasantries, until Aston says, 'I sent you a set of accounts last week. I trust you received them.'

'I did.' But she knows she deleted the email after learning the content. 'Listen, Aston. I want to keep this between you and me, but I'm considering selling some shares in the company.'

'OK. Have you spoken to Paul and April about this?'

'No. And I don't want to tell them just yet. I want to look over some of the figures before I decide. Can you give me access to the accounting software, please?'

'Sure.' There's a pause. 'Can I ask why you don't want them to know?'

'It's a sensitive situation. Again, between you and me, Paul's not going through a good time. So I need to find the right moment. Besides, I haven't made a final decision on what I'm going to do yet. Give me a week or so.'

'Sure. I'll email you the login details.'

'Could you do that today, please?'

'I'll do it right away. Can I help you with anything else? Any advice on a potential sale, perhaps?'

'Just the login details will be fine for now.'

True to his word, within minutes, Aston emails access details for the company's accounting system. After sending them to Ray, Lori returns to the house. She wants to spend a few hours with Molly before taking her and Albert to the station.

Molly has made a jug of fresh lemonade, which they take to the table outside. She pours them both a glass. The sun shines brightly in the clear blue sky, heating their faces. Lori takes a sip of her drink. 'This is perfect. Not too sweet, not too sour.'

Molly smiles. The sunlight has faded her hair a lighter pink. It suits her better. 'Do you remember when Dad used to make it?'

Lori nods. 'I do.' She doesn't want to talk about Howie, but Molly does, so they reminisce about kite-flying, cake-baking, and mountain-biking.

'We need to spend more time together, Mum,' Molly says.

Lori looks at her daughter; how she has desperately tried to convey the same message for so long. 'Nothing would make me happier.'

'I'll make more of an effort. I swear.'

'You've really matured this year.'

'I know.' Molly reaches across the table and takes Lori's hand. 'I'm sorry, Mum. For all the anguish I've caused you.

You didn't deserve all the crap I put you through. You had enough of your own to deal with.'

'You were suffering. I get it. You couldn't help it.'

'I gave you hell. I know I did. I'm going to make it up to you, though. I promise you. You wait and see.' Molly chokes on her words. Where has all this come from? Lori doesn't know, but she's welcoming it with the open arms of forgiveness.

'I took my anger out on you. But Albert has helped me see everything so much clearer. I'm going to make you so, *so* proud of me.'

Lori squeezes her hand back. 'I already am.'

After dropping Molly and Albert at the station, Lori returns to her writing den, where she opens her work in progress. She could spend the afternoon stressing about everything that is going on around her, but she knows it won't get her anywhere. This would be a perfect day if it weren't for her troubles. Her time with Molly has given her comfort. She is finally getting her daughter back. And this story idea is going so well. Her fingers work as fast as her mind, each idea flowing smoothly into the next like the water cascading from the nearby falls. It faintly hums in the distance. She could carry on creating for hours. Not much is more satisfying than the gossipy undertone of her keyboard. The prose is flowing so naturally. Her story is taking shape. For a few hours, she feels so good, lost in getting her story one chapter closer to her readers. And then Ray calls.

36

'I picked a Sauvignon and a Barolo. I didn't know which you'd prefer,' Ray says as he enters the kitchen through the stable door with a laptop bag slung over his shoulder.

Lori can't help feeling a little nervous. It's the first time she has entertained a man in years. She berates herself for being so ridiculous. Ray is just a friend. He was at her house only the other day. But this is different, premeditated, planned. After he called to say he needed to speak to her, she surprised herself by asking him over as if it were an invitation she'd extended many times before.

He holds the two bottles in front of her. 'Red or white?'

'Either suits me,' she says, searching the drawer for a corkscrew. She can't remember when she last needed one. The bottles of wine she buys come with screw tops. Locating it among the kitchen utensils and serving spoons, she hands it to him. He sets to work as Lori finds two wine glasses, thinking he somehow looks different this evening. She glances down at the denim shorts and grubby T-shirt she's been wearing all day and realises it's because he has made an effort with his brushed hair and clean clothes. He has even trimmed his beard.

'Did Molly get off OK?' he asks, opening the bottle of Sauvignon.

She nods, handing him the glasses. 'I dropped them at the station this afternoon. I'm going to miss having her around. She's matured so much since I last saw her. It was like having my old daughter back with me. I think Albert is good for her.'

The cork pops out of the bottle. 'But...'

He reads her so well. Lori bites her lip. 'I don't know. He made himself very much at home.' She elaborates on when Albert took over her desk and the incident in the kitchen.

Ray pours the wine. 'He's a very confident lad, I'll say that.' He hands a glass to Lori.

She takes a sip. It smells citrusy and tastes expensive. 'I know. It's his personality. I just don't think I'd have behaved as presumptuously at his age.' She turns to the stove. 'I've thrown together a pasta sauce. A simple tomato one, with olives and parmesan. I hope that suits you.' All of Lori's dishes are basic. She never was a cook.

'Sounds good. Do you have a wifi code? I'll log in and you can see what I want to show you.' He pulls the laptop out of his bag.

'It's on the back of the router over there,' she says, pointing to the side. She hums along to Classic FM playing a serene piano concerto while he sets up.

'Fortunately, they use Xero, the same accounting software as I do.'

'Shall we chat over dinner?' she asks. 'This is ready to dish up.'

'Suits me.'

Lori serves the pasta. 'This is excellent,' says Ray appreciatively when they tuck in.

'It's the least I could do. I'll be honest with you, I'm not much of a cook. Howie always did the cooking.' Her voice cracks when she mentions her husband's name as if it's reminding her that Ray shouldn't be there. She shouldn't be having dinner with another man. It's wrong. 'So, what have you found?' she asks, wanting this over and done with.

'Well, the good news is that your company seems to be holding its own in the wake of the pandemic. Furlough helped you significantly, I would say.'

'That's what Paul said. All the staff were furloughed. They couldn't have survived the pandemic without it.'

'I don't know how the market is doing, but should you decide to sell, I wouldn't be surprised to see you arouse a lot of interest. You have some outstanding reviews from some big corporate names. And some impressive celebrity names starring in some of their videos.'

'That was Howie's doing. He always chased those reviews.'

'But I think a few anomalies need explaining whatever you decide you want to do.'

'Like what?' Lori takes another sip of the Sauvignon. It's been a long time since she drank wine this delicious.

Not even the bottle Hector ordered at the tapas restaurant the other day was as good. She takes another sip. It's going down as easily as water. She could get used to this.

'Your capital expenditure is relatively high, but I'd expect that with all the equipment and technology needed in your business, I guess. Although I will give that further investigation. I focussed more on the expenditure because it hasn't declined in line with the income streams.'

'Howie was always bemoaning the cost of keeping up with advances in technology,' Lori calls out as she goes to the kitchen to fetch the Sauvignon from the fridge. 'You spend a fortune on a piece of equipment only to find a newer version comes on the market within a year.' When she returns, she refills their glasses and leaves the bottle on the table.

Ray does that looking over the top of his glasses thing. There's something compelling about it, she thinks. Sexy. 'Question for you.' Ray takes a sip of his wine. 'Premises costs are extremely competitive. I would've thought the studios would cost much more. Most of the costs seem to be incurred while out on location.'

'I need to give you a quick history lesson. If you're interested.'

'I am. Carry on.'

'Before they died, Howie's parents owned a house with a chunk of land just outside Chester. Part of it was a disused airfield with an old hangar that passed to Howie when they died. He and Paul slogged close to three years developing it into the studios with the money Howie inherited from his parents' estate. Which is why Howie owns a bigger share than Paul. April and I own ten per cent each, Paul thirty, and Howie fifty.'

Lori recalls the days she hardly saw Howie in those three years. 'He and Paul both grafted so hard to make it work. It was inevitable they were going to succeed. I don't know exactly how they structured it in the accounting records. But that explains why premises costs are low.'

Ray nods. 'That makes a lot of sense. The other observation I have at the moment is overheads.' He turns the laptop to face her and moves around the table next to her. She can smell his woodsy aftershave. He points to a figure on the screen. 'That's your gross profit margin ratio.' He frowns at her. 'Now, I don't know the industry, but even so, that's not what I would call a healthy ratio.'

She looks at him as if he is talking in another language. One she's never heard spoken before. During her journalism days, she always steered away from the financial stories. They didn't interest her. In fact, they bored her. She left them for her colleagues who had a leaning towards money matters.

'If you look here, at overheads.' Another point to the screen from Ray. Another dazed look from Lori. 'The standout number is security costs. You spend a lot on your security firms. Or rather one of them.'

Lori picks up the bottle of wine and empties the last of it into their glasses. 'We have more than one?'

'It appears so. Now, look at this.' He toggles to another spreadsheet. 'The one I would be questioning – James Security – started just over six years ago and has been paid monthly by invoice ever since. If it were my business, for the size of it, I'd have recruited someone onto the payroll rather than paying inflated agency fees. There's probably an explanation, but it seems rather excessive to me. I'm surprised the accountants have never picked up on it.'

A loud noise startles Lori. A drop of wine spills down her T-shirt. Has something fallen over outside? That's what it sounds like. She glances apprehensively towards the stable door. 'What was that?' she says.

'Probably just an animal.' Ray laughs. 'Thought you'd be used to all the nocturnal activities in this part of the world by now. It's probably that scary black panther walkers keep report seeing in the mountains. Some say it's a puma. There's a website with all the sightings.'

Lori bites her bottom lip, staring through to the kitchen.

'Hey, sorry.' He touches her arm. There it is again. That spark of electricity. He feels it as well. She knows he does by the way he instantly withdraws his arm and picks up his wine glass. 'I didn't mean to scare you.'

Her forehead is a frown of worried lines. 'Truth is, I've been a little jumpy lately. A few things have happened that I haven't been able to explain. I sometimes think I'm going mad.'

'You're not going mad. What's been spooking you?'

'Oh, it's nothing, me just being silly. Carry on entertaining me with the accounts.'

Ray laughs. 'You know, I did think when I dropped that milk off the other night that it's very dark around here. You should at least have a security light. Old Parsons should fit one for you.'

'Not him.' Lori shudders. 'The less I have to see of my landlord, the better. I don't want to sound mean, but he gives me the creeps.'

Ray laughs. 'Lots of people seem to give you the creeps.'

She can't argue with that.

'Parsons is all right, just a bit...' Ray raises his hands, curling and uncurling his forefingers as he says, 'Local.' He drops his hands. 'The guy has probably never stepped outside the village. You could get a security camera on the front and back of the house for not a lot of money. All linked to your mobile phone so you can keep an eye on things while you're not here, if you're worried.'

'Good idea.'

'I'll get it sorted for you, if you like. You know, you are brave, living so remotely all on your own.'

Lori laughs. 'I'm used to it. To be honest, I faced more than my fair share of challenges when I was a journalist. So much so that until recently, little fazed me. And then, of course, Howie went missing.' She clears her throat. 'I'll be fine. I have my brutal guard dogs.' Misty and Shadow's tails thump on the sofa as if they can hear her reference to them. She returns her attention to the laptop. 'Let's carry on.'

Ray leans into her to point at the screen again. Lori isn't sure if it's the music or the wine, but the closeness is intoxicating. 'See here, it looks like the contract started mid-2016 and has been going ever since. There've also been regular increases, which seem rather inflated to me. I searched a couple of salary comparison websites, and it just doesn't stack up.'

'I need to speak to Paul about this.'

'Like I said, I'm sure there's an explanation. But you can see where I'm coming from.'

'I've never taken any interest in the company before now. It's going to appear odd.'

'You *are* entitled to do this. You're a company director. You're just taking a healthy interest in your business. In fact, you *should* be taking an interest.'

Lori stares at him. He doesn't get it. Paul will immediately ask why she is suddenly taking an interest. He's not stupid. He'll guess what she is up to and will be distraught that she is serious about selling. What will that say to Howie when he shows up? No, Ray can't possibly understand. No one can.

37

Leaving the dogs an ample supply of water, and after oodles of cuddles and promises of a lengthy walk to the falls that evening, Lori hops into her car. Paul is meeting her at the studios at nine, and she wants to get on the road before the rush hour. But the damn thing won't start. 'Come on, please don't let me down now,' she mutters, turning the key several times. Albert was meant to have fixed it. She tries again. But no signs of life are forthcoming. Thumping her hand on the steering wheel, she sinks into the seat. She's going to hit heavy traffic now. If she ever gets it started, that is. It's so time to get a new car.

She texts Paul to tell him she will be late and notices she has a voicemail. She dials in to listen to her message. Her stomach turns to hear DI Bradford's voice, the detective in charge of the Frankie Evans case. He asks her to call him. He sounds so formal. What does he want from her? Her hands shake as she grabs a pen from her bag and replays the message to jot down the number he has left.

As she waits for him to answer, her stomach takes another turn as she notices a smear of blood on the bottom edge of the driver's seat. Is that Frankie's blood? That wasn't there previously. Surely she would have seen it?

DI Bradford sounds more formal on the phone. 'I'm following up on a few leads regarding vehicles seen around the time of the murder, and I want to clarify a few points with you. We can account for your car and Paul's, but another is still of interest to us. Just checking, has anything else come to mind?'

'No, nothing. If it had, I'd have contacted you.' The call seems a waste of time. Is he simply keeping her on her toes, or is this a genuine question?

'We still can't account for the dark VW Golf seen around the church. You don't remember seeing it?'

'I already told you, no, sorry, I never saw another car there.'

'OK. Please do call me if anything comes to mind. Thanks for your time. I'll be in touch.'

What was the point of that call? Wouldn't his time be better spent looking for Frankie's killer than asking her questions he has already asked? Lori tuts as she tries the ignition again, breathing out a big sigh of relief when the car finally starts. It seems to be ticking over a lot more efficiently. Thank goodness Albert fixed what he did. A wave of guilt pulses through her for what she said about him to Ray. Albert also sorted the blockage in the shower during his stay, which had been annoying her since she'd moved in. And he fixed the curtain pole in the lounge that was sagging in the middle because the fixings had come loose, so the two halves didn't meet properly. She should have asked the landlord to sort all these jobs, but she wanted to avoid inviting Mr Parsons into the house. Ray says she has got Mr Parsons all wrong. He did get the parts for her car. The wave of guilt returns, crashing through a bit harder this time. She was wrong to have had such unkind thoughts about these two men who have shown her such kindness.

The farmhouse Howie's parents once owned sits at the end of a mile-long country lane. They had lived there all their married life until the double-diagnosis of dementia within six months of each other forced them to move to a local nursing home for their final years. Passing the house makes her feel nostalgic. His parents were a spritely couple before their cruel illness took hold and they no longer recognised Howie and her any more. It was heart-breaking to witness, especially for Howie. And tragic for Molly, their only grandchild, who they had adored, and vice versa. Everyone loved Molly. She was that kind of kid.

The entrance to the disused airfield that houses the studios runs alongside the residence. She joins the concrete perimeter that leads to the hangar on the far side. She will never quite get over the vastness of the building that Howie so cleverly designed and developed with Paul over the years. It's been a while since she has been here. After Howie disappeared, she used to stop by regularly. She derived a sense of solace from being around those who knew him so well. But as staff conquered the shock, and the place returned to its usual hive of activity, Lori felt out of place among the workers buzzing around urgently as they caught up on missed work.

Life goes on.

Her visits became less frequent until they dwindled to sporadic drop-ins that always had her leaving in tears.

It has started to rain. Lori looks up at the sky. Dark, bluish-grey clouds hover in the distance. She closes her window. A downpour would be refreshing. Parking the car, she takes a deep breath.

Thankfully, Lori doesn't need to hunt for Paul, locating him in the office he shared with Howie. Or, as Paul would phrase it, "shares with Howie". There's no discussing Howie in the past tense where Paul is concerned. There never has been. The open-plan office sits in an elevated position and is accessed by a steep metal staircase. Howie designed it all, along with the balcony that surrounds it, allowing a bird's-eye view of the six sets below. As the business grew, and they could afford it, Howie installed glass roofs and a sound system on them. Flick a switch, and you can hear what is happening on each set from up on the balcony. 'Found us OK, then?' Paul says, in a lame attempt at humour. They both know why she stopped coming here. The pain that haunted her after each visit became insurmountable.

'Point taken. It's been a while.' Lori looks towards Howie's desk on the other side of the room. It seems like only yesterday she saw him proudly sitting in one of the two expensive director's chairs he sourced cheaply from eBay.

Paul clicks his fingers. 'Penny for them?' He appears to have lost weight, she thinks. His skin is sallow and his cheeks are hollow.

'Any more from April?'

'She sent me a text this morning. I was waiting to see you to tell you. She's coming home.'

Lori dumps her bag on Howie's desk. 'Thank goodness for that. Tell her I miss her and want to see her, won't you?'

He nods. 'What brings you here today, then?'

She shrugs, delaying the inevitable. 'Fancy a coffee?' She walks over to the makeshift kitchen area in the corner of the room. It's looking tired, she notices, like her. The worktop has a burn mark in the centre, and there's a crack in the butler sink Howie salvaged from his parents' house when they refitted their kitchen. He was only twelve, and his mum often relayed to Lori the time her son said, "That'll come in handy one day, Mum". From a young age, he always was a forward-thinker. Lori fills the kettle and flicks the switch.

'I wish you'd given me more time so I could've prepared. Given you a guided tour and introduced you to a few new faces. And showed you those new cameras we bought last month that I told you about. I'm afraid I'm negotiating that new contract for subletting two of the studios to a film production company. It could bring us in a tidy sum, and I'm up against it. I'm meeting the lawyers at ten and the company MD afterwards.'

Lori walks back to his desk and sits in the chair opposite him. 'I'm sorry I'm late. The bloody car wouldn't start. It's ready for the scrapheap, that thing. I won't keep you. I could've done it over the phone, but thought I was overdue a visit.'

'Sure. It's always good to see you here.'

Lori sits forwards and leans her elbows on the desk, clasping her hands tightly. 'Look, Paul. I won't beat about the bush. We've always been honest with each other, haven't we?'

He leans back in his chair. 'And?'

'I've been looking at the company finances. You know I've been toying with the idea of selling.' She sees his pained expression, and she tries to soften the blow that will cause even more distress. 'I'm tired, Paul. I think we all are.'

He lifts his head and glances over at Howie's desk, then back at her. 'What happens when he comes back?'

This is getting a tad irritating. They're going over old ground. She hates herself, especially with everything that has gone on with April. But she can't carry on like this. 'I started by trying to understand the accounts and wanted to ask a few questions.'

'You have been busy.' Someone who didn't know him so well wouldn't be able to detect the hint of sarcasm in his voice.

Lori finds herself fumbling through pre-rehearsed questions. She doesn't want to come across as critical or judgemental in any way. Finally, she spills the question she most wants answered. 'The security overheads look pretty hefty.' Her frown deepens. 'Especially the contract with James Security.'

'It needs to be.'

'Is that market rate?'

'It was Howie who got them in. You remember that break-in we had just before he disappeared? When we lost all that filming and production equipment.'

She nods. 'I do.' It was precisely a month to the day before Howie disappeared. She remembers because both events happened on the twenty-fifth of the month. He'd gone to work early that day – or she should say *earlier*, as he was always at his desk by seven-thirty each morning. As was Paul. They'd gone in an hour early to prepare for a big meeting with a prospective client. Howie was shaken up after it happened. And he was so angry, at the loss they had suffered and at himself for not having addressed the security concerns they'd had for a while. They had insurance for the loss of equipment, but it took them a long time to replace it all, and they lost business in the meantime that they weren't covered for. He knew the crappy CCTV system they had in place wasn't up to the job. And he was proved right when it failed to catch the perpetrators.

'It cost us thousands. Set us back a year, Howie reckoned. He said we couldn't afford to have that happen again. So he hired that company.'

'But the company came on board three months after Howie disappeared.'

The desk starts wobbling intermittently from Paul's leg jigging up and down against the side. It's annoying. Lori removes her elbows from the desk and sits back in the chair.

'That's right,' he says. 'There was a lead time. We had to wait for them to finish some of their other contracts and recruit new staff. I agree with you. I thought they were expensive as well, but Howie spent hours researching different companies and insisted they were the best. Aston pointed the costs out a while back. You would've been copied in on the emails.'

That serves her right for deleting finance-heavy emails.

'From time to time, I've thought of revisiting the whole of our security arrangement, but if I'm honest, every time I set time aside, something more urgent comes up. Better the devil you know, and all that. Plus, I know Howie will be pissed off with me when he comes back and finds out I've gone with another company.'

'So, who's Jimmy?'

Paul repositions himself in his chair. 'Jimmy?'

'There's the contract with James Security, and also Jimmy Blackman.'

'Oh, Jimmy. You've probably never met him. He replaced Wayne. Remember Wayne, our night watchman?'

'Did he leave?'

'He did. I invited you to his leaving do.'

Lori vaguely recollects the invitation. 'Yes, I recall, now you mention it.'

Paul's phone rings. He picks it up and starts a conversation. Lori returns to the kitchenette and opens the cupboard, grabbing the worktop to balance herself when she sees the mug with *Happy Father's Day* printed in a curve above a picture of Molly and Howie. Molly was only about five or six at the time. Lori last saw that mug years ago. She pulls out two different mugs with the company logo, and spoons coffee into each one.

'I'll catch up with you tomorrow,' she hears Paul say to his caller. He ends the conversation and calls over to Lori. 'Hold my coffee. I need to go. Apparently, there are new roadworks in town from a burst water main, and the traffic is hell.' He slips his phone into his chinos pocket and shrugs into a blazer. 'Have a wander around.' He opens a drawer, pulls out a navy silk tie and slips it around his neck. 'There're loads of people who'd love to see you.' Grabbing a file, he waves and gives her a straight-lipped smile. 'Speak soon.'

She tips the coffee from both mugs back into the jar. There are people she'd like to see as well. But she can't face it. She needs to get out of this place. There are too many ghosts, and it's too bloody sad.

After saying a quick hello to staff who might be upset if they knew she had been here and missed her, Lori returns to her car. As she leaves the building, she notices an older guy exiting a small outbuilding used for maintenance equipment. He is dressed in black trousers and a T-shirt with an orange hi-vis sleeveless vest over the top. As he turns to lock the door, she sees SECURITY printed on the back of the vest. She walks over to him. 'Hi.'

The guy spins around, a questioning look on his face.

'I don't think we've met. I'm Lori, Paul's business partner's wife. Howie's wife.' She extends a hand. 'You must work for James Security.'

'James Security? No, sorry, you must be mistaken. I'm Jimmy, not James. Jimmy Blackman.' He holds out a hand to greet her. 'Me and my colleague run security around here. James Security, did you say?'

Lori nods, her stomach tightening.

'I've never heard of them.'

38

The drive home takes forever. Although the Honda seems to have a new lease of life, and the earlier hiccup when it wouldn't start is a distant memory, the traffic proves a nightmare on the outskirts of town. Probably due to the roadworks Paul mentioned. Lori hopes he made it to his meeting on time. She sits at a set of temporary traffic signals, willing the red light to turn green as she replays her conversation with Paul. It's bugging her. Was Howie in some kind of trouble, which is why he hired James Security? She can't recall him saying anything at the time. How come Jimmy Blackman has never heard of James Security? And could the break-in have something to do with Howie's disappearance? Always so many unanswered questions.

Her investigative juices are overflowing. She wants to talk to April. She can't get the sighting of a VW Golf in the vicinity of the church, when Frankie died, out of her mind. And around the business, something smells off. Her senses rarely let her down. James Security. It certainly doesn't have a sizeable corporate name or feel to it. Yet, they are charging corporate rates. It doesn't stack up. Jimmy Blackman seemed genuine, though. Is Paul telling her everything? Does he know something about Howie's existence before he went missing that he is too afraid to reveal? She finds Paul's number, only to get his voicemail. Of course she does. He is in meetings.

The lights turn green. The driver in front edges forwards, as impatient as Lori to get moving. She puts her foot on the accelerator, only to slam on the brakes when the car in front suddenly stops. Banging her fist on the steering wheel, she swears profusely when the lights turn red again. This traffic is so time-consuming. She considers calling Ray to tell him what she has learnt this morning but decides against it. He'll be busy with customers at this time of the day. With the warm weather continuing, hikers will still be venturing out earlier than usual. Besides, she needs to back off from him a bit. He has aroused feelings she hasn't experienced in a very long time. Not since she met Howie. And it's wrong. As if she is being unfaithful. No one should feel such emotions with a wedding ring on their finger.

It takes Lori over two hours to make the forty-minute journey home. Parking up, she can hear the dogs' excitement. She smiles at the sense of belonging they reward her with. What would she do without them? Agitated, she greets their overwhelming mass of enthusiasm and heads to her writing den.

She fires up her iMac and switches on the fan. It whirls around, circulating the unrelenting warm air, but it's better than nothing. After Molly and Albert left, she could have moved back to the snug, but she has taken a liking to the den. There's something peaceful about working down there at the bottom of the garden.

Where to start? She may need Ray's help, but she's positive she can navigate the software from what he showed her last night. She's going to give it a good go, anyway. She finds the log-in details Aston sent her and clicks the link to access the accounting software. Bewildered, she studies the screen. It's like a maze. A network of boxes that link together somehow. Follow the wrong one, and you risk getting lost. Let's keep this simple.

'Now, what – or who – are you, James Security?' Is this an anomaly or something more sinister?

She can't help relishing the charge of excitement she recognises from her journalism days, the thrill of investigating a lead or starting on the trail of an unanswered conundrum. Nothing much tops the highs of solving a mystery. It's partly why she loves her job as an author so much.

Navigating the various drop-down menus, she soon learns it's easy to use, even for a novice like her. She clicks on recent payments. Bingo. Within minutes, she locates the contact details for James Security from an invoice. She grabs her mobile and calls the number, but the line is dead. It must have been added to the account details incorrectly.

Or maybe not?

Lori googles the business name, grimacing when she can't find anything. But she is used to this; the frustration that accompanies the euphoria as she peels away the layers of deceit until she exposes the core of truth. Lori knows there's only one thing for it. She has to keep going.

She searches the company's address attached to the account to see whether that bears any fruit worth getting her teeth into. Five minutes of further investigation reveals that the given address is a virtual company that facilitates receiving and forwarding emails and post. She knows from her journalism days that this is a means used by directors who do not wish to name their home address as their place of work. Or to give the impression their business is a larger concern than it is.

Or to hide something.

39

Lori drums her fingertips on the desk. What would she have done in her journalism days at this stage? She stares out of the den window across the garden, deliberating. Within a minute, she's got it. Grabbing her phone, she hunts for Howie's sister's number. Barbara is a high-flying senior executive at the same bank James Security uses. Barbara takes her work extremely seriously. Howie always said it was the reason why she had never walked down the aisle; she was already married to her job. Lori hasn't spoken to her sister-in-law for a while. But that's fine. They have a solid enough relationship to pick up where they left off as if they spoke only yesterday. Lori knows that what she is going to request of Barbara is a big ask, but she also believes Barbara would do anything if she thought it would lead to her brother's whereabouts.

Barbara answers after a few rings. 'Hey, stranger, what's cooking?'

After catching up on news since they last spoke, Lori

reveals the real reason for the call. 'I need a favour. For Howie.'

'What's happened?'

'Hypothetically, if I gave you a sort code and an account number, could you find the address of the person who owns that account?'

'Is it my bank?'

'Yep.'

'Want to elaborate?'

'Not at this point, if you don't mind.'

'*Hypothetically*, yes,' Barbara says. 'But of course, you never asked me.'

'Of course I didn't.' Lori relays the numbers.

'Leave it with me. I'm on a course all day, but I'll get back to you with what you need as soon as I can.'

Sometimes it's not what you know, but who.

Both dogs rush from under her desk and dart to the door barking, breaking her concentration. Lori stands and stares out of the window, relieved to see Ray appear from the side of the cottage carrying a stack of boxes. He is wearing his cricket hat, the clip strap swinging with his movements. She opens the den door and calls out, beckoning him with her cupped hand to join her.

She tries to suppress her delight at his arrival as his slim frame heads towards her.

'How was your trip?' He removes his sunglasses and hooks them over the pocket of his T-shirt.

'More questions than answers. Come inside; it's cooler. What've you got there?'

'I was at the retail park. As luck would have it, the

video doorbells were on offer.' He unloads the boxes onto her desk. 'I hope you don't mind, but I took the liberty of getting you one for your front door and another monitor for the back of the house, plus a security light – all half price.'

Lori doesn't quite know what to make of Ray's generous gesture. She isn't used to such thoughtfulness and people helping her, like Albert, and Mr Parsons, and now him. Not since Howie disappeared. Ouch. There it is again. The stab of guilt twisting like a knife in her heart. She fumbles for words. 'Oh right, thank you. That's very kind of you. I know how busy you are.'

'It's fine. Teagan is in today, plus two other workers, and I needed to get a couple of things for the café, anyway. The sink is leaking and I needed a washer.' He pauses. 'It troubled me seeing you disturbed last night. I'm not meaning to sound sexist here, but a single woman living in the middle of nowhere shouldn't be without some form of security.'

'How much do I owe you?'

'I'll get them set up for you. It'll take half an hour max, and I'll be off.'

'How much do I owe you?' she repeats.

'Don't worry about that now. We can sort it out later. How did your morning go?'

She shrugs. 'I went to see Paul. It was sad being back there.' Her head drops slightly. 'Too many memories.'

Ray gives her a sad smile. 'I can only imagine.'

'We didn't speak for long as he had to go to a meeting.

He came out with a very plausible explanation for the costs.' She explains the break-in and the mass of expensive equipment that was stolen. 'I remember Howie being really cut up about the incident. He was the one who sourced James Security. I do recall him mentioning something about having to pay above market rate to get a decent company, especially with the studios being out in the sticks. But...'

Ray cocks his head to the side. 'But?'

'As I was leaving, I noticed a security guy coming out of the outbuilding where they store maintenance equipment. I spoke to him, and he said he had never heard of James Security. He sounded straight enough.'

'Strange. Did you ask Paul?'

'I've tried to call him, but there's no answer. He's busy, though. He was meeting our lawyers, and then a company interested in subletting some of the sets. You know, to raise some extra income.'

'I'm sure he'll have a simple answer.'

'So, here's the thing. You'll be proud of me.' Lori grins. 'I went into the accounting software and retrieved the James Security contact information.'

'Very impressive. See, I told you it's not that difficult.'

'I tried to call them.'

'And?'

'The line was dead.'

Ray shrugs. 'The number could've been input incorrectly on the system, or changed, perhaps.'

Lori grins at his perfectly well-balanced voice of reason. 'Exactly what I thought. But on further investigation, I couldn't find anything. And the address is one of those virtual offices. Something seems off.'

'I agree. It's worth looking into. What're you going to do?'

'I need to have it out with Paul.'

'Let me know if there's anything I can do.' Ray picks up the boxes. 'I've got some tools in the Defender if you're up for me doing this now.'

He has put her on the spot. Some security around the place would be a blessing, but she doesn't want to feel she owes him anything other than the money it cost to purchase the equipment. 'Only if you tell me how much I owe you.'

'You drive a hard bargain, Lori Mortimer.'

Lori laughs. 'That's what my old boss used to say to me.'

'I'll promise to tot it up and let you know later.'

She smiles. 'I'll come and open the stable door for you. Can I get you a drink?'

'No, thanks. Give me the keys. I'll open up, and you get on with whatever you need to.'

With nothing further to go on until Paul and Barbara return her calls, Lori opens her work in progress and resumes her story, glancing now and again out of the den door. Ray sets to work, placing the security light strategically on the corner of the cottage by the stable door, where it will be triggered if anyone comes around the back of the house. He calls her name and gives her the thumbs up, asking her to agree to the chosen position.

She can't believe the thought that enters her head. It's

kind of nice having him around. Despite their personalities being very different – he is much calmer than her, and he is too trusting of people – he has become a good friend. Lori is far more worldly, hardened by how cruel people can be to each other. She has seen too much in her line of work to be as trusting as him. Aware that her daydreaming is affecting her word count, she gets up and pulls the den door to and steels herself to focus on her writing.

Just shy of an hour later, Ray taps on the door. 'Sorry, that took a little longer than I thought. The one at the front door was tricky to put up.' He sweeps his hands together to brush off the dust. 'But isn't that always the case? When does any job only take half an hour? Have you got your phone?' Ray holds out his hand.

'Phone?' Lori asks, bewildered.

'You need to upload an app. That way, you can see 24/7 who is at your front door wherever you are.'

Lori laughs, half in jest. 'That's going to scare the life out of me.' She hands him her phone.

'It only takes a few minutes. You get on with what you have to, and I'll sort it.'

Lori bends over and gives Misty and Shadow some attention, while Ray fiddles with her phone. After a few minutes, he turns the screen to her. 'See, all done.' He gives her a rundown on how it works. 'When someone approaches the door, you'll hear a ringing on your phone. As simple as. I tell you what, I'll put it on my phone as well. Extra security for you if you're not around.' He hands over her phone.

She frowns. Does she really want him to do that? It

would be too rude to turn down his kindness. Taking her phone, she places it on the desk.

When he has sorted out his phone, he puts it in the pocket of his shorts. 'I must dash. The lunchtime rush will start soon. Adios.' A chiming sound echoes from Lori's phone as he exits the den. He turns. 'It sounds like you have your first customer.'

She picks up the phone and stares at the screen. A vision confronts her that she barely comprehends at first. But it doesn't take long. On the screen, via the video door-bell Ray has installed, she can see two people standing at her front door. Who can they be? Within seconds the reali-sation strikes. Her free hand shoots to cover her mouth in abject horror at the sight she has prayed she would never have to endure. 'Oh, no, no, please.'

'Who is it?' Ray asks, frowning deeply.

Lori's eyes well up. She looks pleadingly at Ray. 'It's the police.' It only takes a few seconds for the reason for their visit to sink in. 'Oh, no.'

'What's wrong?' Ray asks.

'They're here about Howie.'

40

'How do you know?'

Lori points at the screen, her hand trembling. 'That's the detective who has been working on Howie's case since the beginning. And she's the FLO.'

'FLO?'

'Family Liaison Officer,' Lori whispers. 'Howie's dead.'

Ray puts a hand on her shoulder. 'There could be several reasons they're here.'

'There's only one reason. For any other, they would've phoned.' Her stomach is turning, the nausea overwhelming. 'I know they would have.'

'They could've found him alive.'

'I know, Ray. I just know.'

He squeezes her shoulder. 'You don't. Not for sure. Keep calm until you've spoken to them.'

'I do.' She stands up. The dogs sit to attention and start whining. Lori's eyes are saucer wide. 'Let's get this over with.'

'I'll stay here with the dogs,' Rays say when they reach the kitchen. He grabs hold of Misty and Shadow's collars and bends down to comfort them as Lori heads to the seldom-used front door of the cottage, her face as grey as the slate hallway floor.

Lori opens the door. 'Charlie, Lizabeth,' she says, looking at the man and woman standing on her doorstep. Their forlorn faces confirm they haven't rung her doorbell to deliver news she wants to hear.

'Hello, Lori. May we come in?' says Lizabeth. Lori got to know her well during the weeks following Howie's disappearance. She still looks young, Lori thinks. As if time has stood still. 'We have some news about Howie for you.'

Lori leads the two officers through to the kitchen. The dogs spring towards her, eager to comfort their mistress. She grabs the worktop to anchor herself. Ray has switched on the kettle. One look at Lori's face, and he doesn't wait for introductions. 'I'm Ray. A friend of Lori's. Can I get you a drink?'

Lori is glad to have him here, taking charge. She nods her head towards Ray and then the FLO. 'Whatever you've come to tell me, you can say in front of him.'

Since she first met him, DI Charlie Knowles has never pussyfooted around the truth. It's what Lori has always liked about him. No bullshit, tell it how it is. But now, he appears to be delaying the inevitable. He declines Ray's offer of a drink and asks, 'Can we sit down somewhere?'

Lori leads them into the dining area, beckoning Ray to follow. She hears a small gasp from Lizabeth, as she studies all the photos of Howie and Molly that crowd the walls.

Lori's bottom lip trembles. She can't control it. 'Come on, Charlie, just say it,' she whispers as she sits opposite the officers. Ray stays standing, leaning against the sideboard.

DI Knowles clears his throat. 'A car has been found in Hannfield Quarry. A BMW. It would appear the hot weather has lowered the water levels revealing it to a passer-by this morning.'

The last scrap of hope Lori has hugged tightly around her for so long forces her to ask, 'Is it definitely Howie's car?'

'Lori, I'm afraid to inform you that a body has been found in the boot of the vehicle, and we have every reason to believe it is Howie. We wanted to let you know before the press jump on it.'

She stares at him. 'What happened?'

'The body is with the forensic team as we speak.' DI Knowles pauses, his usual confident manner gone astray in the gravity of his message. 'But it would appear that his neck had been broken.'

Lori exhales a faint whimper. 'Is that how he died?' She needs to know. The thought of him being dumped in the boot of his car alive, knowing his fate, will break her heart even more.

'There'll be a post-mortem which should be able to tell us the cause of death.'

'Will I be able to see him?'

A hand of support squeezes her shoulder. She looks up

to meet Ray's sympathetic face. Her voice breaks. 'I can't, can I?' She turns to the officers. 'There's little left of him, isn't there?'

They don't need to answer her. Their expressions confirm one of the myriad of Google searches she has made over the years. What happens to a body when it's buried? What happens to a body left to rot in a disused warehouse? What happens to a body submerged in water after one year, two years... seven years?

'How will you identify the body? It might not be him.' The final crumb of hope is disintegrating fast.

DI Knowles clears his throat. 'From his dental records, which you know we already have on file.'

'How long will that take?' Lori asks.

'I can't say for sure, but I've asked this to be treated as an urgent case.'

Lizabeth steps in. 'I know nothing can prepare you for this, Lori. Is there anything you can tell us that may be of use?'

'I've told you all I know a thousand times.'

'We know,' says DI Knowles, frowning at his colleague. 'But now circumstances have changed. This is no longer a missing person's case. We're now treating this as a murder enquiry.'

Murder. The word stings. As the hope of finding her husband alive has slowly diminished over the years, Lori has often wondered how she would react if faced with the news of his death. Two scenarios have played out in her head. In one, she breaks down in floods of tears; in the other, she screams and shouts at the bearer of the news.

But neither happens. She is numb, as if the DI's words have thrown her emotions into another world. One she has no access to.

Howie was murdered.

'I need to let Molly know. She can't hear this on the news.'

DI Knowles says, 'Probably better sooner than later.'

'And Paul and April.'

'I can get in touch with them all if you prefer,' Lizabeth says, her voice kind and calm. She must be well-rehearsed in dealing with such tragic circumstances. Although her expression suggests it never gets any easier.

'There's no way I can let that happen,' Lori says.

'Think about it. The offer's there,' says Lizabeth.

'I need to go in person,' Lori says, knowing there's nothing to consider. 'If you'll excuse me. I need to get going.' As kind as they are, she doesn't want these people in her house any longer. She wants to be with her daughter.

Lizabeth glances at Ray. He answers the question before she has time to ask it. 'I'll take care of her.'

As the officers leave, DI Knowles says, 'Again, we're deeply sorry for your loss, Lori. Regardless of the lapse in time, this must be a tremendous shock. We'll be in touch once we've made a formal identification.'

'How long will that take?'

'A few days, maybe more. I'm sure they'll treat it as a matter of priority.'

'And then what?'

'Let us wait for the identification.'

'No. I want to know. What will you do if it's him?'

'We'll have to get everyone in for questioning again. Only when you're ready.'

As Ray sees the officers to the door, Lori stands at the kitchen sink, staring at the A3-sized framed photo of Howie and her on Padstow beach, the year he was last with them. 'Who?' she whispers, looking into her husband's laughing eyes. 'Who did this to you, my darling?'

'He was such a good man,' she says to Ray when he returns to the kitchen. 'A real workhorse, like you. You would've got on well with him. He worked so bloody hard. And all for what? This?'

Ray flicks the switch to re-boil the kettle. 'I'll make you some tea.'

Lori holds up her hand. 'I need to get going. I have to see Molly.'

'You can't drive all the way to Birmingham.'

'I can.'

'Lori, you're in shock. Let me take you.'

'What, in that beaten-up old thing of yours? We'll never make it.'

'We can take your car. I'm insured to drive any car. As long as you give me permission. Get yourself sorted while I make a couple of calls. I'll wait for you outside.'

Lori doesn't have any fight left. When she is alone, she phones Molly. She hears music playing. 'What're you up to?' Lori asks her daughter.

'Packing. Only five days until we move. I can't wait.

Albie has gone out to get some more boxes for me. Since I've been here, I've collected more junk than I thought.'

The happiness and innocence in her daughter's voice is torture. Lori takes a deep breath. 'I need to go to Birmingham, so I thought I'd drop in and see you.'

'You OK, Mum? You don't sound like your usual self.'

'I'm fine. I'll be there in a few hours. I won't stay long.'

Lori ends the call and walks up to the photo of her and Howie. 'I won't give up.' She reaches out her fingers and strokes her dead husband's face. 'But help me out here. Lead me to the bastards who did this to you. Because I won't rest until I find them.'

41

Neither Paul nor April pick up when Lori calls, which doesn't surprise her. Paul could well be in his meeting, and April has yet to answer her calls since she last saw her. She really hopes her friend will come round. Ever since April turned up at her cottage last week, Lori has tried to put herself in April's shoes. Her friend needs space – time to process what has happened. She leaves them each a message saying she needs to speak to them urgently. There's news from DI Knowles that they need to hear. She calls Barbara and leaves the same message.

The journey to Molly's place goes on forever. 'I still can't believe it,' Lori says as Ray parallel parks outside the converted Victorian townhouse where Molly rents a flat. 'What if they've got it wrong?'

He replies with a look of sympathy. 'I'll wait here,' he says. 'Take all the time you need.'

Molly answers the intercom in a fluster. 'Have you forgotten your keys again?'

'It's Mum.'

The lock clunks, and the door grinds as Lori pushes it open. The communal flight of stairs to her daughter's third-floor flat proves a painful struggle with the weight of her husband's death she has to carry. Her mood drops even lower as a waft of weed hits her. She's not going to find Molly smoking, is she? But her fears are allayed when she realises the smell is coming from the neighbouring flat.

Molly knows something is up as soon as she sees Lori. She always was an astute child. 'It's Dad, isn't it?' Her breathing quickens. 'He's dead, isn't he?'

'Let's go inside, love.'

'Oh, Mum!' Molly cries. 'No.' She turns and rushes down the hallway.

Lori follows her daughter to the small lounge which is in disarray with the upcoming move. Rolls of bubble wrap, brown paper and empty and sealed boxes are spread across the room. Molly switches off the radio and collapses on the sofa, dropping her head in her hands, struggling to breathe. The sight claws at Lori's heart. She drops down beside her daughter, cuddling her, as she shares the news DI Knowles has darkened her life with forever. She is as delicate as possible, economical with the details. Molly wails. Lori remains numb. She knows the tears will come. They are there, waiting their turn. They will pour for days, eventually. For now, she needs to delay her own grief to support her daughter.

She also has to find out who murdered her husband.

Lori consoles her daughter with every comforting word in her vocabulary until Molly's cries calm to despairing whimpers. A voice disturbs them. 'Hey, numpty, you left the front door open.' Albert strides in with a stack of flat-packed boxes clenched under his muscled arm. He glances at Molly and then at Lori. 'What...?'

'My father's body has been found. The police are treating it as murder.'

'Oh, babe.' He drops the boxes and rushes to the other side of Molly, who falls into his embrace, the tears coming thick and fast as he kisses her head. 'I'm here for you.' He looks at Lori. 'I'm so sorry.'

'I'll make us a drink,' Lori says, preparing to get up. The sight of her daughter suffering is killing her.

'No. I'll do it.' Albert jumps up. He places a strong, sympathetic hand on Lori's shoulder. 'Strong sweet tea all around.'

The most absurd thought enters Lori's head. She is going to look like a teabag before all this is over. Molly hauls herself to her feet. 'I need to go to the toilet.'

Alone, Lori feels like a spare part. She gets up and goes to the bookcase, half-full of Molly's books. The same as Lori, since she was little, Molly has adored books. The other half of the bookcase has been packed into large plastic containers ready for the move. Lori clears another shelf and loads the contents into an empty box. Busy, keep yourself busy. That's what she learnt after Howie disappeared. She swallows hard with the realisation that she can no longer say disappeared. Murdered is the word from now on.

On the shelf above the one she has emptied, framed photographs decorate the space in front of the row of paperbacks. They are all of Molly with her dad. Lori picks up one of them eating toffee apples nearly as big as their heads the year the three of them went to Disney. She holds it to her chest. This isn't fair. This isn't right. After a few moments, she replaces it, leaving it for Molly to pack.

Albert arrives back in the room. He makes space and places a tray on the table. 'I'm so sorry for your loss.' He walks over to Lori.

'I was just looking at these photos of Molly and her dad.'

'Good idea to get those packed up for her. Can I help?' Albert picks up a sheet of brown paper and wraps the photos until they are protected within a thick bundle. He places the bundle on top of the books she has just packed. 'Please don't worry about Molly, I'll take good care of her,' he says.

Lori hears her phone ringing from her bag. Here we go again. It reminds her of when Howie first went missing. She was glued to her phone, waiting for the call to say he had been found. And as every beat shredded her nerves, she held her breath wondering if it would be the news she wanted. Her jaw clenches as the realisation hits her. This is how she'll spend every day for the rest of her life unless she finds out who murdered him.

Fishing her phone out of her bag, she sees it's Paul. She sends his call to voicemail. She can't face speaking to anyone at the moment. She throws her phone back in her bag as Albert assembles and tapes the flat-packed boxes. He looks towards the door as if checking to see where

Molly is. 'Do they have any idea who could've killed him?' he asks.

Lori shakes her head. 'I will find out, though. If it's the last thing on earth I do. I will...' She stops as Molly returns to the room, her face blotchy and her eyes as red as her flamed cheeks. Molly picks up a cup of tea. Lori pings a text to Paul.

I need to see you urgently. Text me when you're out of your meeting.

Leaving Molly is a wrench. Lori suggests she return to the cottage with her. 'I can't, Mum. I need to get sorted here.'

Albert stops constructing the boxes and gets up off the floor. 'I'll do it for you, babe. I'll get everything packed if you want to go back with your mum.'

'No. I need to stay. This place needs a good clean. The landlord can be tricky. I can't afford to lose my deposit. Unless you want me to come back with you? I'll do that – stay with you for the night and get the train back tomorrow.'

'I'll be fine. Honestly, darling. Get on with what you have to do here.'

Molly sees Lori to the door. 'Please call me with any news. Any time.' She hangs over the banister, waving as Lori descends the stairs until they can no longer see each other. Lori turns and calls up to her, telling Molly she will call her later.

When she leaves the front door, her phone beeps. Paul has messaged.

> Meeting finally finished. Good news. Contracts signed. I tried to call. I'm heading home. What's happened?

Lori replies.

> I'll be there in an hour or so. I'll text when I'm ten minutes away.

Paul phones again. She diverts the call to voicemail. He sends another text.

> You're scaring me. What's happened?

She slips her phone into her pocket.

42

Ray switches off the engine outside Paul and April's double-fronted Edwardian house. Lori touches his arm. 'I don't know what I would've done without you today.'

'Take your time. I'll be here.'

Lori trudges up the pathway and rings the bell, glancing at the long crack in the tiled doorstep. She hasn't been here for a while but can't recall that crack being there before. What a strange observation to make at a time like this. But nothing is making sense.

She couldn't be more shocked to see April open the door. She looks thin, her face pale and drawn. 'It's Howie, isn't it?' April says. She looks so small, standing there in the same pink gingham sundress she was wearing when she confronted Lori at her cottage last week. Her expression is full of despair, sympathy and love, as if that night had never happened.

Words won't come. Lori fixes her eyes on her best friend. April reaches out and grabs her. They embrace, exchanging words of bitter remorse. April about the news of Howie, and Lori for being the bearer of such devastating news, and again for the mistake she made all those years ago, which has resulted in the recent silence between them. 'We need to tell Paul,' says Lori.

April breaks away. 'He only just got home. We were sitting in the garden.'

'Come on. Let's get this over with.' Lori links arms with her friend as they support each other along the hallway. Lori stares at the geometric tiled floor and the scuffed skirting board, thinking how this house has always felt like her second home. When Howie was around, they spent most weekends at each other's houses, and Lori and Molly practically lived in this house for the first few weeks after Howie disappeared… she corrects her thoughts… after Howie was murdered. Will she ever get used to thinking of losing him in these terms? Inexplicably, for the first time, she feels like an intruder. Is it because she hasn't been here for a while? She can't work it out.

They enter the open-plan kitchen with bi-folding doors that look out onto a long and narrow garden. April is proud of her garden. Along with Pilates, spending time with nature is her favourite pastime.

Lori hears Paul's voice. 'You're here.' He appears from the garden, his face as pale as his wife's. He rushes over to Lori and April, sweat running down his forehead. He stands with his hands on his hips, his voice barely audible. 'They've found him, haven't they?'

Lori nods, still remarkably calm. 'In Hannfield Quarry.'

Paul's head dips and swings to the side as if her admission has struck him across the face. He shuts his eyes. His face screws up in pain.

'I didn't want you to hear about it on the news,' Lori says, void of emotion. The proceeding five minutes are surreal. Paul drops to his knees and howls like a wolf. April bawls her eyes out like a baby who can't be consoled. Lori can't connect with them. It's all too much for her. She remains removed from her body. Floating above them as if she is trapped in a balloon of grief that refuses to burst.

'Is it definitely him?' Paul asks between sobs.

'They've not officially identified the body yet, but yes.' Lori remains impassive. 'The police believe it's him.'

She only stays for a quarter of an hour, but that's enough. Suffocated is the only way to describe how she feels sitting at their long dining table drinking a cup of tea that tastes of nothing. 'It might not be him,' Paul says, unconvincingly, when he sees her to the front door. 'We don't know for sure.'

'It's him, Paul.'

'How come you're so calm?'

She shrugs. 'I feel numb. All these years, I've wondered how I'd feel if we found out this is how it ended. But never did I think I'd feel like this. I can't describe it. It's like I'm empty. And I feel bad. I should be bawling my eyes out.' She steps outside. 'Perhaps it's my coping mechanism.'

'You're in shock. Why don't I drive you home?'

Lori points up the street to where Ray is parked. 'My friend drove me. Listen, I need to ask you something.'

'Fire away.'

She knows this isn't the time, but she doesn't care. Finding her husband's killer will remain a priority for as long as she walks this earth. She can't put someone else through the hell she has endured these past seven years. Another wave of nausea hits her at the thought of what Howie must have gone through.

'I know this is something you might have had good reason to keep from the police all this time, but now he's dead, was there something Howie was involved in that he wouldn't have wanted me to know about? I can take it, you know.'

'Absolutely not, Lori. I would've told you.'

'I met Jimmy Blackman when I was leaving the offices this morning.'

'Ah, Jimmy. Nice guy.'

'He said he'd never heard of James Security. And when I tried to google them, they don't appear to exist.'

Lori doesn't like the way he looks at her. She has caught him with his defences down. He gulps like a fish desperate for air. Glancing over his shoulder, he steps outside and pulls the door until it's almost closed.

Lori steps backwards. Her husband's best friend is scaring her. What does he know?

'I can explain,' he says.

43

If he was pale when she arrived, he is now deathly white. 'I should've spoken to you about this long ago.' Paul runs his hands through his lank hair. 'I'm not sure if it was because it was never the right time, or because I was too embarrassed, or too ashamed.'

Lori's chest tightens. Was Howie involved in something Paul hasn't told her about?

'It's April.' He glances over his shoulder at the door.

'What about April?'

He grimaces. 'It's not my place to tell you this, but you've cornered me.'

'Cornered you? What're you talking about?'

'She has an addiction.'

'Addiction?'

He nods. 'A gambling addiction.'

Lori laughs. 'That's absurd. I'd have known.'

'Believe me. She kept it hidden from me for years.'

'How long has this been going on?'

'Looking back, it was always in her personality. Don't you remember how we used to tease her for buying scratch cards all the time?'

Lori slowly nods. There's an uneasiness in her stomach as she recalls the police telling her about a sighting of a black VW Golf the night Frankie Evans was murdered. Is there something else she doesn't know about her best friend?

'I first spotted she had a real problem when Nathan started secondary school. She started buying stuff all the time.'

'All those handbags,' Lori says, nodding.

'That's right. It transpired that while I was working my socks off with Howie building the business, she was blowing what little savings we had on gambling sites.'

Lori exhales a long puff of breath. This doesn't make sense. April tells her everything. Or so she thought. How could April have harboured such a secret all these years? 'April? Gambling?'

'I know, I know. She has hidden it well over the years. One night, she won three grand on this casino site, and it all went downhill from there.' Paul looks so lost standing there. Lori's heart goes out to him. He has been through so much over the years. Third to her and Molly, he has suffered more than anyone else. 'She kept chasing her next big win. And it spiralled after Howie disappeared. I guess it was the stress of it all.'

Lori's eyebrows draw together. 'I can't believe I never knew any of this.'

'Do you remember when you moved away and rented that house in Cornwall for a year?'

Lori nods. How could she forget? Where Molly was concerned, it was the worst mistake she could've made.

'That's when I found out April had racked up a ton of debts. I got her into therapy. She spent a month at a rehab centre.'

Lori puts her hands on her hips. 'How could you keep this from me?'

'You were pretty much off the radar at the time. We hardly heard from you.'

How could she have missed all this? What a terrible best friend she has been.

'I've been so worried that receiving that letter about you and me would send her backwards. That's why I've been a bit of a mess this past week.'

Lori frowns as she recalls how this conversation started. 'What does this all have to do with James Security?'

Paul breathes in deeply and looks at the sky, darkened with black clouds. A storm is on its way. It held off earlier, but it's definitely brewing. 'I'm not proud of this, Lori.' He checks behind him, ensuring the door is pulled to. 'She took out a truckful of loans. We were facing financial ruin. We were going to lose the house. I couldn't even keep up with the interest repayments, let alone thinking about chipping away at any of the debts themselves. So I...' His head drops to his chest.

'So...you...?'

He lifts his head and tells Lori about the repayment

plan he devised to convince the collection agencies they could dig themselves out of the hole April had dug. A hole so deep, he thought they'd never be able to get themselves out of it. 'So I managed to consolidate all the debts into one big loan that I thought I could manage, but then...' His voice breaks. 'But then, after Howie disappeared, and we lost the Bygala contract and we had to reduce our monthly dividends payments, I couldn't afford to pay the loan either. Then there was the cost of rehab.'

'And?'

He looks as if he's going to break down. Lori wants to reach out and help him, but her empathy is mixed with bewilderment. How could all this have been happening with her best friends without her knowing? Has she really been that far removed from reality over the past seven years? If she is honest with herself, the answer is probably yes, she has.

'I set up a ghost company and faked invoices to pay James Security.'

'Which pays your loan.'

'I'll pay it all back at some point. You know that.'

Lori slowly shakes her head. Does she? She feels as if she doesn't know anything any more. 'This is wrong on so many levels. Why didn't you talk to me first?'

'Because you've been unreachable, Lori. And April was too ashamed. She pleaded with me not to tell a soul. You had enough going on with Howie and then all that shit with Molly. You were absent for so long. I didn't want to burden you with it all. I thought I could sort it out. Get it all paid back, so you need never have known. I've been working so hard to make this all good. The loan is nearly paid off. I've got some new clients on board. I can start paying everything back into the business.' His voice cracks. 'I promise I'll make it all good.'

'Does April know you've been defrauding the company?'

He laces his fingers and places them on his head, wincing at her words. 'Don't say it like that. Please. No, she doesn't. Please don't tell her I've told you. It'll destroy her. Let me find the right time, and I will speak to her.'

Lori steps forward. 'I need to talk to April.'

Paul's hand shoots up. 'Please, not now. This isn't the time. She's not in a good place. What with the news of Howie, and us, if she finds out I've told you all this, it'll break her. She has had suicidal thoughts over the years. I was scared I was going to lose her.'

Lori gasps. 'What? When?'

'It's why I got her into rehab. She wanted to kill herself. The spectre of relapsing into her old ways is a constant. It's why I've been so worried about her.'

Lori can't believe what she is hearing. How could her friends, the two people she would have trusted with her life, have behaved this way?

'I'll tell her at some point that you know everything, but let's get over the news of Howie first.' He turns as the door opens.

April appears. She looks at Lori. 'Is everything OK?'

Paul opens an arm and draws his wife into his hold. 'We were just discussing business.'

She looks quizzically at the two of them. 'What about business?'

'I was telling Lori about the new client I signed today.'

April tugs at his arm. 'Business? Paul! I think she has enough going on, don't you?'

'I need to go,' Lori says, blowing her friends a kiss as she usually would when leaving. 'Speak soon.' She turns and walks up the path.

All the deceit.

You don't know anyone.

Not really.

She can't help but include Howie in this equation. What could he have been involved in that led to his broken body being dumped in the boot of his car and left to rot at the bottom of a quarry?

When she gets into the car, she lets out a piercing scream.

Ray squeezes her knee but says nothing. He simply starts the engine and pulls out of the parking spot.

Lori feels she is betraying a confidence, but she has to talk to someone. She explains what Paul has just told her. 'How can I trust them any more as friends, let alone business partners?'

44

Lori stares out of the windscreen, clenching her jaw. 'It's such a betrayal.'

'And one you could've done without discovering today of all days.'

'Why didn't the accountants pick this up? Isn't that what we damn well pay them for?'

'In the grand scheme of things, it's not a huge amount. It could've easily fallen under the radar.'

'How come you picked it up, then?'

Ray shrugs. 'I was coming at it from a different angle, I guess. I was searching for anomalies. The accountants look at the accounts at a higher level; more of a sanity check. Especially if they trust their client. They may well have questioned Paul about it, but he sounds like he can be a pretty convincing guy.'

Ray respects her need for silence, and they travel home, exchanging few words. Lori sends a blanket text to a dozen or so people. Those who should know about the discovery of Howie's body before the media get their claws into the story. She phones DI Knowles and tells him they are free to spread the word. She switches on the radio but immediately switches it off. Sinead O'Connor's 'Nothing Compares 2 U' was one of Howie's favourite songs. He used to serenade her with the words whenever it came on the radio. She closes her eyes as the memory comes back to oppress her.

When they arrive back at her cottage, Ray anticipates her need for privacy. 'You know where I am if you need me. I'll be round here in a jiffy.' He pats her arm before heading off in his Defender.

The dogs are at the lounge window on their hind legs, barking at Lori's arrival. She can only see their heads, but she knows their tails are wagging fifty to the dozen. She hears them dash to greet her as she walks around to the back of the house, where she opens the stable door and squats low to receive their ardent welcome. She wraps herself around them, burying her woes between them as their tails wag vigorously across the slate floor.

But still she can't cry.

Lori stays that way, needing their comfort, until they lose interest and saunter off to sprawl on the floor. Her phone rings. It's Barbara. If it were anyone else she would send the call to her voicemail, but not this one. She needs to speak to her sister-in-law. 'I've just seen the news and picked up your message.' The urgency in her voice is palpable. Barbara is made of steel. As a woman, you don't get to be a senior executive of a major player in the banking industry otherwise. But not even she has been able to hide how much Howie's disappearance has bent her out of shape.

'I'm sorry you found out like that. I did try to call.' Lori updates her on what she knows.

'You must be going through hell. Are there any thoughts on what happened?'

'Not at this point. The police will want to speak to us all again, I guess.'

'You sound remarkably calm.'

Lori's voice dips. But only momentarily. 'Did you manage to get the information I asked for?'

Barbara's voice is strained, as if she is trying to keep strong for Lori when all she wants to do is die like her brother. 'Have you got a pen and paper?'

'Hang on,' Lori says, rifling through the bits and bobs drawer by the kitchen sink and locating a pencil. 'Go ahead.'

'So this account, it's owned by James Security. And the address is number six, Wardener Street, Crisham.' Barbara rattles off the postcode, but Lori can't write any more. The pencil slips out of her hand. It's all coming back to her. The end-of-terrace in a row of two-up two-downs in the village of Crisham that she visited years ago. The small house with the white picket fence and a hoard of colourful flowers in the compact front garden.

She knows who lives at that address.

Or used to live there.

Her eyes dart to the red envelope on the side. It can't be a coincidence. How can David Grove be connected to all of this?

45

How time can change the appearance of a house. Although small, this was once a well-kept family home. That's how Lori recalls it, anyway. She only came here three times. Once to drop Molly off for a playdate Stacy's mum had arranged. Once when she returned a favour and dropped Stacy off because her mum was in a fix. And the third time for Stacy's fourth birthday party. Lori gave the family a wide berth after that. The picket fence is still there, but the paint is peeling so badly you can barely call it white any more, and several pieces are missing. And the garden is an overgrown mess.

Warily, she steps along the path, uneven where the slabs have blown. Weeds and moss grow through the cracks. There is no bell, so she knocks on the PVC door, her stomach in her throat, wondering who is going to answer. Whoever it is, she's ready for them. She fingers the recent letters from David Grove in her pocket, wiping the sweat from her brow. None of this makes sense.

There's no answer, so Lori knocks again, harder this time. Still no answer. She's wondering what to do when a white van pulls up at the end of the lane. Is that him? She squints at the driver but knows it's not David. A young lad in a tracksuit springs out and tugs at the van's side door. It galumphs open with a thud to reveal a mound of parcels. He searches through a pile, grabs a package and checks the address label before slamming the door shut and striding, a man on a mission, up the path towards Lori.

Acting quickly, Lori fishes her keys out of her bag and pretends to open the front door. If someone opens it, she'll deal with them then. Turning to the delivery guy, she takes the parcel he is holding out to her, hoping he doesn't notice how much her hand is shaking. 'Thanks.' She smiles and nods at him. 'We've been waiting for this.'

The young guy gives her the thumbs up. 'Thanks, missus. Have a nice day.'

But Lori can't return the compliment. She is studying the name on the parcel. Robert James, who the hell are you? And what is your connection to David Grove?

A voice startles her. 'Can I help you?' a large woman with a crew cut calls out in a strong Welsh accent from over the fence. The smell of boiled potatoes and green beans wafts from her house. She is wearing a floral apron, which clashes with the multi-coloured maxi dress she is wearing. It doesn't marry with her hair, either. But then again, nothing is holding up around here.

'I'm looking for...' Lori pauses. Does she say David or Robert? She settles on the latter.

'Not seen him for a few days, love. Not that that's unusual. He's a hermit, that one.'

'He lives alone, then?' Lori asks.

'Aye. Like I said, a hermit.'

'Did you know a David who used to live here?'

'Before my time, love. I only moved here at the beginning of the year.'

'Thanks.' Lori raises the parcel. 'I'll come back later.' The woman uproots a few weeds from her garden before returning inside. Lori glances around, wondering what to do. She can't leave without an answer. She has a hunch this Robert James is connected to David Grove. And is he connected to James Security? Is that possible? But the question she can't answer is, how? She gets her phone out of her bag to call Paul, but a nagging doubt tells her not to.

She wanders around to the back of the house. It's in as bad a state as the front. She recalls the well-groomed garden when she brought Molly here to Stacy's birthday party. Now, a manmade path has been trampled through the middle of the overgrown grass for access to a washing line. Tatty boxers and T-shirts that have seen better days gently billow in the slight breeze that has picked up. They look like the clothes of a teenager, though, or someone slim, not the mass of a man she remembers David Grove to be.

When she gets to the back door, she places the parcel beside a bursting refuse sack. Why do some people fill these bags so much that they are almost impossible to tie? It's pure laziness. A black cat appears and sits by the door, meowing, startling Lori as she considers her next move.

She tries the door handle but is not surprised to find it locked. No harm in trying, though. You never know. Cupping her hands to shield her eyes from the light, she peers through the glass section of the door into a galley kitchen so narrow that only one person could work in there at a time. Unwashed crockery and cutlery clutter the worktop beside a stainless-steel sink, but it's tidier than the garden. She stands on tiptoes, straining to see more. A pair of old trainers lie by the door beside a cat bowl caked with crusty pieces of what looks like last week's dinner.

Finding nothing more of interest, Lori sidesteps to the lounge window. Shielding her eyes from the light again, she peers through. Dark curtains, half opened, partly block her view, but she can see two black leather sofas and a large flatscreen TV on a black stand that dominates the small room. So much black, so much darkness. A black coffee table squashed between the two sofas holds folded newspapers, games consoles and several crunched-up cans of beer. There's also an ashtray with half a dozen cigarette butts and what looks like a half-smoked spliff.

She removes her hands, about to call it a day, when her heart misses a beat. No way. Her eyes must be deceiving her. But they're not.

A photograph the size of the one of Howie and Lori in her kitchen sits above the 1960s brick fireplace. It's of a man holding a young girl's hand. And there's no mistaking who they are – David Grove and his daughter Stacy. How could she forget the stern-looking, overweight man with glasses and woolly hair who has told her several times that she can run, but she can't hide forever. Not forever. Her pulse races. How is David Grove wrapped up in all of this?

Bile rushes to the pit of her throat. Lori grabs the window frame to balance herself. What the hell is going on here? It appears David still lives here, but who is Robert? Are they related? Is Robert a lodger? Are they the same person, even? Her phone rings. She locates it in her bag. It's Paul. She stabs the accept button and gets in first with, 'We need to meet. I have more questions.'

'Sure. Come to the studios later. I'll meet you there.' He sounds shaken up, but then who wouldn't be? On a scale of one to ten on how bad a day can get, this would score a dozen.

'Now. I want to meet you now.'

'I can't. I dare not leave April at the moment. I think she's having some kind of breakdown. I don't know what to do with her. She keeps walking around the house, crying her eyes out. I keep trying to get her to talk to me, but she won't. I'll message you as soon as I've calmed her down. I promise.' He sounds so stressed, she wonders if he is having a breakdown too. 'And, Lori?'

'What?'

'I'm so sorry for everything. I've been a fool. I know I should've been more upfront about things, but I didn't want to go behind April's back. She hasn't wanted anyone to know. You didn't need to find out about all this in this way, especially not today.'

Lori doesn't think he quite understands how big a deal this is for her. You can't simply say sorry and expect life to play on as normal when the cards you've been dealt are this rubbish. 'I want you to be honest with me, Paul. When we meet later, I want nothing but the truth. Maybe then, we can all find a way to move on.'

She ends the call and drops the phone in her bag, knowing there is no moving on from this. Things never be the same. Her husband has gone, and so has one of her best friends. Can she salvage her friendship with April? Her heart is heavy with the answer – probably not.

Lori stares at the parcel she left beside the bin bag. She picks it up and shakes it, wondering what's inside. Does it hold a clue? Resisting her better nature, she digs her car keys out of her bag, slices through the tape and opens the parcel, only to be disappointed when she finds a packet of printer ink. She replaces the parcel and glances at the back door. The cat meows again. Can she risk trying to break in? She considers it for a second, but her sensible side says no; a hushed tone telling her she needs to get the hell away from there.

46

Lori drives around the streets of Chester, waiting for Paul's call with a time to meet him. Her head is in a daze. Her phone buzzes. Paul's name flashes on the screen. She pulls into a side street. Taking the phone out of the cradle, she reads his message.

> April's in a bad way. Sorry. Can't meet today. Will call in the morning with a time to meet. P

She screams at the phone. The piercing cry makes a passing woman, pushing a toddler in a buggy, turn and stare. This is not good enough. She can't wait until tomorrow. Frustrated, she dials Paul's number, only to get his voicemail. She screams even louder as she pulls into the road, contemplating returning to April and Paul's house. But she doesn't know what that will achieve, so she heads home.

Back at the cottage, Lori doesn't know what to do with herself. Several text messages deliver condolences and offer support. So many people want to come and visit, including Ray, who calls telling her he is there for her. She kneels on the cold kitchen floor and finds comfort in Misty and Shadow's unflagging affection. Apart from her faithful dogs, the craving for solitude is overwhelming. She has never felt the need to be alone more than now. It will be easier this way. There's a grieving process for her to confront. A new understanding she needs to learn to live with. And she knows she can only do that alone. Besides, she wants time to reconnect with her investigative skills. She refuses to leave the new information solely to the police. Living without knowing what happened to her husband has nearly destroyed her. Living without knowing who murdered him will ultimately kill her.

She trudges to her writing den to move her iMac back to her snug. A heavy mist is rolling down the mountain, engulfing the cottage. The fog gobbles up her view. The hot weather has sucked up the remaining moisture from the land and waterfalls, causing this strange phenomenon. The quietness is eerie. It's as if the local wildlife is holding its breath. Lori remembers Ray saying to expect such occurrences after the heat of the summer; however, this is the first time she has witnessed it first-hand. He said it's due to the microclimate caused by the village being situated between the mountains, the falls, the nature reserve and the Irish Sea. A chill runs through Lori. It's one of those infrequent occasions when solitude is not her best friend.

When settled in the snug, she calls Molly, but Albert answers. 'She's asleep,' he says. 'How're you bearing up?'

'I'm OK. I'm worried about Molly.'

'I'll look after her, Lori. I promise. I'll get her to call you in the morning.'

Lori opens her work in progress, trying to distract her mind. But it's no good. Just as she couldn't stop herself from reading the news about Frankie Evans when she first found out he'd been released from prison, she finds herself googling David Grove. Several faces appear. One by one, she clicks on them all, but recognises none of them. She tries Twitter, Instagram and Facebook, but it looks as if David has stayed away from social media. She tries his daughter, Stacy, but like father like daughter, Stacy doesn't appear to have any presence online either. Not that Lori can decipher, anyhow. When she next sees the police, she is going to show them the letters David Grove has been sending her again.

She turns her attention to Robert James. Does he own James Security? And how is he connected to David Grove? But she learns nothing more than she already knows. There are so many men named Robert James, she would never be able to tell who she is looking for. She relents and surfs all the media reports about the BMW found in a quarry and the body in the boot of the car, even though she knows she'd be better off going to bed. But she wants in on this investigation, and she needs to know everything that is being said. And, although sickening to read, they could lead to closure. It's as if the news of her husband's demise has resurrected the old Lori. The probing and inquisitive Lori she was before he disappeared.

She tries to ignore the vile trolls, baiting readers with hurtful, offensive slurs, suggesting the police look at the wife, look at the family, but she can't. There's even one – using the name 'Katie.with.an-ie' – who speculates that the daughter played a part in her daddy's death and she should rot in hell. This latter one is particularly sickening to digest. To surmise that Molly had something to do with Howie's death is the most savage of insults. Molly needs warning that such slander is out there. She is so young, naive in so many ways. But she may well have read them already. How could anyone think her beautiful Molly could have been involved? How cruel people can be. She sends Molly a text.

> I hope you're bearing up. Please call me as soon as you get this. Love you. Mum x

Repelled, Lori turns to the local news, but learns nothing new. Shortly after one in the morning, she calls it a day. Exhaustion has hit her with a double blow, but sleep is hard to find. She considers popping a sleeping pill, but an inexplicable nagging in her head is telling her not to. A foreboding tells her she needs to stay alert.

Restless, she stares at the faint moonlight sneaking through the curtains, her mind racing. She listens intently, spooking herself, expecting to hear that tapping sound she heard the other night. Nothing. The only sound is the gentle breath of a breeze outside her window. Turning on her side, she hugs the pillow and screams into it. 'I will find out who did this to you, my darling. Even if it costs me my life. They won't get away with it.' And then comes the sentence she has relayed countless times. 'Someone must know something.'

47

Lori awakes to more messages from well-wishers but reads the text from Paul first.

> April is settled. She said she'll call you tomorrow. I'm on set most of the day. Tight deadline Friday. I hope you're bearing up. Come to the studios tonight, and I'll go over everything with you. It's not as bad as it seems. I promise you. I'll text you when I'm free. P

She doesn't want to wait until tonight. She wants to go and see him right now. Lori calls him only to get his voicemail. It's gone eight o'clock. He must already be on set. Trying April's number, Lori swears to get her friend's voicemail too. She leaves a message to say they need to talk.

After whizzing around the village with the dogs, she spends the day drinking endless cups of strong coffee and wandering around the house. Roaming from room to room, she loses herself in the memories every photo of Howie and Molly holds. How life once was. And how it will never be the same. But still, tears remain a stranger she wants to welcome but can't seem to find.

She checks her voicemail. Messages flood in. People want to come and see her. She answers none of them but saves them. She'll get to them at some point. But not today.

Ray sends a text accompanied by a photo of a cup of coffee.

Here for you if you need me. Ray

Lori can't find it in herself to reply so clicks on the emoji to like his message. Molly calls. They have a short conversation. Molly woke in the night and cleaned the flat, so she could come and spend a few days with Lori before she moves. 'I'll get the first train tomorrow morning, Mum.'

'You don't need to,' Lori says.

'I do.'

'I'll come and get you.'

'No way. I'll get the train.'

'Text me the time. I'll meet you at the station.'

Lori ends up in the snug, trawling through the latest news coverage of her husband's death again, but she finds nothing new. They are the same recycled stories from yesterday but with replacement headlines and different photographs. Frustration and resentment overwhelm her. She wants to do something, anything, to find her husband's killer. But first she needs to speak to Paul.

When Paul finally texts late afternoon to say he'll meet her at the studios at seven, she heads out. It's only five o'clock, but she wants to pay David Grove, or Robert James, another visit. Apprehensively, she drives back to his house, wondering if she will get answers this time, but when she gets there, once again, no one is in. She sits restlessly in her car, waiting for over an hour, but doesn't see anyone apart from someone four doors along letting themselves into their house. She gives up. But not for good. Once she has met Paul, she plans to return to call on Robert James, or David Grove, whoever he is.

Arriving at the old hangar, Lori gasps to see April's VW Golf parked beside Paul's car. What is she doing here? Lori drives into the opposite space and gets out. Theirs are the only three cars there. Staff and crew must have left for the day, which doesn't surprise Lori. Most of them are there by eight in the morning, and, unless they have a tight deadline, are gone by six in the evening. It has started to rain. Heavy drops pelt her skin. She is only wearing a sleeveless top and denim shorts and will get soaked. She improvises and slings her bag on top of her head – the next best thing to an umbrella – and runs to the side entrance, taps the code into the keypad and lets herself in.

She shakes raindrops from her arms and legs and brushes them off her bag. It's dark in the small passageway, but she can see light glaring out from the doorway of one of the sets. She walks towards it and enters. Cameras face the stage set with a low-back leather armchair on a small rug beside an antique table. It's been a while since Lori has been here on a film set. When Howie was alive, and she used to visit here regularly, he always showed her around, proudly showing off all the projects they were working on. An old-fashioned lamp sits on the table with a crystal glass and decanter full of golden liquid.

At first, Lori doesn't recognise the scrawny man standing with Paul at the side of the set. The man is not just thin. He is frighteningly gaunt, as if he would blow over in a heavy gust of wind. But it's the glasses that are the giveaway. The tortoiseshell frames holding square lenses that sit lopsided halfway down his nose. As he used to wear them when she knew him all those years ago. 'David,' she says. Her baffled expression, as she glances from him to Paul, seeks answers.

David is smirking, rubbing the grey stubble on his chin. 'You're mistaken, Loret-*ta*. My name is Robert now.' He pauses to deliver another purposeful smirk. 'Because of you.'

The rage rushing through her raises Lori's voice. 'What the hell?' She only remembers one person ever eliciting such anger from her, and that was Frankie Evans before he was put away.

'Don't get all worked up now, Loret-*ta*. It doesn't suit you. And it's not going to help your cause. It's a long time since anyone called me David. I'm Robert now, but you can call me Bob.'

'Fuck off.' How dare this dick play with her head? She looks at him with contempt and then at Paul, who is shaking a plastic bottle half-full of water.

David, or rather Robert, continues, 'Don't be so rude. It doesn't suit you.'

'You don't scare me. You and your pathetic letters all these years.'

He laughs. 'I've never sent you any letters. Must be some other poor sod whose life you ruined.'

'You're a liar.'

He ignores her accusation. 'I had no choice but to change my name. People detested me because of you.'

Lori doesn't look at him. Her focus is on Paul, who remains deathly pale. The glimpse of fear she saw last night when talking to him on his doorstep returns. 'Paul! What the hell is going on?'

David continues. 'I've been looking forward to the day I can finally get even with you.' The eerie way he speaks makes Lori recoil. 'You made me an outcast, you see. After you reported me for supposedly beating up my daughter, I lost everything. You caused the break-up of my family. I lost my wife, my children, my life. No one wanted to know me after all the lies you spread.'

The man is insane. Lori saw the way he treated his daughter with her own eyes. She hadn't heard it second-hand or through idle tittle-tattle from gossiping mums in the nursery school playground. She witnessed it at source.

David spits out a question. 'Have you ever experienced an all-consuming hatred of another human being? Repulsion at the very sight of them? Someone on whom you wish nothing but harm and misery?'

She glares at him but can't answer. The silence antagonises her foe.

'Cat got your tongue, missy? Makes a change. It's not like you to be quiet. Well, let me tell you. You're that person for me, Loret-*ta* Mortimer.'

Lori retaliates. 'You brought it all on yourself. You were the architect of your own suffering. The way you treated your daughter was unforgivable.'

'It was just a story you fabricated to make yourself look good. Just like you did with Frankie Evans.'

'Leave Frankie Evans out of this.'

David gives a nails-down-the-blackboard laugh. 'I can't. You see, you used us. But that's it. You'll never use anyone again.'

Lori takes a step backwards. She doesn't like where all this is going. 'What's Frankie Evans got to do with it?'

'I knew you were on Frankie's case, trying to ruin his life like you did mine. It was all over the papers. Why did you do it?'

Lori doesn't answer. She can see how much this lowlife is enjoying his moment of gloating. She turns to Paul. 'What the hell is going on here?' Paul still won't acknowledge her.

David smirks. 'I thought long and hard about the best way of getting to you – the best way to make you suffer.

And who better to torture you, ridicule you, and make you squirm than Frankie Evans? So I told him I had information about what happened to your husband.'

The day she met Frankie in that café flickers through her mind. The nicotine-stained walls, the smell of cut-price coffee. How he taunted her about knowing what had happened to Howie. She hadn't believed him at the time. She thought he had been bluffing.

David continues. 'We had something in common, you see. And do you know what that was?'

Lori stares at him.

'You. He wanted you off his back, and I wanted you to suffer. Brothers in arms, we were, in more ways than one.'

Lori remains silent. She doesn't want to antagonise him any further. She has started to feel in danger. This man's hatred for her goes back years. That's apparent. And he has been waiting for this moment.

'Oi, you!' David shouts at Paul. 'How do you think it made me feel?'

Paul shrugs, staring at the floor, still shaking the bottle. Why is he doing that? And why is he allowing David to speak to her this way? Lori looks from David to Paul. Fear grips her. 'Paul,' she says. But he still won't acknowledge her. He is mesmerised by the bottle.

'I'll tell you, shall I?' David shouts. 'It made me feel understood.'

Lori puts two and two together, confident she's got her maths right. If what Niamh told her was correct, David is the man who irritated the hell out of Frankie Evans.

'So, what information do you have about my husband?' Another smirk from David, another villainous laugh. Lori gasps loudly. Her hand shoots over her mouth. 'Oh, no. No.' She steps backwards. 'You killed him, didn't you?'

David steps forwards and throws his head back, laughing. 'Me? No. I'd have liked to. Not because he was nasty or anything. Howie was one of the good guys, I'd say. He treated me well.'

'How did you know Howie?'

David ignores her question. 'The only reason I'd have ended Howie's life would've been to get to you. But I was far too much of a coward back then.' He waves for Paul's attention. 'Do you want to tell her, or shall I?'

'Shut it,' Paul growls through gritted teeth.

Lori's posture stiffens. She has never seen Paul act this way.

'I thought we were going to be truthful with her. Tell her what happened to Frankie Evans and her husband.'

'I said, shut the fuck up.' Paul's shouting echoes around the set.

Lori slowly takes another step backwards and then another while the pair argue. The alarm bells of danger are deafening. She needs to get out of there. Fast.

'Don't you tell me to shut up.' David jabs a finger at Paul. 'The day of reckoning is finally here.' David sweeps his hand around the set. 'Rather apt, don't you think? The final scene of a drama played out on stage. Although, it would be more suited to the big screen, even if I say it myself. Shame it'll never get that far, though.'

'I said, that's enough,' Paul shouts.

David dramatically feigns confusion. 'What's so wrong with her going to hell knowing that her dear friend Paul murdered her husband?'

48

The room spins with her twisted thoughts. 'You.' Lori stares at Paul. 'You killed Howie?' It sounds so absurd, she laughs. 'That can't be true.' The scene unfolds in horror. Someone should turn on the camera. David was right. This is worthy of capturing for the big screen. Paul dives for David. He side-jumps out of the way, dodging Paul's grasping hand, and produces a handgun from the inside pocket of his jacket. He points it straight-armed, at Paul, then at Lori.

'Steady on, for fuck's sake!' Paul shouts.

Thoughts of Molly weave their way around Lori's head. Molly can't find out her mother is dead, as well as her father. And if Paul dies, Molly will never know that he killed her father. But did he? Lori can't believe this is true. 'David... Bob... put that away,' says Lori. 'Let's talk about this calmly.' Her whole body is shaking. 'Talk me through what happened.'

David's eyes bulge as he orders the two of them to get

in front of the leather chair. 'Sit!' he bellows so hard his cheeks redden. This man is seriously unhinged.

'For fuck's sake, man!' Paul shouts, getting to the floor. Lori does the same.

'Silence,' David orders, his evil face contorted into a spiteful glare. He points the gun from one to the other of them.

Paul looks at Lori. 'I'm sorry,' he mouths. The pleading in his eyes makes her want to lash out at him. This goes way beyond sorry. He tries to take her hand, but she yanks it away.

'What happened? How did Howie die?' Lori asks. 'Tell me.'

'Actually, perhaps I'd best tell that story,' David says. 'Don't you think, Paul? At the end of the day, I was the one who witnessed the whole thing.' When Paul doesn't answer, David lifts the gun, bellowing, 'Don't you think?'

Paul brings his knees up to his chest, hugging his arms around his shins.

Lori is dumbstruck.

'Your husband employed me. You didn't know that did you, Loret-*ta*?' David's voice is so loaded with glee and spite that it's sickening.

Howie would never have employed this lowlife. She wills herself to stay calm, using the breathing techniques she has learnt over the years to control her anxiety that grew like cancer after Howie went missing. How is she going to get out of here? She surreptitiously peers around the room. There's an emergency exit in the far corner, the green light above the door offering an escape route. But first she needs to work out how to reach it.

'Oh, don't worry about your demise being caught on camera. Paul took care of the CCTV before you got here, didn't you, Paul?'

Paul nods as if he knows he has no choice.

'This is all your fault, Loret-*ta*.' David's eyes blink rapidly. A nervous twitch he hasn't lost since she knew him all those years ago.

She wishes he'd stop calling her by that name. She hates it, and she detests the way he adds emphasis to the 'ta'.

'If you'd never reported me for what I supposedly did to my Stacy, we wouldn't be here. So, in all honesty, you need to take the blame.'

'You're deluded,' she says, her retort like lemon, tart and bitter.

'I wasn't sure how I was going to make it happen at first. But I knew I would. That's how much I've invested in finding a way to ruin you, Loret-*ta*. Just like you ruined me. And what better way than through your husband. Clever, eh? It took me a while to concoct a plan. All the best plans do take a while, don't they? They take time and careful thought. But I got there in the end. Apparently, there was a break-in here one night. That's right, isn't it, Paul?'

Paul doesn't answer, which he soon learns isn't the right approach. David reaches over and thumps his shin with the butt of the gun. 'I said, that's right, isn't it?' Paul nods.

'So I became your night watchman, didn't I?'

Paul nods his head rapidly like a scared schoolboy. He hugs his arms tighter around his legs. David lets out an evil laugh. He turns to Lori. 'No one batted an eyelid at my presence. Not even you. But by then, I had changed. I'd lost loads of weight. All the stress you put me through, you know. I got a new name and grew my hair. I was a different person. Do you know, one day, you came here...' There it is again, the horrendous laugh. 'And you walked straight past me. It was hilarious.'

Lori doesn't know whether to believe him or not. Did he say that to wind her up even more? 'Just spit it out. How did my husband die?'

'Patience, Loret-*ta*. Patience. I've been patient all these years.' He holds up both hands. 'And I got what I wanted in the end, didn't I? I remember that night as if it were happening right now. It was the best night of my life. Until tonight will be, of course, when we're done here.' David points the gun at Paul. 'I had nearly as much fun as I'm having now when I saw this spineless waste of space and your beloved husband arguing. They didn't know I had witnessed it all.' He smirks, the glee on his face sickening. 'I was able to see it all unfold. It was nasty but funny at the same time.'

'You're so fucking sick,' Paul whispers.

'Do you want to tell her what you and Howie argued about, or do you want me to?'

Pure hatred contorts Paul's face. He looks to the ground.

David continues. 'They were arguing over the company, who owned what percentage. You wanted a larger share.' David kicks his dirty trainer in Paul's direction. A piece of dirt flies off and lands at Paul's feet. 'Isn't that right?'

What he is saying sounds dubious to Lori. Paul and Howie never argued. Howie was the calmest person she knew. She turns to Paul for confirmation, but he won't look at her. His head has dropped too far between his knees as if the weight of the shame can't support it any more.

'Then Paul started goading your husband. It seems Paul had a piece of you in the past, is that right?'

Lori's expression scrunches up with shock and contempt. 'What? You told Howie about that?'

'And now we get to the most enjoyable bit. There was a struggle. Yep, the pair of them got their fists out.' He prods the gun in Paul's direction. 'This one sure packs a punch. Poor, poor Howie toppled down the stairs. Crack. That was the sound.' David says it again, louder and with a smirk. 'Crack.'

Lori wants to lash out at him. Both of them. But she finds herself in the out-of-body zone the police sent her to when they arrived at her cottage yesterday.

'He died instantly. There was no mistaking that.' David points at the top of the staircase above them. 'It started right up there.' He pauses and stamps his foot on the ground so hard Lori feels the floor vibrate. 'And it ended down here. Thud. Crack.'

David laughs as he enjoys the show. 'You take it from here, Paul.' He smirks. 'I mean, who better to explain how her dead husband found his way into the boot of his car at the bottom of a quarry?'

49

Paul lifts his head and turns to Lori. 'It was an accident.'

This is not the Paul she knows. The kind, solid person who has been her rock for so long. It's like she is conversing with a different human being. One who is completely insane. All these years, and she never suspected a thing? Lori can't contain her hatred for the man she has considered one of her best friends for more than half her life. She screams at him, 'An accident? Don't take me for an idiot. A body in the boot of a car at the bottom of a quarry is not a damn accident.'

'I mean how he died was an accident – I never murdered him. That was – an accident.' His explanation splutters out of him between sobs and short, shallow breaths. His eyes flicker to David, then back to the floor as if his crime won't allow him to look at Lori. 'What he says is true. Howie and me... we argued.'

'What about?'

'We were struggling to make ends meet at home, and I

wanted a bigger cut of the business. I mean, I worked just as hard. That's how it started out, anyway.'

'And then what happened?'

Paul is silent. Why doesn't he want to answer her? Lori repeats her question. 'Tell me!'

He winces. 'He hit me and I punched him back. He fell. I panicked. I'm sorry, Lori. But it's the truth. It was an accident.'

'All this time, you've acted the grieving friend and business partner. But all along you've known where he was.' Her words come out in a pleading cry. 'You even hired a private detective to find him.' She holds her head in her hands. 'Oh, no. That was all lies as well. You never hired that detective, did you? It was all lies! Who did I meet that time, then?'

Paul doesn't answer.

Lori's voice echoes around the set. 'I fucking hate you!'

Paul shakes his head. 'I'm so sorry.'

'You lied about April as well, didn't you? She doesn't have a gambling problem. You made that up to stop me… delay me… while you thought of a plan to deal with it all.'

'I'm sorry.'

'So what happened next?'

Paul points his finger at David. 'He said it was for the best. He even gave me the directions to the quarry. He helped me. Then he started blackmailing me.'

'And that's what's going through the accounts. You've been paying him all this time to keep quiet about you being a murderer?'

Paul shoves his hands over his ears.

'So where does Frankie Evans come into all of this?'

When Paul doesn't answer, Lori yells at him. 'You killed him as well didn't you? You got to the church before me and murdered him.'

David taps the butt of the gun on his leg. 'Steady on, Loret-*ta*.'

'Stop calling me that.'

'The day after Frankie was released from prison, he contacted me,' David says. 'He had become all righteous. Wanted to repent for his sins, he told me. It was what God wanted.' David points a finger at the side of his head and twirls it one hundred and eighty degrees. 'Prison turned that guy into a fruit loop. A man like Frankie Evans finding God, I ask you.'

Lori stares at him incredulously.

David sniggers. 'Do you know what he wanted me to do?'

Lori fills in the gaps. 'He wanted you to come clean about what you knew about Howie. He wanted you to own up.'

'That's right. Always were a clever girl, weren't you? When Frankie contacted me, he reminded me of the conversations we had just before you put him inside about our common, ungodly goals back then. Would you believe, he wanted me to find my peace?' David laughs loudly. 'The fool wanted me to relay what information I had to unburden myself and release you from your pain and suffering. But we couldn't have that happening could we, Paul?' David delivers another kick, signalling for Paul to remove his hands from his ears. 'When Paul told me you were meeting Frankie, we couldn't risk what he was going to tell you.'

Lori turns to Paul. 'You did, didn't you? Admit it. You killed Frankie Evans as well?'

David interjects. 'Well, that was the plan. But when push came to shove the idiot backed out, leaving muggins here to clean up the crap. He said he got caught in traffic. I still don't know if that's true. Is it?' David steps over to Paul, pointing the gun at his head.

Lori's heart is thumping in her chest. This madman is gaining in confidence. She needs a swift exit out of there. David shoves Paul's head with the barrel of the gun. His hand is on the trigger.

'Tell me the truth. Did you get caught in traffic that night?'

'Yes. It's the truth.' Paul's whole body is shaking. 'The police have proof of that. My car was seen on CCTV.'

Like finishing a complicated jigsaw puzzle, it's finally all slotting into place. 'Whose car is that outside?' She lifts the palm of her hand to David. 'You don't need to tell me. It's yours, isn't it? You drive a black VW Golf, the same as April. That's how you got to the church.'

'Do you know what amused me the most?' David holds the gun up and smiles. 'Where do you think I got this from?'

Lori doesn't need to give any thought to her answer. 'Frankie.'

'Always so smart, Loret-*ta*. Always so savvy. That's how

I first came into contact with Frankie. Because I wanted to source a gun, and I knew the information I had would be a good negotiating tool. The irony of it all is that we had so much in common. But unfortunately for him, he handed me the gun that ended his life. Don't worry. I won't be using it on you, though. We have other, much more appropriate means for your demise.'

'Come on, David. You don't seriously believe you're going to get away with this?' Lori says.

'Of course we will. You know far too much about the two of us to remain on this planet. But, you know what, now you know the truth about what really happened to your husband, it's quite plausible for you to decide you don't want to live any more.' He slams his hand on his chest. 'I can see the headline as clear as you standing in front of me. "Wife takes her own life to be with her husband".' He slaps his chest harder. 'Or how about, "After seven years of living in the dark, wife finds the light to join her husband". Quite good, don't you think?'

'You bastard,' Lori hisses.

David chuckles. 'Now, now. No need for such profanities. Or better still, "Seven Years Missing – woman kills herself after learning her husband is dead". I quite like that one. It might make them think you killed Howie.' He kicks Paul, harder this time. 'That would be good, wouldn't it? Then you and I can get on with our lives.'

'You're insane. Now that Howie is dead, I own the majority of this company. It will all go to Molly if you kill me, and she'll definitely sell.'

'Oh no you don't, Loret-*ta*.' Another kick from David makes Paul lose his balance. Paul's hand shoots to the floor to steady himself. 'Do you want to tell her the next piece or do you want me to?'

Paul closes his eyes.

50

'I thought as much, you coward.' David turns to Lori. 'You should've paid more attention to the papers Paul has given you to sign over the years. And the emails he's sent you. You see, as things stand, upon the death of any managing partner, full control passes to the remaining partner. So with Howie and you out of the picture, Paul and his wife have full control of the company. And with you out of the picture, they will sign shares over to me.'

'You really are an idiot. That'd never stand up in court.'

'It's in the partnership agreement you signed that was witnessed by your lawyers.' David turns to Paul. 'Isn't that right?'

Paul nods. 'It was Howie's idea.'

'Why would he do that?' Lori says.

'He thought that if anything happened to me, my controlling share would pass to April and the kids, and he wanted to keep full control.' Paul shrugs. 'You signed it too, Lori.'

Did she? Lori can't remember. She had trusted Howie and Paul to the extent she would have signed her life away if they had handed her a pen. Pain grips her chest as if someone is squeezing her heart. Thoughts of Ray momentarily come to mind. She has always thought he is too trusting. But here she is, the biggest fool of all.

'Don't worry. Molly won't suffer financially,' Paul says. 'She will still own shares but not the managing shares.'

'She will sell them, and then all your shit will come out,' Lori repeats.

David cackles. 'Not when Paul hands over a chunk of shares to me.' David points the gun at Paul. 'He and I are both safe with each other's secret. We're both murderers. At least I didn't dump Frankie's body in a quarry.' He sniffs loudly. 'Now come on, best we get on with it.' David flicks the gun in the direction of the metal staircase. 'Up you go, hurry, hurry.'

Lori's legs feel like jelly. The fear is real. She's going to die. Defiance overcomes her. 'What if I say no? I won't move from this spot.'

'Then I'll shoot you. Paul, you're good at disposing of bodies, right?' There it is again, a sick chuckle. 'So how would you like to die?' David picks up the bottle Paul was shaking earlier. 'Paul thought it best if you sit in your husband's office chair, write your daughter a goodbye letter, and take an overdose. I'm not as keen on that one. I think it's better if you slit your wrists.'

A noise from somewhere in the building startles the three of them. All three heads turn towards the door. Lori contemplates screaming out for help, but fears David will pull the trigger of the gun. David and Paul exchange glances as they listen intently. 'It was probably just the pipes,' Paul says. 'They sometimes make a clunking sound like that.'

'You sure?' says David.

'No one else is here. I double-checked before she arrived.' She? It's hard to stomach Paul refer to her in this way. They've always had so much respect for each other.

Jabbing the muzzle of the gun in the small of her back, David forces Lori towards the stairs. Lori focuses on Molly's face as she climbs each step, fearing her end is near. And of Ray, standing at his barista machine, his cheeky face brimming with his kind smile. He is waving to her as she sits at the corner table with her laptop, plotting her stories. Is this her life flashing before her? She thinks of her dogs before Howie engulfs her thoughts. Deep down, she has always known she'd never see him again. Not in this life.

She needs to do something. For Molly, for Howie. She can't let the people responsible for such heinous crimes go unpunished. But fear has frozen her ability to think logically. Even a path of least resistance doesn't exist in this situation. David hisses in her ear. 'We'll sit you at your darling husband's desk, and Paul will give you a drink. Don't worry, you'll have time to write a letter to your daughter telling her how sorry you are. It's become impossible for you to live without her dad. You won't feel any pain, just a little drowsy. Then you'll drift off into a lovely deep sleep. See, I'm not that unkind, really, am I?'

Lori stumbles up each step. When she reaches the top,

she glances over her shoulder. Paul is sobbing, following them along the metal walkway to the directors' office. Tears are something she can't afford right now. In her peripheral vision, she catches sight of a head peeping around the door below. Is someone there? Please say they weren't a figment of her distorted imagination. An employee must still be on the premises. The gun rams into her back. She keeps walking along the gantry. How much did they witness? But when she looks again, no one is there. Seeing this as her only chance, she gasps loudly. 'Someone's down there. I saw them.'

David turns. 'Where?' The gun is no longer trained on Lori's back. With all her might, she strikes David's arm. He cries out. Partly from shock, but most likely from pain, David's hand releases the weapon. It falls to the floor. The clang of metal on metal reverberates up to the suspended ceiling. The gun spins out of his reach.

'Get it,' Paul shouts out, motioning for Lori to pick up the gun.

The commotion and fear have a monumental impact on Lori's strength. A force of power she never knew she possessed. It all happens so fast, but she sees it play out in slow motion like an old film. She springs into action and lunges for David, pushing him so hard he smacks into the metal railings. Winded, he doubles over the top of them, clutching the edge to rebalance himself. To Lori's surprise, Paul joins in. His nostrils flare and he bares his teeth, a sobbing wreck transforming into an animal possessed, as his clenched fists land like heavy rocks between David's shoulders. Without thinking, Lori dives for the gun. Grabbing it, she turns to see David's skinny frame hanging over the balcony, his arms flailing as he battles the force of Paul trying to shove him over.

'Don't do it! Don't!' Lori cries, but she is too late. David plunges headfirst towards the set below, taking out the lamp and crystal decanter as he hits the ground. Guttural groans drift upwards as Paul and Lori lean over the railings, watching in shock.

'We need to get out of here,' Paul says, resisting his fate even at the final hour when he knows he has no place left to hide and nowhere left to run.

'Are you serious?'

'Come on, Lori. We just killed a man. We need to find a way out.'

'We? I don't think so.' Lori points the gun at him. The pop-up indicator tells her it's loaded and ready to fire. She knows this from her journalism days when she interviewed an ex-SAS officer. She hovers her finger over the trigger.

A familiar voice booms up from below. 'It's over, Paul.' Lori strains to see April standing in the doorway to the set.

'What are you doing here?' Paul cries.

'I overheard what you told Lori on the doorstep yesterday. And I've just witnessed everything here.'

Paul's resistance to his fate has no mercy. 'Come on, you two,' he says. 'We can find a way out of this.'

April walks to the bottom of the stairs. 'You're nothing but a liar, the lowest of the low. The police are on their way. You're finished.'

· · ·

Sitting in April's VW Golf outside the police station, Lori and her best friend stare into nothingness, trying to process the enormity of the events of the past few days.

'Why didn't you tell me at the time, Lori? I'd never have got back with him.'

Lori clears her throat. 'I'm so sorry.' She can't bring herself to look at April as she tries to explain the biggest mistake of her life. A mistake that has eaten away at her. 'I can't justify my behaviour other than to say I was blind drunk, and I can't even remember most of the night.'

Lori finally looks at April, glassy-eyed. 'All I know is, we all make mistakes, especially when we're young. I was so in love with Howie, I couldn't bear for him to learn what had happened, however it was orchestrated.'

April sighs heavily. 'I need a cigarette. And a bloody large whisky.'

'You and me both.' Lori's eyes turn to watch the comings and goings of the busy police station. Two uniformed officers are standing outside the back entrance, deep in conversation. She doubts it's as deep as the one she is having with her best friend. 'I should never have gone back with him that night. Selfishly, I said nothing. I had too much to lose.'

'What did *you* have to lose?' April says. The lank strands of her pixie-cut hair are stuck to her head in a greasy mess.

'Right or wrong, I didn't think Howie would've stayed around if he'd found out what happened. I was so in love with him; I couldn't bear the thought of losing him. I was still in a mess about losing Mum and Dad that year, and I was scared of losing you... losing our friendship. You've always been the sister I never had. I was vulnerable. Easy prey.'

'I had children with that man!' April cries. 'I married a murderer.'

'I know. I'll never be able to express how deeply sorry I am. But I never could've imagined it would've turned out like this. It's what drew me to journalism, I think. The need to do right. Repent for that one sin.' Lori shrugs. 'Seems I got it wrong in Frankie's case, though.'

'What do you mean?'

'I met with his wife. She swore Frankie was never there when the Bright brothers started the fire that killed Betty Tailor.'

'We can't always get everything right. No one's perfect, Lori. Think of all the good you did over the years. The people you helped. Let me remind you of that trafficker you exposed. Think of all those kids you saved.'

Lori shrugs. 'I guess so.'

They sit silently, lost in their thoughts, until Lori says, 'Thank goodness you turned up when you did. I thought I was a dead woman tonight.'

'All that crap Paul was saying outside our house last night.' April almost laughs. 'Me? A gambling addiction?'

Lori wipes a bead of sweat from her forehead with the back of her hand. 'You heard all that? I can't believe how convincing he was!'

'I was ready to have it out with him, but when he came home and said he had to go out again, I knew something was up. I don't know what made me follow him. Probably all the nonsense he came out with last night. I knew he was up to something. I've never followed him before. All these years, I've had total trust in him.' She pauses to take a deep breath. 'As soon as I got here, I knew something wasn't right. The doors were locked, so I slipped in the back entrance. And as soon as I realised what was going on, I slipped back out and made the call.'

'What now?' Lori asks.

April takes Lori's hand and links their fingers, a bond of unity. 'We move on, I guess.'

'*Can* we move on from this?'

April forces a smile. 'I'll give it my best shot if you can.'

51

THREE MONTHS LATER

Molly shoves a pile of garments into a white refuse sack and picks up another item of clothing. 'I can't believe I ever wore this.'

Lori pulls an amused expression at the florescent pink, sequin-embellished mini skirt. 'We all have our fashion faux pas.' Lori holds up an old jumper of Howie's. 'I remember this one. He used to wear it when I first met him. Perhaps I'll keep it.' She places it on the "to keep" pile, which stands as tall as the "charity" and "recycling" piles.

'No, Mum. You need to move on.' Molly grabs the jumper. 'You were the one who said we need to be ruthless today.' She pokes her finger through an opening in the armpit of the jumper. 'Look, it's got holes. Be ruthless.'

Lori stands up and switches on the light. The sun is setting, and it's growing difficult to see what's left in the attic room where she stored everything she and Molly didn't take to Cornwall.

'I'm getting there,' Lori says. She and April have put the company up for sale. There's a lot of interest. Anti-depression meds are no longer part of her daily diet. She has nearly finished her new book, and she is exchanging contracts on the Chester house next week. However much sadness that brings, she can't deny the relief it has also brought. Lori gestures to the job at hand. 'This is a big step in the right direction, don't you think?'

'Closure,' Molly says. 'I think we'll both feel better when this house is sold. And that's not just because of the financial side of things.'

Lori nods, her lips downturned. 'I guess so.' She stares at her daughter; when did she become so wise and worldly? The sun, low in the sky, has cast a ray of light over Molly's head. It looks like a halo.

'And once Paul's trial goes through. How can it take so long?' Molly says.

'The legal process does, I'm afraid. At least he's behind bars and will be for a very long time.'

'David Grove won't. He'll be pushing up the daisies.'

'Molly!' Lori says, allowing herself to snigger at her daughter's dark humour. She snatches a couple of T-shirts and tosses them onto the "charity" pile, only to slide the turquoise one onto the "to keep" pile. Lori bought that one for Howie the last Christmas they spent together. She could use it as a nightie.

'How's April?'

Lori laughs. 'She has packed Paul's stuff up already.'

'That was quick.'

'Three months? I don't think that's particularly fast. Not considering everything that has happened.'

Molly opens another white bag and discards more of her old clothes into it. 'I guess so. It's not like he disappeared and they spent seven years living in limbo,' she says, her tone dripping with sarcasm. 'What has April done with it all?'

'She chucked it all away. She's put the house on the market as well. At least Paul has done the decent thing and given his blessing for a quick sale and has been allowed to sign his share of the business over to April. Even if it doesn't fetch top dollar, neither of us care. We just want to get rid of it now. I think your dad would understand.'

'He would.' Molly opens a cardboard box and closes it again. 'All this old schoolwork can go down the dump. How's it going with Ray?'

'What do you mean?'

'Oh, come on, Mum. You're blind if you can't see how much he likes you.'

Lori picks up a pair of skiing goggles. Howie and Paul used to go to the Alps every winter together until the business found its feet and they had to support it for what felt like 24/7. 'How's Albert?'

Molly rolls her eyes. 'Change the subject why don't you?' Molly's whole face lights up. 'Albie's good. But he's very busy. What with uni and him working all hours, we don't see much of each other. Never mind. He's booking us a trip to the Canaries for the New Year.'

'Sounds just like your dad. He was a workaholic but was always treating us to breaks away.' Lori picks up a pair of trainers. 'Definitely for the "recycling" pile. I'm so thankful you've got him. It's good to have someone looking out for you.'

'How's your new book coming along?'

Lori claps her hands. She smiles. 'I'm almost done, apart from the ending. I'm trying to write the final few chapters.'

'So all that worry about not making Hector's deadline was unnecessary!'

'I hope so. If I can get the ending right. He didn't like the one I wrote.'

'What's taking you so long?'

'I'm kinda stuck.'

'That's not like you.'

'I know.'

'Are you ready to tell me what it's about?'

Lori laughs. 'You know I don't let anyone read my books until I've finished them. I'll send you a copy when I'm done. By the way, I turned down the two-book deal. Hector wasn't amused, but he understood. I need a break to decide my next move.'

'What're you thinking?'

'I'm mulling over a few ideas.'

Molly sidesteps her knees until she is at Lori's side. 'Oh, Mum. I love you. You'll make the right choice. I know you will.'

52

Lori takes her fourth coffee of the day into the snug and sits back in front of her iMac. She is finding writing the ending to her book impossible. Never before has she had such trouble. She glances towards Misty and Shadow who are lying in front of the log burner. Since the change of seasons, and Lori started lighting the burner every morning, they have taken this spot in favour of the cushion beside her desk. 'You two will burn if you get any closer.' Their tails lazily thump on the rug as they acknowledge their mistress.

Sipping her drink, she gazes out of the window, looking for inspiration for the end of her novel that she can't seem to find. Day by day, winter has taken a firm hold. The days have grown shorter, and snow tops the crest of the mountains. She remembers the vast number of spiders she saw spinning their webs in the cottage in early autumn, suggesting this winter is set to be a harsh one.

Thankfully, she was wrong about Mr Parsons. He

acquired a vast supply of logs from a local farm and delivered a pile to her doorstep a few weeks ago. And knowing how fond Lori is of the den in the garden, he even installed a radiator out there, proving Ray right. He always maintained her landlord wasn't the creep she made him out to be. Mr Parsons even berated Ray for installing the video doorbells. He said he would have done it himself and insisted on reimbursing Ray for the cost and for his time. Yet another by-product of her paranoia. As summer drew to a close, Mr Parsons asked Lori if she was considering renewing the lease for another year. She told him she was definitely considering it. Despite the inclement weather at this time of year, she loves the cottage and the area. But something isn't right. She doesn't know if it's the cottage or her. She's still finding it hard to completely move on. Perhaps it's time to buy a place of her own, settle somewhere more permanently. When she nipped into town to run some errands last week, she stopped at the estate agent's window and perused the properties for sale in the local area. There's a cottage for sale in the village. Perfect for her and the dogs, and it has two double bedrooms, useful for when Molly wants to come and stay. But she's got to finish her book first, and then she will decide.

An hour later, she still hasn't hit a key.

She checks her emails. Again. Her inbox hasn't been so clean since she started trying to write the ending of this story. Procrastination at its worst. Even the boring emails regarding finance she has read in detail and filed away in the new folders she set up for all money matters. Molly has replied to the email Lori sent last night. The sixty thousand pounds from Howie's estate that Lori transferred yesterday has arrived safely. When her first term at uni ends, Molly will pay off her debts and move the remainder to an easy-access high-interest savings account to see her through her uni course. It's an immense relief that she won't have money worries while she is studying. She signs off: *Thanks for everything, Mum. I love you.*

After skimming the news and taking a quick scroll through Facebook, Lori returns to her novel. She types a sentence that leads to another, only to delete them both. She tries again and again, but it's no good. It's not happening. Staring at the rain thrashing the window, she shivers at the thought but accepts there is only one way to free herself from the stagnation of writer's block. She needs to get outside. Fresh air always helps. She stands up and pats her thighs. The dogs sit to attention. 'Come on, you two. If we don't go now, it'll be dark by the time we get back. Let's do it.'

In a strange way, there's something invigorating about walking in the wind and the rain. It's certainly a contrast to the heat and droughts of the past summer. The legs of her waterproof trousers brush against each other, as do her sleeves against her knee-length coat, making a mesmerising sound as she heads to the mountains.

Last minute, Lori decides to pop into the café to see Ray on the way. Business in this weather is slow. Partly because the locals stay at home more, and partly because there's a dramatic drop in visitors to the nature reserve and falls. Not many people are as bold as Lori to brave the elements. Ray fills such days with making dishes and baking cakes that freeze well, dealing with maintenance issues and catching up with paperwork. And, it goes without saying, trying out new recipes to add to his extensive coffee menu.

'You're not going up there in this weather?' he says when he sees her arctic attire.

'I need to clear my head. I've got a deadline.'

'I thought deadlines were a thing of the past for you?'

'*My* deadline.' After discovering how Howie met his end, she told Hector she wanted to keep working with him, but his tight deadlines had to go. And she needs time out to work at her own pace. He wasn't happy, but Lori thinks he felt sorry for her. Given the news of Howie, he is giving her some breathing space. For now, anyway. It's far more relaxed and enjoyable. She still can't stop committing to tight schedules. But the knowledge they can slip, if she chooses, has increased her productivity. Until she came to writing the end of this book, that is. She sniffs the fragrant air. 'What's that smell – vanilla?'

'I'm working on a new coffee.' Ray smiles. A smile she has found incredibly addictive as the weeks have rolled into months. 'I found a website with this recipe that has over thirty different ingredients I can play with. I'll have a cup ready for when you get back from your walk. I think I'm going to name this one Winter Woolly.'

Lori laughs. 'Very apt.'

'Are you still OK for Christmas Eve?' he asks. 'I've had

about a dozen confirmations so far. The usual bunch who always turn up.'

'Sure. Eight o'clock. I can't believe it's only a week away. Molly said she's up for it as well.'

'Be watchful up there in the mountains. Those winds can get draconian on days like these.'

Negotiating the gate and the slippery slate path leading up into the hills is more challenging with the extra layers of clothing. The exertion is exhausting. However, Misty and Shadow strive to haul Lori up the sharp incline. She looks up through the torrential rain driving diagonally from left to right. She can barely make out the base of the mountains carpeted with bracken and undergrowth, let alone the top of the falls. Who says walking isn't a workout?

A flock of sheep line the barren grassy track. They stare her out like they are drugged, hallucinating. The one nearest to her, although remarkably mobile, appears to have been attacked. Lori winces. She knows this is a regular occurrence in the mountains, but the sight upsets her. Fresh blood cakes the sheep's fleece along its chest. She ties the dogs up on a lopsided handmade fence post joined to a turnstile and reaches out her hand to the sheep. She doesn't know why, other than her desire to comfort it. 'Hey, little fellow. Are you OK?' But it doesn't trust her. Every moving being is its foe. It flees the scene. The others funnel after it, tottering off like teenage girls in their first pair of stilettos.

While she could easily turn back, she unties the dogs

and gently tugs their leads to carry on. 'Come on, you two. Let's get a sweat on.' True to her personality, once she has a final destination in sight, she has to reach it.

Finally, after what seems an age, the three of them arrive at the large rock she often rests on when she comes up to the falls. She loves the feel of its polished surface, achieved through millennia of attrition. There's a peacefulness up there, high in the mountains, even with the weather like it is today. She stares at the falls cascading over the landscape and hammering the rocks below. The rain has abated, but freezing spray slaps her cheeks. She wonders if the falls have ever frozen over. One for Google when she gets home; or perhaps Ray can tell her.

Misty and Shadow start leaping around on their leads excitedly, confusing her. The unexpected voice from behind shocks her. 'One hundred and twenty feet. The mortality rate from falling at this height and smashing onto those rocks below is one hundred per cent. Fact.'

53

Lori tries to swing around, but her bottom slips on the wet rock, unbalancing her. The dogs' leads fly out of her hands. She grabs the edge of the rock to support herself and gasps. 'Albert. What on earth are you doing here?'

Albert squats down, spoiling Misty and Shadow with fuss. 'I kept on asking myself, when will she see it? When will Miss Clever Clogs work it out?' He laughs, sending panic racing through her. She recognises that evil laugh. Fear cuts through to her bones. 'But you haven't. Right up to this point, you've not worked it out. Bit slow on this one, hey, Loret-*ta*?'

She glares at him. The man who has made her daughter so happy. There's a pause, a realisation. 'You're his son. You're Albert Grove.' Adrenaline kicks in, urging her to escape from danger. She needs to get away. Fast. Her eyes flick from side to side, searching for an escape route. But there isn't one. He is in front of her, and a perilous drop down the mountains is behind her. He has cornered her at the edge of the falls.

Albert claps. His gloved hands make little noise in the whirling wind. 'At last. Good try. But not quite! I have to say I'm most disappointed in your investigative skills. The famous journo always looking for a scoop but couldn't see what was happening right before her eyes.'

'What do you mean?'

'I'm not Albert Grove. I'm Albert James. I took my dad's surname.'

Lori tries to think. Has Molly ever mentioned his surname? She can't recall hearing it.

'I've been playing with you, Loret-*ta*. It's been so much fun. The sightings up here. The strange goings on: hiding your dogs' leads, noises in the night, blood in your car, stalking you in the mountains.'

Lori gasps. 'But you were with Molly the whole time.'

'That's where you're wrong. I had that new client I claimed I was seeing.' He throws his head back and laughs. 'Fictitious. I made him up like you make up your stories. It's rather fun, isn't it? I can see why you enjoy your occupation.' Albert's evil laugh sounds exactly like his father's. 'It doesn't matter now.'

'And all the letters. You sent them, didn't you? And that letter to April?'

'Yep, all me. You're catching up now. Clever girl.'

'How did you find me every time?'

'Your daughter needs to be more careful about what she puts on social media. It hasn't been that hard to find you at all.'

Lori feels sick with fear.

'My mum walked out on my dad because of you.'

'I know what I saw, Albert. Your dad always was evil. He beat your sister.'

He ignores her. 'So I missed seeing my dad when I was growing up. It was only when my mum died that I got to meet him again. I ended up going to live with him. My sister wouldn't come with me.'

'I wonder why.'

'So you broke up my family. Twice. And now my dad is dead.'

'It was already broken.' Lori pauses, shaking her head. 'So, all this time, you've been sending those letters to me. You're as rotten as your dad.'

His nostrils flare. His fists clench. 'Don't talk about my dad like that.'

'What do you plan to do?'

Albert steps forwards. 'I'll finish off what my dad started. Suicide. You take a little tumble off the edge there. "Local woman who couldn't live without her husband takes her own life." Who's going to know?'

'There's CCTV in the village. You won't get away with it.'

'Don't take me for a fool. Don't you think I have CCTV covered? With such a remote location, it wasn't that difficult.' He takes another step closer to her.

'What about Molly?'

'What about her? Collateral damage, I'm afraid. Poor gullible Molly. She'll be heartbroken, of course. Losing her

328

mum. Her boyfriend vanishing with her sixty thousand pounds. Thanks for that, by the way.'

'No. That's her inheritance.' Fear and coldness shiver through Lori's body. 'A chance for her to get through uni. You bastard! Don't you dare touch that money.'

Again, that laugh. The grating laugh of a madman. 'Too late. It's in my bank account.'

'You've played her. You absolute bastard.'

'I fly off tonight. No one will ever hear of me again.'

'You're deluded. Just like your father. People can't just disappear these days.'

He strokes his chin, smirking. 'Judging from what happened to your husband, I believe it is possible. I have new documents ready and waiting for me.'

It happens so quickly. Lori glances over the precipice to the rocks below. Albert rushes for her. Her leg muscles tighten, preparing for flight. But his two firm hands are pushing on her chest. He takes another step forwards. Her legs turn weak as if they're going to give up on her. She tries to squirm away from his reach, but he is too strong. This isn't how it's all meant to end. She struggles to breathe. She has to stop him. Molly's face when she receives a visit from the police to tell her that her mother is dead flashes before her.

Suddenly a figure appears in the distance, walking towards them. Is that Ray? She screams out to them. 'Help!'

But it's too late. Albert pushes her again, determined to finish what he came there to do. The fall is imminent. She screams at him; tells him he is making a mistake. He won't get away with it. Albert laughs at her.

She loses her footing.

She's going.

Her life flashes before her. Just as it is described in literature when death is a few breaths away.

She sees her dad cooking breakfast while she reads an Enid Blyton or a Roald Dahl.

The day she met Howie in the student union bar. He was standing watching a game of pool, his hands wrapped around a half-finished pint of Guinness. The head had left a creamy line above his top lip. He kept looking over at her and catching her eye. When he finally smiled at her, she fearlessly approached him. That was it. There was no looking back for either of them.

She recalls the elation of giving birth to Molly, the sheer exhaustion, the overwhelming love.

Molly growing up, the sweetest of kids with her girly pigtails and love of dressing up like a princess.

Her life with Howie; how he treated her like gold.

Frankie Evans appears next. The turning point in her career. Not that it turned in the direction she had hoped it would. The calls rushed in from all the major players in the media world. She could've had any job she wanted. But Howie disappeared. And so did her motivation to get out of bed in the morning. Molly went off the rails. So much sadness that was out of her control.

All this in a split second.

She is free falling to her death, the black rocks below rushing to meet her at breakneck speed. Her bones feel like they are rattling within her. In the distance, she hears Misty and Shadow's faint whining. She reaches out to grab something, but there's nothing in reach. The weightlessness is a peculiar feeling. She thinks about the adjectives she can use to describe it.

The white light is bright. She can see Howie. He is smiling, and his arms are open wide, his hands beckoning her towards him with overwhelming love exactly how she remembers it.

And then she is gone from this life. Perished among the black uncompromising rocks at the bottom of the falls.

54

It's the first time she has been out on Christmas Eve in seven years. She has even bought a new dress for the occasion. A burgundy feather-trimmed shift dress that stops just above the knee. She found it in a small boutique in Bangor, next to the hairdressers where she spent a couple of hours that afternoon. She gave the crazy stylist strict instructions to chop the lot off. 'Are you insane, woman?' The flamboyant hairdresser, dressed in a multi-coloured trouser suit, laughed. 'I know it's Christmas, but you may regret asking me to go that far when you wake up and look in the mirror in the morning.'

'Not at all. Just get on with it,' she replied. 'Before I change my mind.'

They compromised on an inverted bob. 'Try it at least,' the stylist said, holding a hand mirror to show her the back of her new hairdo. 'See what you think. I can always chop off more next week if you're not happy.' She had to admit, he was right, and she left him a ten-pound tip for a job well done and his skilful insight.

She opens her wardrobe door and poses in front of the full-length mirror. Something else she realises she hasn't done for seven years. It feels strange to look at herself for so long. What with the makeup and the new hairstyle she doesn't think she looks too shabby. The dress, though. It's too short. She can't possibly go out in that. Perhaps her black maxi dress would be more appropriate. Her phone pings with a text. It's from Ray.

I've finished your book.

Lori replies:

And?

Ray immediately texts back:

Confused...

Lori sends another one.

Let's talk when I get there.

'Misty, Shadow, what do you think? Not too bad for an old girl, eh?' Lori asks her faithful friends when she gets to the kitchen. The dogs' tails wag in unison. She could be saying anything. They are only trying to decipher if her words will lead to a treat, a walk, or food. Lori smiles at them. It sure is a dog's life!

Two glasses and a bowl of Twiglets – Molly's favourite Christmas snack – are waiting on the side. Molly pounds downstairs. She still wears the grief of a broken relationship and the hurt of a double-crossed heart. They show in the sadness of her sombre expression and the loss of her usual energetic spirit. But she'll get there. Lori has faith. 'Mum! Where did you get that dress? I've not seen it before.'

'I found it in a little boutique in town. I wasn't sure whether to wear it. You think it's OK?'

'OK? It's more than OK. What with the haircut, you look ten years younger.'

'You're only saying that because you're my daughter.'

Molly throws a palm up to Lori. 'Stop right there. I'm saying it because it's the truth.'

'You're such a sweetie.'

'No, Mum. I'm an honest friend. Listen, would you mind if I didn't come tonight?'

Lori finds the champagne she put in the fridge earlier. Her lips turn downwards. 'I do mind.'

'I'm not in the mood for socialising.' Molly's voice wobbles. 'How could I have let another bastard get the better of me? I'm done with guys.'

'At least we managed to save your money, and Albert is behind bars.' Lori pops the cork and fills the glasses. 'It's time to move on, Molly. For both of us.' She hands her daughter a glass of champagne. 'Put him behind you. He's not worth your energy or your tears. Every experience we face makes us stronger.' Lori lifts her arm and flexes her bicep.

Molly laughs and clinks her glass against Lori's. 'Cheers, Mum. Merry Christmas.'

'And here's to a happy new year too. Now, let's enjoy this evening.'

Ray's split-level apartment sits above the café. It's the first time Lori has been in there.

Ray steps backwards when he opens the door. His jaw drops as he does a double take. 'Wow.' His eyebrows rise high. 'I nearly didn't recognise you.'

'You like the new look?' Lori feels her cheeks blush.

He takes their coats. 'One hundred per cent. The haircut makes you look so much younger.'

Molly prods Lori's shoulder. 'See? What did I tell you?'

As Lori expected, the apartment is tastefully decorated and immaculately tidy. Several people have already arrived, and the air is heavy with the festive spirit of Christmas. Chatter is buzzing, and Mariah Carey is belting out, *All I Want for Christmas is You*. Teagan is passing around entrées; another café worker fills glasses with prosecco.

The waft of warm buttery pastry plays havoc with Lori's tastebuds. 'Something smells delicious.'

'That'll be a new homemade sausage roll recipe I thought I'd try out.'

Lori laughs. 'We're guinea pigs, then?' She follows Ray into the kitchen. 'So why are you confused?'

Ray is checking the oven, pulling out a baking tray of sausage rolls using a red and white checked tea towel. 'Sorry?'

'You said you finished my book, but you're confused.'

He bangs the oven closed and slings the tea towel over his shoulder. 'Yes – a couple of questions.' Ray's tone is soft. It awakens emotions in Lori she didn't know still existed. 'I'm surprised you didn't write what really happened. I was expecting my moment of fame. The hero who saved the day. But you wrote that part out.' A twinkle in his eye assures Lori he is kidding. 'And how much of the story is actually true? I recognise a lot of what has happened but not all of it, and of course, not the ending.'

'All of the story is true apart from Albert pushing me into the falls. And, of course, I've changed names. It's been a cathartic experience. A kind of memoir, I suppose, but I've turned it into a suspense story. I'll never stop saying it, you know. Thank you for saving my life. If you hadn't followed Albert to the falls that afternoon, the book would

336

never have got finished. I'd be a dead woman, and Albert would be a free man.'

'I understand now.'

'I know I keep saying it but thank goodness you arrived when you did. I could never have fought him off. He would've had me over the edge in the blink of an eye. But he didn't. And you *are* my hero. That's why I've dedicated the book to you, as well as Howie and Molly.'

His hand flies to his chest. 'I'm honoured. But why did you kill yourself off?'

'Can't you see? It's my way of closing this chapter of my past. I've been missing for seven years too. I need to get my old self back.' With that, Lori steps over to Ray and pecks him on the cheek. 'I'm putting the past behind me.' Her eyes glow with resolution. 'This is the new me.'

THE END

Dear reader

For me, building a relationship with my readers is one of the joys of writing. Please keep in touch by following the link below to get your free copy of my novella *Choices*.

www.ajcampbellauthor.com/download

CHOICES

Warning signs presented themselves from the start. Flashing like the neon displays in Piccadilly Circus, they couldn't have advertised things more clearly. But Abbie was too troubled to see clearly. Too damaged to see the dangers Tony Sharpe brought into her life. Until the day he pushed her too far.

PLEASE LEAVE A REVIEW

As for all authors, reviews are the key to raising awareness of my work. If you have enjoyed Her Missing Husband, please leave a review on Goodreads and from your purchase on Amazon to help others find it too.

All my novels undergo a rigorous editing process, but sometimes mistakes do happen. If you have spotted an error, please contact me, so I can promptly get it corrected.

www.ajcampbellauthor.com/contact

Thank you for choosing to read my books. AJ x

I hope you enjoyed reading my sixth published book *Her Missing Husband* as much as I adored writing it. If you haven't read my other novels, check them out on Amazon.

THE WRONG KEY

A mother's love. A daughter's life. A race against time.

London-based Steph Knight faces the challenge of a lifetime when she's sent to New York to cover for a colleague involved in a tragic car accident. Recently divorced, Steph sees it as an opportunity for a fresh start and to spend time with her teenage daughter, Ellie, a talented musician, before she leaves for university.

Soon after arriving, Steph crosses paths with Edward, a

corporate lawyer, who introduces Ellie to Jack, a bioethics
student enjoying his summer break. As both relationships
intensify, Steph begins to uncover a web of corruption within
her company that seemingly reaches right to the top. Feeling
increasingly threatened, she has no idea who she can trust. Not
even the men they've fallen for are beyond suspicion.

And then the unthinkable happens. Ellie disappears.

Steph receives a menacing text message. Ellie has been
kidnapped.

The clock is ticking. Ellie's life is in danger. And so is Steph's.

Terrified, far from home, and with no one to trust, Steph must
draw on her inner strength to save her daughter... even if it
kills her.

THE PHONE CALL

SHORTLISTED FOR THE ADULT PRIZE FOR
FICTION: THE SELFIE BOOK AWARDS 2023

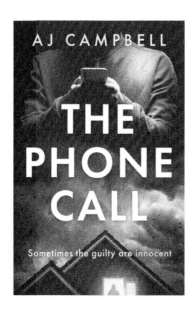

Joey Clarke was just fifteen when his dad died, leaving him
to raise his much younger siblings as his mum dealt with
the trauma of bereavement and her failing health. Ten

years on, Joey's only pleasure is spending time with his friend Becca, the love of his life. It's the one escape from his dead-end job, his ever-increasing debts and the fear that enforcement agents will knock on his front door any day.

So when a phone call brings Joey the chance to ease the burdens of his life, he grabs the opportunity, even though he knows things are not entirely as they should be. He justifies it to himself as a way to get back on his feet. But when he finds himself party to a crime linked to Becca, he panics.

As catastrophic events unfold, Joey becomes further embroiled in a web of secrets, lies and deceit. He is now faced with the impossible. Should he confess to the police? Tell Becca? Or should he keep quiet and say nothing?

So, when the next job comes in, Joey wants out. But this time he's in way too deep to say no...

LEAVE WELL ALONE

A broken family. Skeletons in the closet. Lives in danger.

How far would you go to protect your family?

When Eva's brother Ben announces he has found their mother, Eva is determined to have nothing to do with the woman who abandoned them eighteen years ago to a traumatic childhood in foster care. Eva is happy now, in a loving relationship with rich and dependable Jim, and she is pregnant.

Nothing can change Eva's mind. Her eyes are firmly on the future. But when her baby is born with a serious hereditary illness, she is forced to confront both her mother and her past. Eva begins to find forgiveness. But as old secrets and layers of deceit emerge, she makes a shocking discovery, leaving her fearing for her baby's, Jim's, and her own life.

DON'T COME LOOKING

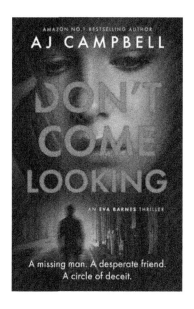

A missing man. A desperate friend. A circle of deceit.

Would you refuse your best friend's plea for help?

Marc O'Sullivan has disappeared.

His wife Sasha is frantic, and Eva is baffled.

They were blissfully married with three kids. The perfect couple... or so everybody thought.

Sasha begs Eva to help her find Marc. But he has given a written statement at the police station where Eva works. It's on record –

when his family report him missing, Marc does not want to be found. But why?

Ultimately, friendship and loyalty override Eva's professional integrity, and she is compelled to use her resources to delve into Marc's life, even if it means breaking the police code of conduct and jeopardising her career.

As each day passes, the mystery deepens. Murky goings-on from Marc and Sasha's neighbours heighten the tension. What dark secrets are they hiding? And what drove Marc's inexplicable actions in the weeks leading up to his disappearance? Behaviour so out of character that Eva struggles to tell Sasha about it.

Will Eva uncover the truth before it's too late and lives are destroyed forever?

SEARCH NO FURTHER

Cara De Rosa is the heart of her large family and community in London. Her restaurant business is booming. She's found a second chance at love, and marriage is on the horizon. But there's no such thing as a perfect life. And the good times never last forever.

When Cara's health suddenly falters, her family's world turns upside down in the blink of an eye. In a bed-ridden haze, she confides in Sienna, her favourite

grandchild, that her rapid decline may be at the hands
of one of her own.

Sienna, a young, single mother, is reeling in the wake of her
husband's unsolved death. She is haunted by crippling anxiety
and misplaced guilt, heightened by suddenly finding herself in a
race against time to save Cara's life. As she begins to pull at the
strings of a tangled family web, she reveals disturbing secrets,
decades of deceit and shockingly serious crimes.

ACKNOWLEDGMENTS

The inspiration for this book came in the summer of 2022 when I visited one of my close friends, who owns a café in North Wales. My son spent a week working in his café while my husband and I toured the local area. It was while we were walking in the mountains one morning that I thought, it's so desolate around here. I wonder what it would be like to live so remotely. Lori Mortimer sprung into my imagination, and I began plotting. During the journey home, I started writing Lori's story. It has been so much fun!

Thank you to my brilliant editor, Louise Walters, for guiding me to make this book the best it can be, and to AJ McDine for your proofreading skills. And thank you, Tim Barber, for working patiently with me to produce the perfect cover.

To my savvy beta readers – Mr C, Christine Henderson, Maddie Standen, John Black, Mel Vout, Collie Loveday, Dawn Harland and Sally Riordan – your help is invaluable! Your observations and suggestions have helped me to make this story so much better.

To my ARC team and all the fantastic book bloggers and media people who support my work, thank you! Most of you have been by my side since my debut novel. I'm blessed to have you.

A special extra thank you to Christine Henderson for your unwavering support in championing my work.

And, last but not least, thank you, Mr C and my boys, for the endless cups of tea and support to help me write. I love you to the moon and back.

ABOUT THE AUTHOR

AJ CAMPBELL is an Amazon bestselling author of six psychological suspense novels and promises stories full of twists, turns and torment. Her fourth book, *The Phone Call,* was released in July 2022. It topped the Amazon charts for several months and was shortlisted for the Adult Prize for Fiction at the Selfie Book Awards 2023. She released her fifth novel, *The Wrong Key,* in January 2023, and her sixth, *Her Missing Husband,* in May 2023.

AJ lives in the UK on the Essex / Hertfordshire border with her husband, sons, and cocker spaniel, Max. She is a dog lover, Netflix junkie, and a wine and Asian food enthusiast. And, either reading, watching TV or writing, AJ enjoys nothing more than getting stuck into a twisty story!

Find AJ here:

www.ajcampbellauthor.com
www.facebook.com/AJCampbellauthor
www.instagram.com/ajcampbellauthor/

Printed in Great Britain
by Amazon